THE
WHITE HOUSE
CONNECTION

JACK HIGGINS

BERKLEY BOOKS, NEW YORK

THE WHITE HOUSE CONNECTION

A Berkley Book / published by arrangement with
Michael Joseph, a publishing division of Penguin Books, Ltd.

PRINTING HISTORY
G. P. Putnam's Sons edition / May 1999
Berkley edition / July 2000

The Penguin Putnam Inc. World Wide Web site address is
http://www.penguinputnam.com

ISBN: 0-425-17541-3

BERKLEY®
Berkley Books are published by The Berkley Publishing Group,
a division of Penguin Putnam Inc.,
375 Hudson Street, New York, New York 10014.
BERKLEY and the "B" design are trademarks belonging to
Penguin Putnam Inc.

PRINTED IN THE UNITED STATES OF AMERICA

13 12 11 10 9 8 7 6

To my mother-in-law, Sally Palmer.
Thanks for the idea.

PROLOGUE

NEW YORK

MANHATTAN, WITH AN east wind driving rain mixed with a little sleet along Park Avenue, was as bleak and uninviting as most great cities after midnight, especially in March. There was little traffic—the occasional limousine, the odd cab—hardly surprising at that time of the morning and with such uninviting weather.

In a stretch of mixed offices and residences, a woman waited in an archway, standing in the shadows, a wide-brimmed rain hat on her head and wearing a trench coat, the collar turned up. An umbrella was looped to her left wrist. She carried no purse or shoulder bag.

She felt for the gun in the right-hand pocket of her trench coat, took it out, and checked it expertly by feel. It was an unusual weapon, a Colt .25 semiautomatic, eight shot, relatively small but deadly, especially with the silencer on the end. Some people might have thought it a woman's gun, but not when used with hollow-point cartridges. She replaced it in her pocket and looked out.

Slightly to her right on the other side of Park Avenue was a splendid town house. It was owned by Senator Michael Cohan, who was attending a fund-raiser at the Pierre, a function due to finish at midnight, which was why she waited here in the shadows with the intention, all things being equal, of leaving him dead on the pavement.

She heard the sound of voices, a drunken shout, and two young men came round the corner on the other side and started along the sidewalk. They were dressed in identical woolen hats, reefer coats, and jeans, and they were drinking from cans. One of them, tall and bearded, stepped into the flooded gutter and kicked water, grinning, but as the rain increased, the other one wrapped his jacket tighter. Spotting the entrance to a covered alley, he swallowed the rest of his beer and dropped the can into the gutter.

"In here, man." He ran for the entrance.

"Damn!" the woman said softly. The alley was next to Cohan's house.

There was nothing to be done. They had disappeared into the shadows, but she could hear them clearly, their laughter loud. She waited impatiently for them to move on, and then a young woman turned the same corner the men had come from and moved along the sidewalk. She was small and, except for her umbrella, unsuitably dressed for such weather, in high heels and a black suit with a short skirt. She heard the raucous laughter, hesitated, then started past the alley.

A voice called, "Hey, where are you going, baby?" and the bearded man stepped out, his friend following.

The girl started to hurry, and the bearded man dashed after her and grabbed her arm. She dropped her umbrella and struggled, and he slapped her across the face.

"Fight as much as you want, sweetheart. I like it."

His friend grabbed her other arm. "Come on, let's get her inside."

The girl cried out in terror, and the bearded one slapped her again. "Now you be good."

They dragged her into the alley. The older woman hesitated, and then she heard a scream. "Damn!" she said for the second time, stepped out into the rain, and crossed over. It was dark in the alley, with only a little diffused light from the streetlamp outside. The girl tried to struggle against the man holding her from behind, but the bearded man had a knife in his right hand and touched it to her cheek, drawing blood.

She cried out in pain, and he said, "I told you to be good." He reached for the hem of her skirt and sliced upwards with the sharp blade, parting it. "There you go, Freddy. Be my guest."

A calm voice said, "I don't think so."

Freddy's face, as he looked beyond his friend, registered astonishment. "Jesus!" he said.

The bearded man turned and found the woman standing in the alley entrance. She was carrying the rain hat in her right hand. Her hair was silvery white, highlighted by the back light from the streetlamp. She looked to be in her sixties, but it was hard to tell anything about her face in the dark.

"What the hell is this?" the one holding the girl said.

"Just let her go."

"I can't tell you what she wants, but I know what she's going to get," the bearded man said to his friend. "The same as this bitch. You feel like some company tonight, Grandma?"

He took a step forward and the woman shot him in the heart, firing through the rain hat, the sound muted. He was thrown against the wall, bounced off, and fell on his back.

The girl was so terrified that she didn't utter a word. It was the man holding her who reacted. "Jesus!" he moaned. "Oh, God," and then he took a knife from his pocket and sprang the blade. "I'll cut her throat," he said to the older woman. "I swear it."

The woman stood there, the Colt in her right hand, down against her thigh now. Her voice, when she spoke, was still calm and controlled. "You never learn, you people, do you?"

Her hand swung up and she shot him between the eyes. He fell backwards. The girl leaned against the wall, breathing heavily, blood on her face. The woman removed her light woolen scarf and passed it across, and the girl held it to her face. The woman leaned over, checked the bearded man first, and then the other.

"Well, neither of these gentlemen will be bothering anyone again."

The girl exploded. "The bastards." She kicked the bearded man. "If you hadn't come along . . ." She shuddered. "I hope they rot in hell."

"It's a strong possibility," the woman said. "Do you live near here?"

"About twenty blocks. I was having dinner at a place around the corner, had a fight with my date, and walked out hoping to find a cab."

"You never can find one when it's raining. Let me look at your face."

She pulled the girl to the entrance. "I'd say you'll need two or three stitches. St. Mary's Hospital is two blocks that way." She pointed. "Go to the emergency room. Tell them you had an accident. You slipped, cut your cheek, tore your skirt."

"Will they believe me?"

"It doesn't matter. It's your business." The woman shrugged. "Unless you want to go to the police."

"Good God, no!" the girl replied, a kind of agony there. "That's the last thing I want."

The woman stepped out, picked up the fallen umbrella, and gave it to her. "Then go, my dear, and don't look back. It didn't happen, none of it." She stepped back and picked up the girl's purse where it had fallen. "Don't forget this."

The girl took it. "And I won't forget you."

The woman smiled. "On the whole, I'd rather you did."

The girl managed a small smile. "I see what you mean."

She turned and hurried off, clutching the umbrella. The woman watched her go, examined the bullet hole in her hat, put it on, then opened her own umbrella and walked away in the opposite direction.

Two blocks north, she found the Lincoln parked at the curb. The man behind the wheel was out and waiting for her as she approached, a large black man wearing a gray chauffeur's suit.

"You okay?" he asked.

"I'm here, aren't I?"

She got into the front passenger seat. He closed the door, went round, and got behind the wheel. She strapped herself in and tapped his shoulder. "Where's that flask of yours, Hedley, the Bushmills whiskey?"

He took a silver flask from the glove compartment, unscrewed the cap, and passed it to her. She swallowed once, twice, then handed it back.

"Wonderful."

She took out a silver case, selected a cigarette, and lit it with the car lighter, then blew out a long stream of smoke. "All the bad habits are so pleasurable."

"You shouldn't be doing that. It's not good for you."

"Does it matter?"

"Don't say that." He was upset. "Did you get the bastard?"

"Cohan? No, something got in the way. Let's head back to the Plaza and I'll tell you." She was finished by the time they were halfway there and he was horrified.

"My God, what are you trying to do? Clean up the whole world now?"

"I see. You mean I should have stood by and waited while those two animals raped the girl and probably cut her throat?"

"Okay, okay!" he sighed and nodded. "What about Senator Cohan?"

"We'll fly back to London tomorrow. He's due there in a few days, showing his face on what he pretends is Presidential business. I'll get him then."

"And then what? Where does it end?" Hedley grunted. "It all seems unreal."

He pulled up at the Plaza and she smiled mischievously like a child. "I'm a great trial to you, Hedley, I know that, but what would I do without you? See you in the morning."

He went round and opened the door for her and watched her go up the steps.

"And what would I do without you?" he asked softly, then got behind the wheel and drove away.

The night doorman was waiting at the top. "Lady Helen!" he said. "It's wonderful to see you. I heard you were in."

"And you, George." She kissed him on the cheek. "How's that new daughter of yours?"

"Great, just great."

"I'm going back to London in the morning. I'll see you again soon."

" 'Night, Lady Helen."

She went in, and a man in a raincoat who had been waiting for a cab said, "Hey, who was that woman?"

"Lady Helen Lang. She's been coming here for years."

"Lady, huh? Funny, she doesn't sound English."

"That's 'cause she's from Boston. Married an English Lord ages ago. People say she's worth millions."

"Really? . . . Well, she seems quite something."

"You can say that again. Nicest person you'll ever meet."

IN THE BEGINNING

LONDON
NEW YORK

ONE

BORN IN BOSTON in 1933 to one of Boston's wealthiest families, Helen Darcy's mother had died giving birth to her, and she was raised as an only child. Fortunately, her father truly loved her, and she loved him just as much in return. In spite of his enormous business interests in steel, shipbuilding, and oil, he took the time to lavish every attention on her, and she was worth it. Enormously intelligent, she went to the best private schools, and later, Vassar, where she found she had a special flair for foreign languages.

To her father, only the best was good enough and, himself a Rhodes Scholar as a young man, he sent her to England to finish her graduate education at St. Hugh's College at Oxford University.

Many of her father's business associates in London put themselves out to entertain her, and she became popular in London society. She was twenty-four when she met Sir Roger Lang, a baronet and onetime lieutenant colonel in the

Scots Guards, now chairman of a merchant bank with close associations with her father.

She adored him at once and the attraction was mutual. There was one flaw, however. Although he was unmarried, there was a fifteen years' age difference between them and, at the time, it simply seemed too much for her.

She returned to America, confused and uncertain about the future, for business held no attraction for her, and she'd had enough of academia. There were plenty of young men, of course, if only for the wrong reason—her father's enormous wealth—but no one suited her, because in the background there was always Roger Lang, with whom she stayed in touch once a week by telephone.

Finally, one weekend at their beach house on Cape Cod, she said to her father across the breakfast table, "Daddy, don't be mad at me, but I'm thinking of moving back to England . . . and getting married."

He leaned back and smiled. "Does Roger Lang know about this?"

"Dammit, you knew."

"Ever since you came back from Oxford. I was wondering when you'd come to your senses."

She poured tea, a habit she'd acquired in England. "The answer is . . . he doesn't know."

"Then I suggest you fly to London and tell him," and he returned to his *New York Times*.

And so, a new life began for Helen Darcy, now Lady Helen Lang, divided between the house in South Audley Street and the country estate by the sea in North Norfolk, called Compton Place. There was only one fly in the ointment. In spite of every effort to have a child, she was bedeviled by miscarriages year after year, so that by the time her son, Peter, was born when she was thirty-three, it seemed a major miracle.

Peter proved to be another great joy in her life, and she took the kind of interest in his education that her father had taken in hers. Her husband agreed he could go to an American prep school for a few years, but afterwards, as the future Sir Peter, he had to finish his education at Eton and the Sandhurst Military Academy. It was the family tradition—which was fine with Peter, for he had only ever wanted to be one thing, a soldier like all the Langs before him.

After Sandhurst came the Scots Guards, his father's old regiment and, a few years later, a transfer to the SAS, for he had inherited his mother's ability with languages. He saw service in Bosnia and in the Gulf War, where he was awarded the Military Cross for an unspecified black operation behind Iraqi lines. And in Ireland, of course, the one place which never went away. Hand-in-hand with his ability for languages was a flair for dialects. He spoke not with some stage Irish accent but as if he were from Dublin or Belfast or South Armagh, which made him invaluable for undercover work in the continuing battle with the Provisional IRA.

Because of the life he led, women figured little. The odd girlfriend now and then was all he had time for. The fear was real, the burden immense, but Helen bore it as a soldier's wife and mother should, until that dreadful Sunday in March 1996 when her husband answered the phone at South Audley Street, then replaced the receiver slowly and turned, his face ashen.

"He's gone," he said simply. "Peter's gone," and he slumped into a chair and cried his eyes out, while she held his hand and stared blankly into space.

If there was one person who understood her grief that rainy day in the churchyard in the village church of St. Mary and All the Saints at Compton Place, it was Lady Helen Lang's chauffeur, Hedley Jackson, who stood behind her and Sir Roger, immaculate in his gray uniform as he held a large umbrella above them.

He was six feet four and originally from Harlem. At the age of eighteen, he'd joined the Marine Corps and gone to Vietnam, emerging at the other end with a Silver Star and two Purple Hearts. Posted to the American Embassy Guard in London, he'd met a girl from Brixton, who was house-keeper to the Langs at South Audley Street. They had mar-ried, Hedley had left the service and been appointed the Langs' chauffeur, and had lived in the spacious basement flat and had a child, a son. It was an ideal life for them both, and then tragedy struck: Jackson's wife and son were in-volved in a multicar pileup in the fog on the North Circular Road, and were killed instantly.

Lady Helen had held his hand at the crematorium, and when he had disappeared from South Audley Street, she had hunted him down through one bar after another in Brix-ton until she found him, sodden with drink and nearly sui-cidal, had taken him to Compton Place, and slowly, patiently, brought him back to life.

To say that he was devoted to her now was an under-statement, and his heart bled for her, particularly since Sir Roger's words to her, "Peter's gone," had hidden a horrific truth. The IRA car bomb which had killed him had been of such enormous strength that not a single trace of his body remained and, standing there in the rain, all they could com-memorate was his name engraved in the family mausoleum.

MAJOR PETER LANG, M.C., SCOTS GUARDS, SPECIAL AIR
SERVICE REGIMENT
1966–1996
REST IN PEACE

Helen held her husband's hand. He had aged ten years in the past few days—a man once spry and vigorous now seemed old as if he'd never been young. Rest in peace, she thought. But that's what it was supposed to have been for. Peace in Ireland, and those bastards destroyed him. No trace. It's as if he's never been, she thought, frowning, unable to weep. That can't be right. There's no justice, none at all in a world gone mad. The priest intoned: "I am the resurrection and the life, saith the Lord."

Helen shook her head. No, not that. Not that. I don't believe anymore, not when evil walks the earth unpunished.

She turned, leaving the astonished mourners, taking her husband with her, and walked away. Hedley followed, the umbrella held over them.

Her father, unable to attend the funeral because of illness, died a few months later and left her a millionaire many times over. The management team that controlled the various parts of the corporation were entirely trustworthy and headed by her cousin, with whom she'd always been close, so it was all in the family. She devoted herself to her husband, a broken man, who himself died a year after his son.

As for Helen, she gave a certain part of her activities to charitable work and spent a great deal of time at Compton Place, although the one thousand acres that went with the house were leased out for large-scale farming.

To a certain extent, Compton Place was her salvation because of its fascinating location. A mile from the coast of the North Sea, that part of Norfolk was still one of the most rural areas of England, full of winding, narrow lanes and places with names like Cley-next-the-Sea, Stiffkey, and Blakeney, little villages found unexpectedly and then lost, never to be found again. It was all so timeless.

From the first time Roger had taken her there, she had

been enchanted by the salt marshes with the sea mist drifting in, the shingle beaches, and sand dunes, and the great
wet beaches when the tide was out.

From her days as a child growing up in Cape Cod, she
had loved the sea and birds, and there were birds in plenty
in her part of Norfolk: brent geese from Siberia, curlews,
redshanks, and every kind of seagull. She loved walking or
cycling along the dikes, none of them less than six feet high,
that passed through the great banks of reeds. It gave her re-
newed energy every time she breathed in the salt sea air or
felt the rain on her face.

The house had originally been built in Tudor times, but
was mainly Georgian with a few later additions. The large
kitchen was a post-war project, lovingly created in country
style. The dining room, hall, library, and the huge drawing
room were paneled in oak. There were only six bedrooms
now, for others had been developed into bathrooms or dress-
ing rooms at various stages.

With the estate leased to various farmers, she had re-
tained only six acres around the house, mainly woodland,
leaving two large lawns and another for croquet. A retired
farmer came up from the village from time to time to keep
things in order, and when they were in residence, Hedley
would get the tractor out and mow the grass himself.

There was a daily housekeeper named Mrs. Smedley, and
another woman from the village helped her with the cleaning when necessary. All this sufficed. It was a calm and or-
derly existence that helped her return to life. And the
villagers helped, too.

The laws of the British aristocracy are strange. As Roger
Lang's wife, she was officially Lady Lang. Only the daugh-
ters of the higher levels of the nobility were allowed to use
their Christian names, but the villagers in that part of Norfolk were a strange, stubborn race. To them she was Lady

Helen, and that was that. It was an interesting fact that the same attitude pertained in London society.

Any help anyone needed, she gave. She attended church every Sunday morning, and Hedley sat in the rear pew, always correctly attired in his chauffeur's uniform. She was not above visiting the village pub of an evening for a drink or two, and there, too, Hedley always accompanied her and, though you might not think it, he was totally accepted by those taciturn people ever since an extraordinary event some years past.

An incredibly high tide combined with torrential rain had caused the water to rise in the narrow canal that passed through the village from the old disused mill. Soon it was overflowing into the street and threatening to engulf the village. All attempts to force open the lock gate which was blocking the water proved futile, and it was Hedley who plunged chest-deep into the water with a crowbar, diving under the surface again and again until he managed to dislodge the ancient locking pins, and the gate burst open. At the pub, he had never been allowed to pay for a drink again.

So, although it had lost its savor, life could have been worse—and then Lady Helen received an unexpected phone call, one that in its consequences would prove just as catastrophic as that other call two years earlier, the call that had announced the death of her son.

"Helen, is that you?" The voice was weak, yet strangely familiar.

"Yes, who is this?"

"Tony Emsworth."

She remembered the name well: a junior officer under her husband many years ago, later an Under-Secretary of State at the Foreign Office. She hadn't seen him for some time. He had to be seventy now. Come to think of it, he hadn't been at either Peter's funeral or her husband's. She'd thought that strange at the time.

"Why, Tony," she said. "Where are you?"

"My cottage. I'm living in a little village called Stukeley now, in Kent. Only forty miles from London."

"How's Martha?" Helen asked.

"Died two years ago. The thing is, Helen, I must see you. It's a matter of life and death, you could say." He was racked by coughing. "My death, actually. Lung cancer. I haven't got long to go."

"Tony. I'm so sorry."

He tried to joke. "So am I." There was an urgency in his voice now. "Helen, my love, you must come and see me. I need to unburden myself of something, something you must hear."

He was coughing again. She waited until he'd stopped. "Fine, Tony, fine. Try not to upset yourself. I'll drive down to London this afternoon, stay overnight in town, and be with you as soon as I can in the morning. Is that all right?"

"Wonderful. I'll see you then." He put down the phone.

She had taken the call in the library. She stood there frowning, slightly agitated, then opened a silver box, took out a cigarette, and lit it with a lighter Roger had once given her made from a German shell.

Tony Emsworth. The weak voice, the coughing, had given her a bad shake. She remembered him as a dashing Guards captain, a lady's man, a bruising rider to hounds. To be reduced to what she had just heard was not pleasant. Intimations of mortality, she thought. Death just round the corner, and there had been enough of that in her life.

But there was another, secret reason, something even Hedley knew nothing about. The odd pain in the chest and arm had given her pause for thought. She'd had a private visit to London recently, a consultation with one of the best doctors in Harley Street, tests and scans at the London Clinic.

It reminded her of a remark Scott Fitzgerald had made about his health: *I visited a great man's office and emerged with a grave sentence.* Something like that. Her sentence had not been too grave. Heart trouble, of course. Angina. No need to worry, my dear, the professor had said. You'll live for years. Just take the pills and take it easy. No more riding to hounds or anything like that.

"And no more of these," she said softly, and stubbed out the cigarette with a wry smile, remembering that she'd been saying that for months, and went in search of Hedley.

Stukeley was pleasant enough: cottages on either side of a narrow street, a pub, a general store, and Emsworth's place, Rose Cottage, on the other side of the church. Lady Helen had phoned before leaving London to give him the time, and he was expecting them, opening the door to greet them, tall and frail, the flesh washed away, the face skull-like.

She kissed his cheek. "Tony, you look terrible."

"Don't I just?" He managed a grin.

"Should I wait in the Merc?" Hedley asked.

"Nice to see you again, Hedley," Emsworth said. "Would it be possible for you to handle the kitchen? I let my daily go an hour ago. She's left sandwiches, cakes, and so on. If you could make the tea . . ."

"My pleasure," Hedley told him, and followed them in.

A log fire was burning in the large open fireplace in the sitting room. Beams supported the low ceiling, and there was comfortable furniture everywhere and Indian carpets scattered over the stone-flagged floor.

Emsworth sat in a wing-backed chair and put his walking stick on the floor. A cardboard file was on the coffee table beside him.

"There's a photo over there of your old man and me when I was a subaltern," he said.

Helen Lang went to the sideboard and examined the photo in its silver frame. "You look very handsome, both of you."

She returned and sat opposite him. He said, "I didn't attend Peter's funeral. Missed out on Roger's, too."

"I had noticed."

"Too ashamed to show my face, ye see."

There was something here, something unmentionable, that already touched her deep inside, and her skin crawled.

Hedley came in with tea things on a tray and put them down beside her on a low table. "Leave the food," she told him. "Later, I think."

"Be a good chap," Emsworth said. "There's a whiskey decanter on the sideboard. Pour me a large one and one for Lady Helen."

"Will I need it?"

"I think so."

She nodded. Hedley poured the drinks and served them. "I'll be in the kitchen if you need me."

"Thank you. I think I might."

Hedley looked grim but retired to the kitchen. He stood there thinking about it, then noticed the two doors to the serving hatch and eased them ajar. It was underhanded, yes, but all that concerned him was her welfare. He sat down on a stool and listened.

"For years I lived a lie as far as my friends were concerned," Emsworth said. "Even Martha didn't know the truth. You all thought I was Foreign Office. Well, it wasn't true. I worked for the Secret Intelligence Service for years. Oh, not in the field. I was the kind of office man who sent brave men out to do the dirty work, and they frequently died doing it. One of them was Major Peter Lang."

There was that crawling feeling again. "I see," she said carefully.

"Let me explain. My office was responsible for black operations in Ireland. The people we were after were not only IRA, but Loyalist paramilitaries who, because of threats and intimidation of witnesses, escaped legal justice."

"And what was your solution?"

"We had undercover groups, SAS in the main, who disposed of them."

"Murdered, you mean?"

"No, I can't accept that word. We've been at war with these people for too many years."

She didn't pour the tea but reached for the whiskey and sipped some. "Am I to understand that my son did such work?"

"Yes, he was one of our best operatives. Peter's ability to turn on a range of Irish accents was invaluable. He could sound like a building site worker from Derry if he wanted to. He was part of a group of five. Four men, plus a woman officer."

"And?"

"They all came to an untimely end within the same week. Three men and the woman shot . . ."

"And Peter blown up?"

There was a pause as Emsworth swallowed the whiskey, then he got up and lurched to the sideboard and poured another with a shaking hand.

"Actually, no. That's just what you were told." He swallowed the whiskey, spilling some down his chin.

She drank the rest of her whiskey, took out her silver case, selected a cigarette, and lit it. "Tell me."

Emsworth reached the chair again and sank down. He nodded to the file. "It's all in there. Everything you need to know. I'm breaking the Official Secrets Act, but why should I care? I could be dead tomorrow."

"Tell me!" she said, her voice hard. "I want to hear it from you."

He took a deep breath. "If you must. As you know, there are many splinter groups in Irish politics, both Catholic and Protestant. One of the worst is a nationalist outfit called the Sons of Erin. Years ago, it was run by a man called Frank Barry, a very bad article indeed, and almost unique—he was a Protestant republican. He was eventually killed, but he had a nephew, named Jack Barry, who had an American mother. He'd been born in New York, then gone to Vietnam in 1970, when he was eighteen, on a short-term commission. There was some kind of scandal—apparently he shot a lot of Vietcong prisoners, so they turfed him out quietly."

"And then he joined the IRA?"

"That's about it. He took over where his uncle left off. He's a murdering psychopath, who's been doing his own thing for years now. Oh, and another bizarre thing. Jack's great-uncle was Lord Barry. He had a place on the Down coast in Ulster called Spanish Head. It's part of the National Trust now. His father died when he was a child, and Frank Barry was killed just before his old uncle died."

"Which leaves Jack with the title?"

Emsworth nodded. "But he's never attempted to claim it. He could be proscribed as a traitor to the Crown."

"I wonder. I think executions on Tower Hill went out some years ago. But Tony, please, get to the point."

He closed his eyes for a moment, then sighed and continued. "There was a man called Doolin, who used to drive for Barry. He ended up in the Maze Prison, and we put an informer in his cell. Our man had an ample supply of cocaine and eventually had Doolin telling his life story from birth."

"My God." She was horrified.

"It's the name of the game, my dear. Doolin had not been with Barry during the time in question, but his story was that Barry was on a high as he drove him north to Stramore, on pills and whiskey. He told Doolin he'd just taken out an entire undercover British group thanks to the New York branch of the Sons of Erin, and with a little help from someone he called the Connection. Doolin asked who this Connection was, and Barry said no one knew, but that he was an American, and then he started acting all coy, and talking about the detectives who'd operated out of Dublin Castle for Mick Collins in the old days."

"So the implication was that this Connection was someone very high up and on the inside? But where? How?"

"For years, British Intelligence has had a link with the White House, especially because of the developing peace process. Information has been passed to what were supposed to be friends on a need-to-know basis."

"Including information on my son's group?"

"Yes. I thought that was going too far, but those more important than I, people such as Simon Carter, Deputy Director of the Security Services, ruled against me. And then Doolin was found hanged in his cell."

She went and poured another whiskey and turned. "It gets more like the Borgias every minute. And as you've avoided explaining your remark about Peter not being blown up, I think I'm going to need this." She swallowed half the whiskey. "Get on with it, Tony."

"Yes, well, the Sons of Erin. They passed on information obtained from the Connection. They all had contacts in Dublin and London." He was in agony and showed it. "It's in the files. Everything's in there, all the players, photos, the lot. I copied the Top Secret file and . . ."

"Tell me about Peter."

"They snatched him coming out of a pub in South Armagh, Barry and his men. They tortured him, and when he wouldn't talk, beat him to death. They were building a new bypass road nearby, down to the Irish Republic. It had one of those massive concrete mixers that works all night. They put his body through it."

She sat there, staring, silent, then suddenly swallowed the rest of the whiskey.

He carried on. "They blew up his car with the heavy charge to make it look as if he'd gone that way. I mean, they needed us to know he'd gone but couldn't send us a postcard saying how."

He was a little drunk now. She cried out and put a hand to her mouth as she stood and ran for the door. She made it to the toilet in the hall and vomited into the basin again and again. When she finally wiped her face and came out, Hedley was there.

"You heard?"

"I'm afraid so. Are you okay?"

"I've been better. Tea, Hedley, hot and strong."

She went back into the sitting room and sat down. "What happened? Why was nothing done?"

"They decided to keep it black, which was why you weren't told the truth. We had operatives check Republican circles in New York and Washington. We discovered there was indeed a New York dining club called the Sons of Erin. The names of the members are all in the file, along with their photos. They're prominent businessmen, one's even a US Senator. It all fit. There had already been examples of privileged information from London to Washington ending up in IRA hands."

"But why was nothing done?"

Emsworth shrugged. "Politics. The President, the Prime Minister—no one wanted to rock the boat. Let me tell you something about intelligence work. You think the CIA and the FBI keep the President informed about everything? Hell, no."

"So?"

"It's just the same in the UK. MI5 and MI6 have their own dark secrets, and they not only hate each other, but also Scotland Yard's antiterrorist unit and Military Intelligence. For proof of that, you'll find two interesting entries in the file, one American, the other Brit."

"And what do they refer to?"

"There's a man called Blake Johnson at the White House, around fifty, a Vietnam veteran, lawyer, ex-FBI. He's Director of the General Affairs Department at the White House. Because it's downstairs, it's known as the Basement. It's one of the most closely guarded secrets of the administration, passed from one President to another. It's totally separate from the FBI, the CIA, the Secret Service. Answers only to the President. The whispers are so faint people don't believe it exists."

"But it does?"

"Oh, yes, and the British Prime Minister has his own version. It's there in the file. Brigadier Charles Ferguson runs it."

"Charles Ferguson? But I've known him for years."

"Well, I don't know what you thought he was, but his outfit is known in the trade as the Prime Minister's private army. It's given the IRA a bad time for years. Ferguson has a sizable setup at the Ministry of Defence and is responsible only to the P.M., which is why the other intelligence outfits loathe him. His right hand is an ex-IRA enforcer named Sean Dillon; his left, a Detective Chief Inspector named Hannah Bernstein, granddaughter of a rabbi, if you can believe it. Quite a bunch, huh?"

"But what has this to do with anything?"

"Simply, that the Secret Intelligence Service didn't want Ferguson and company involved, because Ferguson might have told the Prime Minister, and Ferguson has a private contact with Blake Johnson, which meant the President would have been informed and SIS couldn't have that."

"So what happened?"

"SIS started to send the White House mild and useless information and disinformation. There was no way of implicating the members of the Sons of Erin. And then the file was lost." He reached for the folder and held it up. "Except for my copy. I don't know why I took it at the time. Self-disgust, I suppose. Now, I think you should have it."

He started to cough, and she passed him a napkin. He spat into it and she saw blood. "Should I get the doctor?"

"He's calling in later. Not that it'll make any difference." He gave her a ghastly smile. "That's it, then, now you know. I'd better lie down."

He rose, picked up the stick, and walked slowly into the hall. "I'm sorry, Helen, desperately sorry."

"It's not your fault, Tony."

He heaved himself up the stairs and she watched him go. Hedley appeared behind her, holding the file. "I figured you'd want this."

"I surely do." She took it from him. "Let's move on, Hedley. There's only death here."

Back in the Mercedes, as they drove through the narrow lanes, she read through the file, every detail, every photo. Strangely enough, she dwelt on Sean Dillon longer than anyone: the fair hair, the self-containment, the look of a man who had found life a bad joke. She closed the file and leaned back.

"You okay, Lady Helen?" Hedley asked.

"Oh, fine. You can read the file yourself when we're back at South Audley Street."

She felt a flutter in her chest, opened her purse, shook two pills into her hand, and swallowed them. "Whiskey, please, Hedley," she said.

He passed back the silver flask. "What's going on? Are you okay?"

"Just some pills the doctor gave me." She leaned back and closed her eyes. "No big deal. Just get me to South Audley Street."

But Hedley didn't believe her for a moment and drove on, his face troubled.

TWO

At South Audley Street, she sat in the study and worked her way through the file again, studying the text, the photos.

The composition of the Sons of Erin was interesting. There was Senator Michael Cohan, aged fifty, a family fortune behind him derived from supermarkets and shopping malls. Martin Brady, fifty-two, an important official in the Teamsters' Union. Patrick Kelly, forty-eight, a construction millionaire, and Thomas Cassidy, forty-five, who had made a fortune from Irish theme pubs. All Irish Americans, but there was one surprise, a well-known London gangster named Tim Pat Ryan.

She passed the file to Hedley in the kitchen, got a pot of tea, returned to the study, and started on her computer, a recent acquisition and something with which she'd become surprisingly expert, thanks to help from an unexpected source.

She'd asked for advice from the London office of her

corporation, and their computer department had jumped to attention and recommended the best. She'd mastered the basics quickly, but soon wanted more and had consulted the corporation again. The result was the arrival in South Audley Street of a strange young man in a very high-tech electric wheelchair. She'd seen him from the drawing room window, but when she went into the hall, Hedley already had the door open.

The young man on the sidewalk had hair to his shoulders, bright blue eyes, and hollow cheeks. He also had scar tissue all over his face, the kind you got from bad burns.

"Lady Helen?" he said cheerfully as she appeared behind Hedley. "My name's Roper. I'm told you'd like your computer to sit up and do a few tricks." He gave Hedley a twisted smile. "Turn me around, there's a good chap, and pull me up the two steps. That's the one thing these gadgets can't manage."

In the hall, Hedley turned him and she said, "The study."

When they reached it, he looked at her computer setup and nodded. "Ah, PK800. Excellent." He glanced up at Hedley. "I'm not allowed to eat lunch, but I'd love a pot of tea to wash my pills down, Sergeant Major."

Hedley smiled slowly. "Do I say 'Sir'?"

"Well, I did make captain in the Royal Engineers. Bomb disposal." He held up his hands. They saw more scar tissue.

Hedley nodded and went out. Helen said, "IRA?"

Roper nodded. "I handled all those bombs so slickly, and then a small one caught me by surprise in a car in Belfast." He shook his head. "Very careless. Still, it did lead me to a further career, fatherhood being out." He eased his wheelchair to the computer bank. "I do love these things. They can do anything, if you know what to ask them." He turned and looked up at her. "Is that what you want, Lady Helen, for them to do anything?"

"Oh, I think so."

"Good. Well, give me a cigarette and let's see what you know, then we'll see what I can teach you."

Which he did. Every dirty trick in the computer book. By the time he'd finished, she was capable of hacking into the Ministry of Defence itself. And she continued to be an apt pupil until the morning she got yet another phone call—that was three, she thought: these things always seemed to travel in threes—the phone call that said Roper was in the hospital with kidney failure. They'd managed to save him, but he'd gone to a clinic in Switzerland to convalesce, and she'd never heard from him again.

Now, typing from memory, she started trawling through files, entering names as she went. Some were readily available. Others, such as Ferguson, Dillon, Hannah Bernstein, and Blake Johnson, were not. On the other hand, when she cut into Scotland Yard's most-wanted list, there was Jack Barry, complete with a numbered black-and-white photo.

"They got you once, you bastard," she mused. "Maybe we can do it again."

Hedley came in from the kitchen with the file and put it on the desk. "The new barbarians."

"Not really," she said. "Very old stuff, except that in other days we did something about it."

"Can I get you anything?"

"No. Go to bed, Hedley. I'll be okay."

He went reluctantly. She poured another whiskey. It seemed to be keeping her going. She opened the bottom drawer in the desk in search of a notepad and found the Colt .25 Peter had brought back from Bosnia, along with the box of fifty hollow-point cartridges and the silencer. It had been a highly illegal present, but Peter had known she liked shooting, both handgun and shotgun, and often practiced in the improvised shooting range in the barn at Compton Place. She reached down and, almost absentmindedly, picked it up, then opened the box of cartridges, loaded the gun, and screwed the silencer on the end. For a while, she held it in her hand, then put it on the desk and started on the file again.

Ferguson fascinated her. To have known him for so many years and yet not to have known him at all. And the Bernstein woman—so calm to look at in her horn-rimmed spectacles, yet a woman who had killed four times, the file said, had even killed another woman, a Protestant terrorist who had deserved to die.

And then there was Sean Dillon. Born in Ulster, raised by his father in London. An actor by profession, who had attended the Royal Academy of Dramatic Art. When Dillon was nineteen, his father had gone on a visit to Belfast and been killed accidentally in a firefight with British paratroops. Dillon had gone home and joined the IRA.

"The kind of thing a nineteen-year-old would do," she said softly. "He took to the theater of the street."

Dillon had become the most feared enforcer the IRA ever had. He had killed many times. The man of a thousand faces, intelligence sources had named him, with typical originality. His saving grace had been that he would have no truck with the bombing and the slaughter of the innocent. He'd never been arrested until the day he had ended up in a Serb prison for flying in medicine for children (although Stinger missiles had also apparently been involved). It was Ferguson who had saved him from a firing squad, had blackmailed Dillon into working for him.

She went back to the Sons of Erin and finally came to Tim Pat Ryan. His record was foul. Drugs, prostitution, protection. Suspected of supplying arms and explosives to IRA active service units in London, but nothing proved. He had a pub in Wapping called The Sailor, by the river on China

Wharf. She took a London street guide from a shelf, leafed through it, and located China Wharf on the relevant map.

She lit a cigarette and sat back. He was an animal, Ryan, just like Barry and the others, guilty at least by association, and the thought of what had happened to her son wouldn't go away. She stubbed out her cigarette, went to the couch, and lay down.

The great psychologist Carl Jung spoke of a thing called synchronicity, the suggestion that certain happenings are so profound that they go beyond mere coincidence and argue a deeper meaning and possibly a hidden agenda. Such a thing was happening at that very moment at Charles Ferguson's flat in Cavendish Square. The Brigadier sat beside the fireplace in his elegant drawing room. Chief Inspector Hannah Bernstein was opposite, a file open on her knees. Dillon was helping himself to a Bushmills at the sideboard. He wore a black leather bomber jacket, a white scarf at his neck.

"Feel free with my whiskey," Ferguson told him.

"And don't I always," Dillon grinned. "I wouldn't want to disappoint you, Brigadier."

Hannah Bernstein closed the file. "That's it, then, sir. No IRA active service units operating in London at the present time."

"I accept that with reluctance," he told her. "And of course our political masters want us to play it all down anyway." He sighed. "I sometimes long for the old days before this damn peace process made things so difficult." Hannah frowned and he smiled. "Yes, my dear, I know that offends that fine morality of yours. Anyway, I accept your findings and will so report to the Prime Minister. No active service units in London."

Dillon poured another Bushmills. "Not as far as we know."

"You don't agree?"

"Just because we can't see them doesn't mean they're not there. On the Loyalist side, we have the paramilitaries like the UVF, and then the LVF, who've been responsible for all those attacks and assassinations, we know that."

"Murders," Hannah said.

"A point of view. They see themselves as gallant freedom fighters, just like the Stern Gang in Jerusalem in forty-eight," Dillon reminded her. "And then on the Republican side, we have the INLA and Jack Barry's Sons of Erin."

"That bastard again," Ferguson nodded. "I'd give my pension to put my hands on him."

"Splinter groups on both sides. God knows how many," Dillon told them.

"And not much we can do about it at the moment," Hannah Bernstein said. "As the Brigadier says, the powers that be say hands off."

Dillon went to the terrace window and peered out. It was raining hard. "Well, in spite of all that, there are bastards out there waiting to create bloody mayhem. Tim Pat Ryan, for example."

"How many times have we turned that one over," Hannah reminded him. "He's got the best lawyers in London. We'd have difficulty getting a result even if we caught him with a block of Semtex in his hand."

"Oh, sure," Dillon said. "But he's definitely supplied active service units with material in the past, we know that."

"And can't prove it."

Ferguson said, "You'd like to play executioner again, wouldn't you?"

Dillon shrugged. "He wouldn't be missed. Scotland Yard would break out the champagne."

"You can forget it." Ferguson stood up. "I feel like an

early night. Off you go, children. My driver's waiting for you in the Daimler, Chief Inspector. Good night to you."

When they opened the door, it was raining hard. Dillon took an umbrella from the hall stand, opened it, and took her down to the Daimler. She got in the rear and put the window down a little.

"I worry about you when things get quiet. You're at your most dangerous."

"Be off with you before I begin to think you care." He grinned. "I'll see you at the office in the morning."

He kept the umbrella and walked rapidly away. He had a small house in Stable Mews only five minutes away and, as he walked in the front door, he felt strangely restless. The place was small, very Victorian: Oriental rugs, polished wood block floors, a fireplace with an oil painting by Atkinson Grimshaw, the great Victorian artist, above it, for Dillon was not without money, mostly nefariously obtained over the years.

He poured another Bushmills, stood with it in his hand, gazing up at the Grimshaw, thinking of Tim Pat Ryan. He had too much nervous energy to sleep, and he checked his watch. Eleven-thirty. He walked to the sideboard, took the stopper out of the decanter, and poured the glass of whiskey back.

He went to the shelves of books in an alcove, took three out, and opened a flap behind, removing a Walther PPK with a silencer already fitted. He replaced the books, checked the weapon, and put it into the waistband of his jeans, snug against the small of his back.

He took the umbrella when he left the house, for the rain was relentless, and lifted the garage door, where an old Mini Cooper in British racing green waited. The perfect town car, so small and yet capable of over a hundred with the foot down. He got in, drove to the end of the mews, and paused to light a cigarette.

"Right, you bastard, let's see how you're doing," and he drove away.

At the same moment, Helen Lang, dozing on the couch, came awake, aware of Tim Pat Ryan's face, the last photo she had looked at in the file. She sat up, face damp with sweat, aware that in the dream, he had been hurting her, laughing sarcastically. She stood up, went to the desk, and stared down at the open file, and Tim Pat Ryan looked back at her.

She picked up the Colt and weighed it in her hand. There was an inevitability to things now. She stood in the hall, pulled on a trench coat and rain hat, opened the shoulder bag that hung on the hall stand, found some cash, then put the Colt in her pocket, took down her umbrella, and let herself out.

She hurried along South Audley Street, the umbrella protecting her from the driving rain, intending to go to the Dorchester nearby. There were always cabs there, but as it happened, one came along on the other side of the road. She waved him down and darted across.

"Wapping High Street," she said as she climbed inside. "You can drop me by the George," and she sat back, tense and excited.

Hedley had retired with no intention of sleeping, had simply sat in an armchair in the basement flat in the darkness, for some reason afraid for her. He had heard her footsteps in the hall, was up and waiting at the foot of the stairs. As the front door opened and closed, he grabbed his jacket, went up and had the door open. He saw her hurrying along the pavement, the umbrella bobbing, the wave of the hand for the cab. He'd left the Mercedes at the curb and was at it in an instant and switched it on. As the cab passed on the other side of the road, he went after it.

Dillon reached the Tower of London, St. Katherine's Way, and moved into Wapping High Street. He passed the George Hotel, turned into a maze of side streets, and finally parked on a dead-end turning. He got out, locked the door, and walked rapidly between the tall, decaying warehouses, finally turning onto China Wharf. There were few ships now, only the occasional barge, long-disused cranes looming into the sky.

The Sailor was at the end beyond the old quay. He checked his watch. Midnight. Long past closing time. When he paused in the shadows, the kitchen door at one side opened, light flooding out. Tim Pat Ryan and a woman.

"See you tomorrow, Rosie."

He kissed her cheek and she walked away rapidly, passing Dillon safe in the shadows. He moved to the nearest window and peered in. Ryan was sitting at the bar with a glass of beer, reading a newspaper, totally alone. Dillon eased open the kitchen door and entered.

The saloon was very old-fashioned and ornate with a mahogany bar and gilded angels on either side of a great mirror, for *The Sailor* dated from Victorian times, when sailing ships had moved up the Thames by the dozen each day to tie up and unload at the quay. There were rows of bottles on glass shelves, beer pumps with ivory handles. Ryan was proud of it and kept it in apple-pie order. He loved it like this at night, all alone, reading *The Standard* in the quiet. There was a slight eerie creaking of a door hinge, a draft of air that lifted the paper. He turned and Dillon entered the bar.

"God save the good work," Dillon said cheerfully. "There's hope for the world yet. You can actually read."

Ryan's face was like stone. "What do you want, Dillon?"

" 'God save you kindly' was the answer to that," Dillon said. "And you an Irishman and not knowing."

"You've no right to be here. I'm clean."

"Never in a thousand years."

Ryan stood and opened his jacket. "Try me. I'm not carrying."

"I know. You're too clever for that."

"You've no right to be here. You're not even Scotland Yard."

"Granted, but I'm something more. Your own worst nightmare."

"Get out now."

"Before you throw me out? I don't think so." Dillon lifted the bar flap, went behind, reached for a bottle of Bushmills and a glass, and filled it. "I won't drink with a piece of dung like you, but I'll have one for myself. It's cold outside."

Without a flicker of emotion, Ryan said, "I could call the police."

"What for? I'm not carrying myself," Dillon smiled as he lied. "You see, old son, this is a new agenda, what with the Northern Ireland Secretary, Sinn Fein, and the Loyalists with their heads together in Belfast working away at the peace process. I mean, who needs guns anymore? My boss wouldn't like it."

"What do you want?" Ryan asked. "What is this? You've been on my back for years."

"Just making my rounds," Dillon said. "Just to let you know I'm still on your case. The Semtex you supplied the Birmingham and London units—how many bombings was it used for? Three? Four housewives in that shopping mall in Birmingham. We know it was you, we just can't prove it. Yet."

"You can talk. How many did you kill for the cause? For nearly twenty years, Dillon, until you turned traitor."

"But I never sold drugs or used young girls for prostitution," Dillon said. "There's a difference." He swallowed the rest of the Bushmills and put the glass down. "It's cold outside and dark, and I'll always be there in the shadows. To vary an old IRA saying, my day will come."

He turned and walked to the kitchen door and Ryan exploded. "Fuck you, Dillon, fuck you. I'm Tim Pat Ryan. I'm the man. You can't treat me like this," but the kitchen door was already closing softly.

Ryan, beside himself with rage now, hurled back the flap, opened the old-fashioned cash register, fumbled at the back of the drawer, and found the Smith & Wesson .38 pistol he always kept there fully loaded, turned, and headed for the kitchen.

Lady Helen Lang had paid off the cab outside the George Hotel in Wapping High Street. Remembering the street map, she crossed the road and turned into a narrow lane. Hedley, caught behind two cars at a red light, saw her go. He swore softly, took off on the green, and moved into the same lane. But there was no sign of her, even when he turned his lights on fully. It was a maze of decaying warehouses and narrow crisscrossing streets. What in the hell was she playing at in a place like this? Frantic with worry, he started to cruise slowly.

Lady Helen, her umbrella high against the teeming rain, found China Wharf with no trouble. There was a light at the pub window and an old-fashioned gas lamp bracketed to the wall above the painted sign that said "The Sailor." It threw a diffused light to the edge of the wharf, the river black beyond, lights on the far side. She hesitated, uncertain now. A large Range Rover was parked close to the pub entrance, Ryan's, probably.

She stood in the umbrella's shelter, and the kitchen door opened and Dillon came out. She recognized him at once from the file, and, surprised, she drew back. She watched him walk across the wharf and light a cigarette, then the kitchen door opened again and Tim Pat Ryan, also unmistakable, rushed out.

"Dillon, you bastard," he called, and in the light she saw the Smith & Wesson. "Here's for you."

Dillon laughed. "You couldn't hit a barn door, you never could. Someone always had to do it for you."

His hand found the butt of the Walther and he drew it, crouching as Ryan fired wildly. Dillon put a foot forward to steady himself, but there was a puddle of spilled oil there, and he slipped, falling headlong, the Walther skidding away.

Ryan laughed triumphantly. "I've got you now," and he fired again.

Dillon rolled frantically and went over the edge of the wharf, plunging into the dark waters below. It was bitterly cold, and he surfaced to find Ryan peering down.

"So there you are."

He raised his Smith & Wesson, and then Dillon heard a voice call: "Mr. Ryan."

Ryan turned. Dillon heard a muted cough that he recognized as the sound of a silenced pistol, then Ryan came backwards over the edge of the wharf, hit the water beside Dillon, and surfaced with a hole between his eyes. Dillon pushed him away and grabbed for a ring bolt. There was a footfall above, but no one looked over. When the voice spoke again, it was with an Irish accent.

"Are you all right, Mr. Dillon?"

"As ever was, ma'am, and who in God's name might you be?"

"Your guardian angel. Take care, my friend."

He heard her walk away as he swam to a wooden ladder and climbed up. As his head rose above the edge of the wharf, he caught a brief glimpse of her disappearing into the shadows, a dark shape under an umbrella that was gone in a moment.

He pulled himself over and stood up, streaming water. His Walther lay where it had fallen, and Ryan's weapon was close by. He pushed the Walther into his waistband and picked up the Smith & Wesson, went to the edge of the wharf, looked down at Ryan's half-submerged body, then hurled the gun far out into the river.

"And you can chew on that, you bastard," he said, and hurried back to the Mini Cooper.

He had a mobile phone in the glove compartment, got it out, and dialed Cavendish Square. Ferguson sounded irate. "Who is this?"

"It's me," Dillon told him.

"Good God, do you know what time it is? I'm in bed. Can't it wait until the morning?"

"Not really. An old friend just passed on."

Ferguson's voice changed. "Permanently?"

"Very much so."

"You'd better come round, then."

"I need to go home first."

"What on earth for?"

"Because I've been swimming in the Thames, that's why," and Dillon switched off and drove away.

Ferguson thought about it and then phoned Hannah Bernstein. She answered at once. "Are you in bed?"

"No, reading actually. One of those nights. Can't sleep."

"Phone through for one of the emergency cars and get

round here. It would appear our Sean has been involved in some sort of mischief."

"Oh, dear, bad?"

"The graveyard variety, or so it would seem. I'll see you soon."

He put down the phone, got out of bed, and pulled on a robe, then he phoned through to Kim, his Ghurka manservant, woke him up, and ordered tea.

Hedley had almost given up when he saw her at the end of the sidewalk in front of him, and as he coasted toward her, three youths came round the corner wearing bomber jackets and jeans, young animals of the kind to be found anywhere in the world, from New York to London. Hedley heard the ugly laughter and then they were on to her, one of them yanking her purse away. His anger was instant; he braked at the curb and jumped out.

"Leave it."

One of them pushed Helen against the wall and they all turned. The one with the purse said, "Hey, nigger, get out of here, this is none of your business."

They moved in on him and it all came back: 'Nam, the Delta, every dirty trick he'd ever learned. He grabbed the wrist of the one holding the purse, twisted the arm straight, and delivered a hammer blow that snapped the bone. His right elbow went back into the face of the one behind, breaking the nose, and his left foot scraped down the leg of the third, dislodging the kneecap.

They were on the sidewalk, crying in pain. He picked up the purse and took her arm. "Can we go now?"

"My God, Hedley, you don't take prisoners."

"Never could see the point."

"What are you doing here?"

"I heard you leave, so I followed. Then I lost you when you went on foot."

He held the door for her, she slipped in, and he got in behind the wheel. Sounding a little breathless, she opened her purse, took out a bottle, and shook a couple of pills into her palm.

"The flask, Hedley."

"Lady Helen, you shouldn't."

"The flask." Her voice was insistent, and he passed the flask over reluctantly. She drank, washing the pills down, a warm glow spreading through her. "We'll go back to South Audley Street now and pack. Compton Place in the morning."

As he pulled away, he said anxiously, "Are you okay?"

"Never better. You see, I just executed Tim Pat Ryan."

He swerved slightly, then regained control. "You've got to be kidding me."

"Not at all. Let me tell you about it."

Kim opened the door to let Dillon in, and when the Irishman went into the drawing room, he found Hannah Bernstein, wearing a track suit, opposite Ferguson, who wore a robe over his pajamas.

"God bless all here," Dillon said.

"Enough of the stage Irishman, Dillon. Just tell us the worst," Ferguson said wearily.

Dillon did, in a few brief sentences, then went and helped himself to the Bushmills.

"For God's sake, what am I to do with you?" Ferguson demanded. "You know the present political situation. Hands off, no trouble, and yet out of some strange perversity, you went looking for it."

"I only intended to lean on the bastard."

For once it was Hannah Bernstein who spoke up.

"It's no great loss, sir. Ryan was like something from under a stone."

"Yes, I admit to a certain satisfaction," the Brigadier told her. "But how does that fine Special Branch mind intend to handle it?"

"By leaving it alone, sir. Someone will find Ryan down there by the wharf soon enough. That leaves Scotland Yard and a Murder Squad investigation. Let's face it, a piece of filth like Ryan had more enemies than you could count. It's not our problem, sir."

"I agree," Ferguson said.

Dillon shook his head. "Jesus, 'tis the hard woman you are. Whatever happened to that nice Jewish girl I fell in love with?"

"Comes of working with you." She turned to Ferguson. "To business, sir, our business. This woman with the Irish accent may have done us a favor, but I'd like to know who she is. With your permission, I'll trawl all intelligence sources on the computer at the Ministry of Defence and see what I can see."

"Be my guest, Chief Inspector. There may be a Loyalist link here."

"I don't think so," Dillon said. "Most Loyalists have the Ulster accent like my own. Hers was different."

"No matter." Ferguson stood. "You can stay in one of the spare bedrooms, Chief Inspector. I don't want to turn you out again in the rain at this time in the morning."

"Thank you, sir."

He turned. "You, of course, can walk home, Dillon. I mean, you Irish are used to the rain, aren't you?"

"God save your honor, 'tis the grand man you are. I'll take my shoes off at your door, tie them round my neck, and walk barefoot to Stable Mews to save the leather."

Ferguson laughed out loud. "Just go, you rogue, go," and Dillon went out.

In the study at South Audley Street, Lady Helen sat at the desk examining the file, and Hedley came in with tea on a tray. He put the tray down and poured tea into a cup.

She added milk, English style, and sipped it. "Lovely." She leaned over the file. "Strange. Tim Pat Ryan was the last on the list, but the first to go."

"Lady Helen, this can't go on."

"Oh, yes, it damn well can. What's my money buy me that's worth anything, Hedley? Those bastards, all of them, were directly responsible for the butchery of my son. As a result, my husband died an early and unnecessary death, and I'll tell you another thing, old friend. I don't have much time. The pills I've been taking—I have a damaged heart."

He was deeply shocked and sat down. "I didn't realize."

"You do now, so are you with me or against me? You could phone Dr. Ingram and tell him I've gone mad. You could call Scotland Yard and they'd arrest me for murder. It's up to you, isn't it?"

He stood up. "You've been good to me, more than anyone else in my life." He sighed. "I still don't like it, but one thing's for sure. You need someone you can count on, and I'll be there for you, just like you were there for me."

"Bless you, Hedley. Get some sleep and we'll leave for Compton Place in the morning."

He left the room and she sat there, wondering how Dillon was getting on, then she went and lay on the couch and pulled a comforter over herself.

LONDON
WASHINGTON
ULSTER
LONDON

THREE

AT THE MINISTRY of Defence, Hannah Bernstein's efforts at trawling the computer proved useless. She even tried Dublin and British Army Headquarters at Lisburn, in Northern Ireland, but nothing. So, the matter was shelved. Ryan's death was a seven-day wonder; the newspapers spoke of rivalry between gangs in the East End and other parts of London. No one at Scotland Yard was shedding tears, underworld contact proved useless, the case was shelved. Left open, of course, but shelved.

At Compton Place, Helen ate well, took long walks, and got plenty of fresh air. She also practiced at the pistol shooting range in the old barn, a reluctant Hedley giving her the benefit of his expertise. She had never realized how good he was until one afternoon, after supervising her, he picked up a Browning, one of many handguns her husband had accumulated over the years, and loaded it. There were seven cardboard targets at the far end of the barn, each a facsimile of a charging Chinese soldier, a legacy of the old colonel's time in the Korean War.

"I want you to watch."

He was about thirty feet away. His hand swung, he fired rapidly, and shot each target through the head. She was amazed and showed it as the sound died away.

"Incredible."

"But I'm a trained soldier. Now, you, you're good, but handguns are unreliable unless you get close."

"How close?"

He slammed a fresh clip into the butt of the Browning and handed it to her. "Come with me." He led her to the large center target. "Right, put it against his heart and pull the trigger." She did as he ordered. "Now you get it, that close."

"I was about twelve feet away from Ryan."

"Sure, but you could have missed, and he might have got you."

"All right, but I'd still like to return to the table and try again from there."

"Be my guest." The mobile phone on the table rang.

He opened it and passed it to her, and she said, "Helen Lang." After a while, she nodded. "My thanks. I'm so sorry." She closed the phone and looked at Hedley. "Tony Emsworth just died."

"That's a shame. When is the funeral?"

"Wednesday."

"Are we going?"

"Of course." She was calm, but there was pain in her eyes. "I've had enough, Hedley. I think I'll go back inside," and she walked away.

It was a fine sunny morning for the funeral at Stukeley. As it was no more than an hour's drive from London, the church was full, and Helen Lang, sitting on one side of the aisle, was almost amused to find Ferguson, Hannah Bernstein, and Dillon on the other. On her way out, she paused to shake hands with Tony Emsworth's nephew and his wife, who had organized things.

"So nice of you to come, Lady Helen," they chorused. "We've arranged a reception at the Country Hotel just outside the village. Do come."

Which she did. The hotel lounge was crowded. She accepted a glass of indifferent champagne, and then Charles Ferguson saw her and barreled through the crowd.

"My dear Helen." He kissed her on both cheeks. "My God, you still look fifty and that's on a bad day. How do you do it?"

"You were always a charmer, Charles, a glib charmer, but a charmer." She turned to Hannah at his shoulder. "Beware of this one, my dear. I remember when he had an affair with the Uruguayan Ambassador's wife, and her husband challenged him to a duel."

"Now Helen, that's very naughty. This gorgeous creature is my assistant, Detective Chief Inspector Hannah Bernstein, and this Irish rogue is one Sean Dillon, who knew Tony quite well. Lady Helen Lang."

Dillon wore an easy-fitting Armani suit of navy blue. Helen Lang took to him at once as they shook hands. At that moment, someone called to Ferguson, who turned and moved away. Dillon and Hannah went with him.

Ferguson said hello to the man who'd called him and Dillon pulled him around. "Lady Lang, who is she?"

"Oh, I soldiered with her husband in Korea. Her son, Major Peter Lang, was Scots Guards and SAS. One of our best undercover agents in you-know-where. Someone in the IRA got on to him the other year and blew him up. Car bomb."

Hannah Bernstein was talking to someone, and Ferguson was hailed again. Suddenly, it was all too much for Helen Lang and, slightly breathless, she went out onto the terrace in the February sunshine. Dillon saw her go. There was something about her, something he couldn't define, so he went after her.

She was at the terrace balustrade tossing a couple of pills back when Dillon arrived. "Can I get you a glass of champagne?"

"Frankly, I'd rather have whiskey."

"Well, I'm your man. Will Irish do?"

"Why not?"

He was back in a few moments with two glasses. She put hers down, got out her silver case, and held it out. "Do you indulge?"

"Jesus, but you're a wonderful woman." His old Zippo flared and he gave her a light.

"Do you mind if I say something, Mr. Dillon?" she said. "You're wearing a Guards tie."

"Ah, well, I like to keep old Ferguson happy."

She took a chance. "I should mention that I know about you, Mr. Dillon. My old friend Tony Emsworth told me everything, and for very special reasons."

"Your son, Lady Helen." Dillon nodded. "I'm surprised you'd speak to me."

"I believe war should still have rules, and from what Tony told me, you were an honorable man, however ruthless and, may I say, misguided."

"I stand corrected."

He bowed his head in mock humility. She said, "You rogue. You can get me that champagne now, only make sure they open a decent bottle."

"At your command."

He joined Ferguson at the bar. "Lady Helen," he said. "Quite a woman."

"And then some."

The barman poured the champagne into two glasses. "There's something about her, something special. Can't put my finger on it."

"Don't try, Dillon," Ferguson told him. "She's far too good for you."

It was a week later that they flew from Gatwick to New York in one of her company's Gulfstreams, and stayed at the Plaza. By that time, she knew the file backwards, every facet of every individual in it, and had also used every facility available in the company's computer. She had the Colt .25 with her. In all her years flying in the Gulfstreams, she had never been checked by security once.

She knew everything. For example, that Martin Brady, the Teamsters' Union official, attended a union gym near the New York docks three times a week, and usually left around ten in the evening. Hedley took her to a place a block away, then she walked. Brady had a red Mercedes, a distinctive automobile. She waited in an alley next to where he had parked it and slipped out only to shoot him in the back of the neck as he leaned over to unlock the Mercedes.

That had been Hedley's suggestion. He'd heard that the mob preferred such executions with a small-caliber pistol, usually a .22, but a .25 would do, and this would make the police think they had a mob-versus-union problem.

Thomas Cassidy, with a fortune in Irish theme pubs, was easy. He'd recently opened a new place in the Bronx and parked in an alley at the rear. She checked it out two nights running and got him on the third, at one in the morning, once again as he unlocked his car. According to the *New York Times*, there had been a protection racket operating in the area, and the police thought Cassidy a victim. She'd known about all that and his complaints to the police from the computer.

Patrick Kelly, the boss of the construction firm, was even easier. He had a house in Ossining, with countryside all around. His habit was to rise at six in the morning and run five miles. She checked out his usual route, then caught him on the third morning, running with the hood of his tracksuit up against heavy rain. She stood under a tree as he approached, shot him twice in the heart, then removed the gold Rolex watch from his wrist and the chain from around his neck, again at Hedley's suggestion. A simple mugging, was all.

So, everything worked perfectly. She hadn't needed the pills as much, and Hedley, in spite of his doubts, had proved a rock. Am I truly wicked? she would ask herself, really evil? and then recalled reading that in Judaism, Jehovah was not personally responsible for many actions. He employed angels, an Angel of Death, for example.

Is that me? she asked herself. But needing justice, she could not be sorry. So she continued until that rainy night in Manhattan, when she waited for Senator Michael Cohan to come home from the Pierre and was sidetracked.

At the same time that Helen Lang was returning to the Plaza, consoling herself with the thought that she would get Cohan in London, other events were taking place there that would prove to have a profound influence not only on her but on others she already knew.

A few hours after Lady Helen went to bed, Hannah Bernstein entered Charles Ferguson's office at the Ministry of Defence, Dillon behind her.

"Sorry to bother you, sir, but we've got a hot one."

"Really?" He smiled. "Tell me."

She nodded to Dillon, who said, "There's an old mate of mine, Tommy McGuire, Irish American. Been into arms dealing for years. He was caught with a defective brake light in Kilburn last night, and a rather keen young woman probationer insisted on checking the boot of his car."

"Surprise, surprise," Hannah Bernstein said. "Fifty pounds of Semtex and two AK47s."

"How delicious," Ferguson replied. "With his record, which I'm sure he has, that should draw ten years."

"Except for one thing," Hannah told him. "He says he wants a deal."

"Really."

"He says he can give us Jack Barry," Dillon told him.

Ferguson went very still, frowning. "Where is McGuire?"

"Wandsworth," Hannah said, naming one of London's bleaker prisons.

"Then let's go and see what he has to say," and Charles Ferguson stood up.

Wandsworth Prison was one of the toughest in the country, what was known as a hard nick. Ferguson saw the governor and served him with the kind of warrant that made that good man sit up. No one was to see McGuire except those designated by Ferguson, not even Scotland Yard's antiterrorist section, and certainly not any from Military Intelligence in Northern Ireland or the Royal Ulster Constabulary. Any deviation from such a ruling could have sent the governor himself to prison for breaching the Official Secrets Act.

Ferguson, Hannah Bernstein, and Dillon waited in an interview room and a prison officer delivered McGuire and withdrew on Ferguson's nod. McGuire almost had a fit when he saw Dillon.

"Jesus, Sean, it's you."

"As ever was." Dillon offered him a cigarette and said to the others, "Tommy and I go back a long way. Beirut, Sicily, Paris."

"IRA, of course," Ferguson said.

"Not really. Tommy was never one for direct action, but if there was a pound or two in it, he could get you anything. Automatic weapons, Semtex, rocket launchers. Got away with a lot because of his Yank passport and the fact that he always acted as an agent for foreign arms firms. German, French." He gave McGuire a light. "Still fronting for old Jobert out of Marseilles, but then you would. He has the Union Corse protecting him." He turned to Hannah. "Worse than the Mafia, that lot."

"I know who they are, Dillon." She looked at McGuire with total contempt. "Two AK47s and fifty pounds of Semtex were found in your car last night. Samples, I presume? Who were you going to see?"

"No, you've got it wrong," McGuire told her. "I mean, I didn't know they were there. I was told there would be a car waiting for me at Heathrow when I got in. The key under the mat. It must have been a setup."

Ferguson said coldly, "We'll leave now."

"Okay, okay," McGuire said. "You were right about the stuff in the car being samples. They were from Jobert to Tim Pat Ryan. When I flew in, I phoned to arrange the meet and discovered he was dead."

"Indeed he is," Ferguson said. "But there was some mention of Jack Barry."

McGuire hesitated. "Barry used Tim Pat Ryan as a front man in London. It was Ryan who fixed things up. I can give you Jack Barry. I swear it. Just listen."

"Get on with it, then."

Hannah said, "So you know Jack Barry?"

"No, I've never met him."

"Then why are you wasting our time?"

"Let me," Dillon said and offered McGuire another cigarette. "You've never met Jack Barry? That's good, because I have, and he'd cut your balls off for fun if you crossed him. Let me speculate. Jack inherited the Sons of Erin from dear old Frank Barry, alas, no longer with us. The Sons of Erin would kill the Pope, which isn't surprising as our Jack is one of the few Protestants in the IRA. However, he's had a falling-out with Dublin, Sinn Fein, and the peace process. Probably thinks they're a bunch of old women."

"So I hear."

"So let me speculate again. His source of arms from Dublin has dried up. However, there's family money in his background, he's rich in his own right, so he's dealing direct with Jobert. Semtex, guns, whatever, and you're the middleman. Ryan was in London, but alas, no more."

"That's right," McGuire said eagerly. "I'm supposed to meet Barry in Belfast in three days."

"Really?" Ferguson said. "Where exactly?"

"I'm to book in at the Europa Hotel and wait. He'll send for me when he's ready."

"Send for you where?" Hannah Bernstein asked.

"How the hell would I know? I've already told you, I've never even met the guy."

The room went very still. Ferguson said, "Is that really true?"

"Of course it is."

Ferguson stood up. "Serve the warrant on the prison governor, Chief Inspector. Deliver the prisoner to the Holland Park safe house."

She pressed the bell and the prison officer entered. "Take him back to his cell and get him ready to leave."

McGuire said, "Have we got a deal?" but the prison officer was already hauling him out.

Dillon said, "Are you thinking what I am, you old bugger?"

"You must admit it would be a wonderful sting," the Brigadier said. "When is McGuire not McGuire? This could lead us directly to Barry and, oh, how I'd love to lay hands on that one."

"There is one thing, sir," Hannah Bernstein said. "McGuire is an American, and it's too easy to spot a phony American accent. Who are we going to get to play him? We need someone who can pass as American and who can handle himself."

Ferguson said, "That's a good point. In fact, it would seem to me there's an American dimension to all this. I mean, the President wouldn't be too happy to find out in the middle of peace negotiations for Ireland that there was an American citizen trying to sell arms to one of the worst terrorists in the business."

Dillon, devious as usual, was ahead of him.

"Are you suggesting that I speak to Blake Johnson?"

It was Hannah who said, "Well, that's what the Basement is for, sir."

"Who knows?" Dillon said. "Blake might feel like a holiday in Ireland. Who better to play an American than an American—especially one who can shoot a fly at twenty paces?"

"Sometimes you really do get it right, Dillon." Ferguson smiled. "Now let's get out of this dreadful place."

Blake Johnson was still a handsome man at fifty, and looked younger. A Marine at nineteen, he'd left Vietnam with a Silver Star, a Vietnamese Cross of Valor, and two Purple Hearts. A law degree at the University of Georgia had taken him into the FBI. When President Jake Cazalet had been a Senator and subject to right-wing threats, Blake had managed to get to him when a police escort had lost him, shoot two men trying to assassinate him, and taken a bullet himself.

It had led to a special relationship with the man who became President, and an appointment as Director of the General Affairs Department at the White House, a cloak for the President's private investigation squad, the Basement. Already during the present administration, Johnson had proved his worth, had engaged in a number of black operations, some of which had involved Ferguson and Dillon.

It was hot that afternoon, when Blake arrived at the Oval Office and found the President signing papers with his chief of staff, Henry Thornton. Blake liked Thornton, which was a good thing, because Thornton basically ran the place. It was his job to make sure the White House ran smoothly, that the President's programs were advancing through Congress, that the President's image was protected. The pay was no big deal, but it was the ultimate prestige job. Besides, Thornton had enough money from running the family law firm in New York before joining the President in Washington.

Thornton was one of the few men who knew the true purpose of the Basement. He looked up and smiled. "Hey, Blake, you look thoughtful."

"As well I might," Blake said.

Cazalet sat back. "Bad?"

"Let's say tricky. I've had an interesting conversation with Charles Ferguson."

The President sat back. "Okay, Blake, let's hear the worst."

When Blake was finished, the President was frowning and so was Thornton. Cazalet said, "Are you seriously suggesting you go to Belfast, impersonate this McGuire, and try to take Barry on his own turf?"

Blake smiled. "I haven't had a vacation for a while, Mr President, and it would be nice to see Dillon again."

"Dear God, Blake, no one admires Dillon more than I do. The service you and he did for me—rescuing my daughter from those terrorists—I'll never forget that. But this? You're going into the war zone."

Thornton said, "Think about it, Blake. You'd be going into harm's way, and is it really necessary?"

Blake said, "Gentlemen, we've worked our rocks off for peace in Northern Ireland. Sinn Fein have tried, the Loyalists have talked, but again and again it's these terrorist splinter groups on both sides who keep things going. This man, Jack Barry, is a bad one. I must remind you, Mr. President, that he is also an American citizen, a serving officer in Vietnam who was eased out for offenses that can only be described as murder. He's been a butcher for years, and he's our responsibility as much as theirs. I say take him out."

Jake Cazalet was smiling. He looked up at Thornton, who was smiling, too.

"You obviously feel strongly about this, Blake."

"I sure as hell do, Mr. President."

"Then try and come back in one piece. It would seriously inconvenience me to lose you."

"Oh, I'd hate to do that, Mr. President."

In London, in his office at the Ministry of Defence, Ferguson put down the red secure phone and touched the intercom button.

"Come in."

A moment later, Dillon and Hannah Bernstein entered.

"I've spoken to Blake Johnson. He'll be at the Europa Hotel the day after tomorrow, booked in as Tommy McGuire. You two will join him."

"What kind of backup will we have, sir?" Hannah asked.

"You're the backup, Chief Inspector. I don't want the RUC in this or Army Intelligence from Lisburn. Even the cleaning women are Nationalists there. Leaks all over the place. You, Dillon, and Blake Johnson must handle it. You only need one pair of handcuffs for Barry."

It was Dillon who said, "Consider it done, Brigadier."

"Can you guarantee that?"

"As the coffin lid closing."

FOUR

As frequently happened in Belfast, a cold north wind drove rain across the city, stirring the waters of Belfast Lough, rattling the windows of Dillon's room at the Europa, the most bombed hotel in the world. He looked out over the railway station, remembering the extent to which this city had figured in his life. His father's death all those years ago, the bombings, the violence. Now the powers that be were trying to end all that.

He reached for the phone and called Hannah Bernstein in her room. "It's me. Are you decent?"

"No. Just out of the shower."

"I'll be straight round."

"Don't be stupid, Dillon. What do you want?"

"I phoned the airport. There's an hour delay on the London plane. I think I'll go down to the bar. Do you fancy some lunch?"

"Sandwiches would do."

"I'll see you there."

It was shortly after noon, the Library Bar quiet. He ordered tea, Barry's tea, Ireland's favorite, and sat in the corner reading the *Belfast Telegraph.* Hannah joined him twenty minutes later, looking trim in a brown trouser suit, her red hair tied back.

He nodded his approval. "Very nice. You look as if you're here to report on the fashion show."

"Tea?" she said. "Sean Dillon drinking tea, and the bar open. That I should live to see the day."

He grinned and waved to the barman. "Ham sandwiches for me, this being Ireland. What about you?"

"Mixed salad will be fine, and tea."

He gave the barman the order and folded the newspaper. "Here we are again then, sallying forth to help solve the Irish problem."

"And you don't think we can?"

"Seven hundred years, Hannah. Any kind of a solution has been a long time coming."

"You seem a little down."

He lit a cigarette. "Oh, that's just the Belfast feeling. The minute I'm back, the smell of the place, the feel of it, takes over. It will always be the war zone to me. The bad old days. I should go and see my father's grave, but I never do."

"Is there a reason, do you think?"

"God knows. My life was set, the Royal Academy, the National Theater, you've heard all that, and I was only nineteen."

"Yes, I know, the future Laurence Olivier."

"And then my old man came home and got knocked off by Brit paratroops."

"Accidentally."

"Sure, I know all that, but when you're nineteen you see things differently."

"So you joined the IRA and fought for the glorious cause."

"A long time ago. A lot of dead men ago."

The food arrived. A young waitress served them and left. Hannah said, "And looking back, it's regrets time, is it?"

"Ah, who knows? By this time, I could have been a leading man with the Royal Shakespeare Company. I could have been in fifteen movies." He wolfed down a ham sandwich and reached for another. "I could have been famous. Didn't Marlon Brando say something like that?"

"At least you're infamous. You'll have to content yourself with that."

"And there's no woman in my life. You've spurned me relentlessly."

"Poor man."

"No kith or kin. Oh, more cousins in County Down than you could shake a stick at, and they'd run a mile if I appeared on the horizon."

"They would, wouldn't they? But enough of this angst. I'd like to know more about Barry."

"I knew his uncle, Frank Barry, better. He taught me a lot in the early days, until we had a falling out. Jack was always a bad one. Vietnam was his proving ground and the murder of Vietcong prisoners the reason the army kicked him out. All these years of the Troubles, he's gone from bad to worse. Another point, as you've read in his file, he's often been a gun for hire for various organizations around the world."

"I thought that was you, Dillon."

He smiled. "Touché. The hard woman you are."

Blake Johnson entered the Library Bar at that moment. He wore black Raybans, a dark blue shirt and slacks, a gray tweed jacket. The black hair, touched by gray, was tousled. He gave no sign of recognition and moved to the bar.

"Poor sod. He looks as if he's been traveling," Dillon said.

"I've said it before and I'll say it again, Dillon. You're a bastard." She stood up. "Let's go and wait for him."

Dillon called to the barman. "Put that on room fifty-two," and followed her out.

Rain rattled against the window as Dillon got a half bottle of champagne from the fridge and opened it. "The usual Belfast weather, but what can you expect in March?" He filled three glasses and took one himself. "Good to see you, Blake."

"And you, my fine Irish friend." Blake toasted him and turned to Hannah. "Chief Inspector. More fragrant than ever."

"Hey, I'm the one who gets to make remarks like that," Dillon said. "Anyway, let's get down to it."

They all sat. Blake said, "I've read the file on Barry. He's a bad one. But I'd like to hear your version, Sean."

"It was his uncle I knew first, Frank Barry. He founded the Sons of Erin, a rather vicious splinter group from the beginning. He was knocked off a few years ago, but that's another story. Jack's been running things ever since."

"And you know him?"

"We've had our dealings over the years, exchanged shots. I'm not his favorite person, let's put it that way."

"And we're certain that he hasn't met McGuire?"

"So McGuire says," Hannah told him. "And why would he lie? He wants an out."

"Fine. I've memorized all that stuff you sent on the computer. McGuire's past, this French outfit he works for, Jobert and Company, and this Tim Pat Ryan who nearly finished you off in London, Sean. Intriguing that—a woman as executioner. But as for Barry, I'd like to hear about him from you, everything, even if it is on file."

Dillon complied and talked at length. After a while, Blake nodded. "That's about it, then. I'm going to need my wits about me with this one."

"There's one more thing you should know about the Barrys. First of all, they're an old Protestant family."

"Protestant?" Blake was incredulous.

"It's not so unusual," Dillon said. "There are plenty of Protestant nationalists in Irish history. Wolfe Tone, for example. But in addition to that, his great-uncle was Lord Barry, which made Frank Barry the heir, except that he's dead, as you know."

Are you trying to tell me Jack Barry is the heir apparent?" Blake asked.

"His father was Frank's younger brother, but he died years ago, which only leaves Jack."

"Lord Barry?"

"Frank didn't claim the title, and Jack certainly hasn't. It would give the Queen and the Privy Council problems," Hannah told him.

"I just bet it would," Blake said.

"But Jack takes it seriously," Dillon nodded. "An old family, the Barrys. Lots of history there. There's a family estate and castle, Spanish Head, on the coast, about thirty miles north of Belfast. It's owned by the National Trust now. Jack used to rhapsodize about it years ago. So—our Jack's a complicated man. Anyway, let's get down to it. McGuire is to wait in the bar between six and seven for a message that his taxi is ready."

"Destination unknown?"

"Of course. I figure he'll be waiting somewhere in the city, with lots of ways out in case of trouble. The dock area, for example."

"And you'll follow?"

"That's the idea. Green Land Rover." Dillon passed him a piece of paper. "That's the number."

"And what if you lose me?"

"It's not possible." Hannah Bernstein put a black briefcase on the table and opened it. "We've got a Range Finder in here."

"Follow you anywhere. The very latest," Dillon told him.

The Range Finder was a black box with a screen. "Watch this," Hannah said and pressed a button. A section of city streets appeared. "The whole of Northern Ireland's in there."

"Very impressive," Blake told her.

"Even more so with this." She opened a small box and took out a gold signet ring. "I hope it fits. If not, I've got another bug that you can pin anywhere you want."

Blake tried the ring on his left hand and nodded. "Feels good to me."

"No weapon," Dillon said. "There's no way of fooling Barry's people in that respect."

"Then you'd better be right behind me."

"Oh, we'll be there and armed to the teeth."

"So the general idea is I lead you to Barry and you jump him? No police, no backup?"

"This is a black one, Blake. We snatch the bastard, stick a hypo in him, and get him to the airport, where a Lear jet will take us to Farley Field."

"And afterwards?"

"Our Holland Park safe house in London, where the Brigadier will have words," Hannah put in.

"Grand drugs they have these days," Dillon said. "He'll be telling all before you know it, although the Chief Inspector doesn't like that bit."

"Shut up, Dillon," she said fiercely.

Blake nodded. "No need to argue, you two. I'm happy to

be here and the President's happy. No problem. I'm in your hands, and that's good enough for me."

The Library Bar was a popular watering hole for those in business who liked a drink before going home, and was quite busy when Blake went in just after six. Blake sat at the bar, ordered a whiskey and soda, and lit a cigarette. Tense, but in control. For one thing, he had enormous faith in Dillon. It got to six-thirty. He ordered another small whiskey, and as the barman brought it to him, a porter came in with a board saying McGuire.

"That's me," Blake told him.

When he went down the steps to the red taxi, it was raining hard. He got in the back and noticed to his astonishment that the driver was a gray-haired woman.

"Good night to you, sir," she told him in the hard Belfast accent. "You just sit back and I'll tell you where you're going."

She drove away, and Dillon, at the wheel of the Land Rover parked nearby, Hannah beside him, followed.

The woman didn't say a word, simply drove down to the docks, passing through an area of desolation and decaying warehouses. She pulled into a space beside an old Ford Transit van.

"There you are, sir, out you get."

Blake did exactly as he was told. She drove away. Blake stood there in the rain, waiting, and the rear door of the Transit opened and two men jumped out. One was in a bomber jacket, the other, a bearded man, wore an Australian drover's coat down to his ankles. Both carried handguns.

"Mr. McGuire?" the bearded one said. "I'm Daley and this is Bell, Daley and Bell. Sounds like a cabaret act, only it isn't. One wrong move, as they say on television, and you're dead. Assume the position."

Blake put his hands on the Transit and spread his legs. He was thoroughly checked. Satisfied, Daley said, "In the back and let's go."

The bench seats were comfortable enough. Daley sat opposite him and Bell locked the door and got behind the wheel. He drove away.

Blake said anxiously, "Look, what is this? I'm here in good faith and I expected to see Mr. Barry."

"And he can't wait to see you," Daley told him, "but it'll be a while yet, so have a cigarette and enjoy the trip."

Dillon, having seen the taxi turn in before, had pulled into a side turning, gotten out, and approached on foot. Now he ran back to the Land Rover and got behind the wheel.

"They've transferred him. White Ford Transit," he told Hannah, and a few moments later was following it through the evening traffic.

The rain was relentless, and as night fell, it was obvious that they were moving out of town.

"So it's not Belfast," Hannah observed.

"So it would appear."

They came to a place where temporary lights had been set up because of roadworks. The traffic had turned from two lanes to one.

"Damn!" Hannah said.

"Just open the box, girl. We'll be all right."

She had the briefcase on her knee, lifted the lid, and went to work. The map was clear, even more so as it grew darker. The Transit had disappeared, but that didn't matter. Time passed, and they were still going north.

Hannah said, "Where in the hell are we going?"

"God knows," Dillon told her. "But I do have the glimmering of an idea."

"Such as?"

"We're heading north and the Antrim coast is close. What about Spanish Head?"

"But that's crazy. You told us it was owned by the National Trust."

"Yes, but these places don't open to the public 'til Easter."

"You can't be serious."

"Just keep your eye on that screen and we'll see."

There were a couple of windows in the Transit. They were proceeding along a coast road and, for the moment, the rain had stopped, and the sky was stormy with a half-moon. They finally turned into a side road and paused at the gate. A notice said "Spanish Head National Trust."

There was a cottage on the other side, a light at the window. Bell sounded the horn, and a door opened and an old man appeared. He hesitated, and Bell called, "Punch the bloody button, Harker, and let us in."

The gate was obviously electronic. The old man opened a box by the door, fiddled inside, the gate swung back, and Bell drove through. Blake saw a castle above steep cliffs, towers, battlements, all very spectacular. It was only as they got closer that Blake saw that it was only a large country house built in nineteenth-century Gothic style. The Transit came to a halt, Bell got out, came round, and opened the door. Blake followed Daley out and found himself in a courtyard.

"This way, Mr. McGuire," Daley told him.

Bell opened a massive oak front door and led the way in. There was a huge entrance hall, a flagged floor, an open fireplace, and flags draped from poles: the Irish Republican tricolor, the Union Flag, and, surprisingly, an old flag of the Confederate States of America.

"This way."

Daley led the way up the sweeping stairs and Blake followed, Bell bringing up the rear. They passed along a wide corridor, portraits everywhere, and Daley finally opened a great mahogany door. They passed into a library. There were more portraits, a log fire in a great fireplace, book-lined walls, and French windows standing open. A man stood there, looking out, a glass of wine in his hand. He was tall, with good shoulders, wearing a black sweater and jeans. When he turned, the face was handsome enough, dark, brooding, and yet cruel.

"Mr. McGuire? Jack Barry."

The voice was still American, and Blake said, "My pleasure." He tried to sound a little weak and shaken. "I was kind of worried."

"Oh, stuff all this pretense, Mr. Johnson. I know very well who you are. Blake Johnson, President Jake Cazalet's personal minder. You run the Basement, isn't that what you call it? Here, have a glass of Sancerre." He took a bottle from an ice bucket, filled a glass, and offered it. "There you go. I have it on good authority that the real McGuire is in the hands of Brigadier Charles Ferguson and Sean Dillon. And that my other dealer in London, Tim Pat Ryan, is very dead indeed."

Blake savored the wine. "Eighty-six, maybe eight."

"Seven," Barry said. "So you know my old friend Sean Dillon?"

"Friend?"

"A slight exaggeration. However, let's get down to facts. I have excellent sources, but there are things you could tell me, including details about that old bastard Charles Ferguson's operations."

"Well, I guess you can kiss my ass," Blake told him.

Barry poured another glass of Sancerre. "I thought you might take that attitude." He nodded to Daley. "I think the

Soak Hole might do here, Bobby. It's cold out there and starting to rain again. Try him for an hour and see where it gets us."

It was raining hard as Daley and Bell took Blake down through the grounds toward the cliffs, and sheet lightning flickered over the water, the waves raging below. They started down a track, Bell leading the way, a lamp in his hand. Halfway down, he paused.

"This is it."

White spray erupted with a hollow roar. Daley pushed Blake forward. "In you go. There's a ledge ten feet down. You'll be okay. As it's a cold night, I'll let you keep your clothes on."

Blake hesitated, then started down. There were steps of a kind, then a platform. The spray cascaded up and he caught his breath. God, but it was cold.

Daley said to Bell, "Watch him, I'll be back."

He started up to the castle.

"I was right, then," Dillon said as he and Hannah approached the castle. "Spanish Head it is."

He coasted up to the gate and paused, the engine still ticking over. Hannah got out and tried to open the gate without success.

"No joy, it must be electronic. Give me a moment."

There was a small stile to one side intended for pedestrians. As she climbed over, the cottage door opened and an old man appeared. "Here, you can't do that. This is private."

"Not anymore it isn't." She took her Walther from her shoulder bag and put it under his chin. "Do whatever you have to to open the gate and be quick about it."

He was terrified and showed it. He went to the box and pressed the button and the gate opened. Dillon drove through, pulled in to a parking spot to one side, and switched off.

He got out and pushed the old man onto the porch. "Now let's see if I've got this right. You'll be the caretaker. Is anyone else in the cottage?"

"I'm a widower."

"And your name?"

"Harker, John Harker."

"Well, I think you've been a naughty boy, Mr. Harker. Closed from September 'til Easter, and you allow unauthorized guests like my old friend Jack Barry."

"I don't know what you mean." The old man was shaking.

Dillon produced his Walther and said cheerfully, "Maybe your memory will improve if I stick this behind your right kneecap and pull the trigger."

Harker gave in instantly. "His lordship's at home, I'll grant you that, and what can I do about it, an old man like me?"

"His lordship, is it?" Dillon laughed. "How often is he here?"

"On and off during the winter months, and there are others who know, estate workers from the village."

"Who will keep their mouths firmly shut, I shouldn't wonder," Hannah said.

"What else can we all do?" the old man said. "These are desperate times, and his lordship is not a man to cross."

"A bullet in the head, is it?" Dillon asked.

"No need for that, not with the Soak Hole to teach a man a lesson. Tim Leary died in it last year."

"And what would the Soak Hole be?"

"It's a kind of funnel in the cliffs. The sea explodes up through it. His lordship puts people down there to teach them a lesson."

"Good God!" Hannah said.

"I shouldn't imagine he's got anything to do with it," Dillon told her and turned to Harker. "To business. A white Ford Transit van. It arrived a little earlier, right?"

Harker nodded. "It went down to Belfast this afternoon. Came back about forty minutes ago."

"Who was in it?"

"Bobby Daley and Sean Bell, two of his lordship's men, when it went, just Bell at the wheel when it came back."

"And you were curious and went up the drive to see what was what."

Harker was startled. "How did you know?"

"I know everything. What happened?"

"I was some distance away, but I saw Bell open the van's rear door and Bobby Daley got out with another man, and the three of them went inside."

"And you, being curious, went closer, stood under a tree or whatever, and waited."

Again, Harker was astonished. "And how would you be knowing that?"

"Because I'm Irish, you daft bugger, I'm from County Down, I have the second sight. There's also the fact that you're wet through because you were standing in the rain. Now who does Barry have up at the castle?"

"Only Daley and Bell."

"Good man. Now we'll walk up there nice and quiet and you lead the way. Some suitable back path would do nicely."

"Anything you say, sir."

Lamps set in various parts of the grounds gave a certain amount of light as they walked along a narrow path through shrubbery and lush woodland, the castle battlements looming beyond. Suddenly, Harker paused.

"I think someone's coming," he whispered.

They moved into the trees, and a moment later, Daley moved out of another path and started toward the castle. "That's him," Harker whispered. "That's Bobby."

Daley carried on toward the castle and Dillon said, "Where's he been, that's the thing?"

"There're only the cliffs and the Soak Hole down there."

Dillon turned to Hannah. "Why would Barry not make the meet in Belfast? Why go to all the trouble of hauling Blake up here? It doesn't make sense."

"Only if it stinks," she said.

"I agree." Dillon turned to Harker. "The Soak Hole it is, and be discreet."

Sean Bell sheltered under a tree at the side of the track, the lamp on the ground at his feet. He was distinctly unhappy, already wet from driving rain, and couldn't even smoke, since the cigarettes disintegrated in seconds. There came a hollow booming sound like some dinosaur in pain, as the Soak Hole erupted high into the air. He wondered how the American was doing. He wouldn't last long on a night like this.

There was a click as the silencer on the end of Dillon's Walther nudged Bell's right ear, and Dillon said, "The hard way, Mr. Bell, is to blow your brains out, so be good."

"Who the fug are ye?" Bell gasped, as Dillon ran his hands over him and recovered a .38 revolver.

"Webley .38. Long past its sell-by date. You must be hard up, you lot," and he stuffed the weapon in a pocket of his bomber jacket. "Dillon's the name."

"Oh, my God!"

"Tonight's bad news for you. I suspect you've got an American friend of mine somewhere nearby."

He ground the Walther in again, and Bell cried out in

pain. "He's in the Soak Hole. The entrance is just down the track."

"And why would he be in there?"

"Barry knew he wasn't what he seemed. We were waiting for him."

"Really? Well, lead the way."

Bell picked up the lamp and walked down the track, stepping back as the Soak Hole thundered white spray high into the night.

"Watch him," Dillon told Hannah, and walked to the edge of the steps leading down. "Are you still there, Blake? It's Dillon."

Blake, on the platform and hanging on to a rusting iron bolt, colder than he had ever been in his life, shouted back, "What kept you?"

"Come away up," Dillon called.

A couple of minutes passed, and then Blake appeared, climbing slowly. "Jesus, Dillon, that was bad. I feel terrible. Takes me back to a tidal swamp I once spent six hours in back in Vietnam."

"What happened?"

"Barry knew everything. My name, the President, the Basement. He said he had excellent sources but wanted any facts I had to disclose about you and Ferguson."

"Let's go up to the castle and oblige him."

"Only too happy," Blake said. "Just one thing." He turned to Bell, who was standing at the top of the steps. "Here's for you, you bastard." He punched Bell very hard, and he went backwards headfirst with a cry. A moment later, the Soak Hole fountained.

"Can we go now?" Dillon asked.

"My pleasure."

Blake led the way up to the courtyard and paused at the massive front door. Dillon said to Harker, "Down to the gate, Da, sit inside and hold your tongue. Do that and I won't shoot you. Is it a bargain?"

The old man scuttled away. Blake said, "Has anyone got a spare pistol here?"

Dillon produced the Webley. "I think this should be in a museum, but it will probably do the job."

"Then let's get on with it," Blake said and opened the door.

In the library, Daley put another log on the fire, and Barry stood by the French windows staring out as the rain drove against them. "A desperate night, Bobby. I wonder how Mr. Johnson is getting on."

"Better than you think," Blake said, easing the door open and leading the way in.

They all stood in a kind of tableau, and Barry threw back his head and laughed. "Dear God, it's you, Sean."

"As ever was, Jack, come to haunt you. Charles Ferguson wants words, even more so after what I've heard from my friend here. An inside source of information? It could only be at White House level. You really are a naughty boy."

"Always was, Sean, always was. I presume Bell has gone the way of all flesh?"

"Absolutely."

"Ah, well, comes to us all. Pour Mr. Johnson a brandy, Bobby, a large one. I expect he needs it." He raised his glass to Blake. "One old Vietnam hand to another."

"Not really. I killed, but not in the way you did." Blake took the brandy from Daley and looked at the paintings on the wall. "Would that be a Confederate uniform there?"

Barry looked at the portrait. "Yes. The stout gentleman on the end there was Francis the First. Made his money in Barbados in the eighteenth century. Sugar and slaves. Came back and bought a title. They were all called Francis. That's where Frank comes from."

"Until you?"

"Yes, Jack for John. The one who fought for the Confederacy was killed at Shiloh. In letters home he said he'd chosen that side because gray suited his eyes."

"That would figure, if he's anything like you," Blake said. "But let's get down to business. You knew I was coming in place of McGuire."

"What happened to him?"

"As you well know, he's in a safe house in London emptying his guts," Hannah said.

"The dog."

"Yes," Dillon told him. "But they usually are. So, you know everything, it appears."

"Always did, you know that, always one step ahead. That's what keeps me going."

"And you wanted information about Brigadier Ferguson, so we hear," Hannah said.

"Well, I would, wouldn't I. Always the old fox, that one."

"You'll be seeing him soon enough," Dillon told him. "I'm sure you'll have an interesting conversation."

"I'm certain we will." Barry turned to the ice bucket and poured more Sancerre. He moved and stood at one side of the fireplace. "Give Mr. Johnson another brandy, Bobby. I'm sure he could do with it."

Daley went to the sideboard and reached for the brandy decanter, then he pulled open a drawer and turned, a gun in his hand.

"There you go. Tables turned, I think," Barry said.

But Dillon's hand was already under the back of his bomber jacket; his hand swung up, and there was a dull thud as he shot Daley in the heart, hurling him back against the sideboard, still clutching the decanter as he crashed to the floor.

Hannah cried out, and Dillon turned to see a section of the wood paneling beside the fireplace swing open, and Barry simply stepped back. There was a click as Dillon ran to it, but the paneling was immovable.

"Damn his eyes!" Blake said.

"I should have known," Dillon told him. "He'd never have used this place without an escape route or two. It's a rabbit warren. We'll never catch him now."

Hannah looked down at Daley. "What about him? Should we call the RUC?"

"That's the last thing we need." There was an Indian rug on the floor, and Dillon rolled the body up in it. "Help me get him on my shoulder."

Blake did as he was told. "Now what?"

"Let's get out of here. I'll dispose of the evidence. He can join Bell in the Soak Hole."

He led the way down to the hall, and Blake got the massive door open. Rain dashed in and Dillon said, "The grand night it is for dirty work. I'll see you at the gate," and he strode away.

When Blake and Hannah reached the cottage, there was no sign of Harker, although the light was still on. They got into the Land Rover out of the rain, and Dillon appeared a few minutes later.

"All done and dusted. The paths of the wicked all reach a sticky end." He went to the cottage door and kicked on it. It opened and Harker peered out. "We lost them," Dillon told him. "His lordship and Daley took off through some secret passage."

"There's a few of those up there."

"Anyway, no need for Barry to know of your part in this.

Keep your mouth shut and you'll be all right. It never happened."

"Damn right I'll keep my mouth shut. I'll open the gate for you."

Dillon got behind the wheel of the Land Rover and drove out and started along the coast road.

"Now what?" Hannah demanded.

"You can call the Lear jet to pick us up in the morning. Ferguson likes to hear bad news as soon as possible, you know that." He spoke over his shoulder to Blake. "What about you? Is it back to Washington?"

"No, I think I should follow this through. I'll come to London with you and help you brave Ferguson's wrath."

"Right, then next stop the Europa and some decent room service."

FIVE

THE LEAR JET flew over at midnight and they found Flight Lieutenants Lacey and Parry waiting for them, ready for a seven o'clock departure. It was all very official. The Lear carried RAF rondels, and Lacey and Parry wore RAF flying overalls with rank insignia.

"Nice to see you again, Mr. Johnson," Lacey said and turned to Dillon, who was last up the steps. "Are we going into action again, Sean?"

"Well, let's put it this way. I wouldn't book that holiday in Marbella," Dillon said and went up the steps.

They took off and climbed to thirty thousand and turned across the Irish Sea. Hannah found the tea and coffee flasks and Dillon three cups.

"You said Ferguson expects us like yesterday at the Ministry of Defence?"

"That's what he said."

"How did he sound?"

"Neutral."

Dillon poured tea into his cup. "Oh, dear, that's when he's at his worst."

The big surprise was Ferguson in the Daimler limousine waiting at Farley Field. Lacey took them across, providing what shelter he could with a large golf umbrella.

"Get in, for heaven's sake, and let's get on with it. Nice to see you, Blake. Sit beside me." Hannah and Dillon took the jump seats, and she pressed the button to close the dividing window. "Right, let's hear the worst," Ferguson carried on. "You do the talking, Dillon, the Irish are good at that."

"You'd never believe his sainted mother was from Kerry," Dillon told Blake, "but there you go and here I go."

He went through the events in Belfast and at Spanish Head, leaving nothing out. Ferguson listened, his face grave until Dillon was finished.

"What a mess. He actually knew you weren't McGuire, and that was only arranged within the last few days."

"More than that, Brigadier. He knows about the Basement, boasted about his inside source."

"But what could that be?"

"Has to be someone in the White House. A lot of people operate out of there one way or another."

"But the Basement is supposed to be very hush-hush," Ferguson said.

"Just like your outfit, Brigadier, but how many people know about it?" Blake observed. "Computer accessing is another problem. We've even had kids hack in."

"So have we," Ferguson agreed.

"And we do ourselves when we can, sir," Hannah pointed out. "Paris, Moscow . . ."

"Even Washington," Dillon said.

"So, you've no clues?" Ferguson asked Blake.

"Not really. I had to use the Travel Bureau, that's a polite name for the Forging Department. I wanted a passport as Tommy McGuire in case Barry wanted to see it. Then there were travel arrangements. Plane tickets, the room at the Europa, all as McGuire."

"And all on computers," Hannah said.

"But it still leaves the one incontrovertible fact that he knew who you were. I don't like it." Ferguson showed a spark of anger. "Don't like it at all. And you can bet the President won't like it either."

"You can say that again," Blake said with feeling.

Ferguson nodded. "So what's to be done?"

It was Dillon who said, "I've been thinking about McGuire. There might be more than he's told us."

"What makes you think that?" Hannah asked.

"There always is with people like him. You've been a copper long enough to know that." He turned to Ferguson. "Let me have a go at him."

"Does that mean beating it out of him?" Hannah demanded.

"No. Just putting the fear of God in him."

Ferguson nodded. "Right, it's all yours."

"Good," Dillon said. "This is what we'll do . . ."

The safe house at Holland Park was a mid-Victorian mansion behind high walls. It looked innocuous enough but had the kind of security that made it impregnable. McGuire had been amazed at the comfort. His own room, en suite, television, excellent food. What he didn't know was that he was on screen even when he went to the toilet.

Occasionally he was taken down to a drawing room that was very pleasantly furnished with an open fire, and an even larger television. He was served a more than decent meal. There was even a bottle of Chablis. The guard was just as decent, Mr. Fox, who didn't wear a uniform, just a navy blue suit. Of course, McGuire didn't realize that Fox carried a .38 Smith & Wesson Magnum in a holster under his left arm, just as he didn't appreciate that the large gold-framed mirror provided a perfect view for those in the next room, which on this occasion were Ferguson, Blake, and Hannah Bernstein.

They watched McGuire finishing his lunch, Fox standing against the wall. There was a knock at the door, Fox unlocked it, and Dillon walked in.

"Well, you seem to be doing all right, Tommy," he said.

McGuire stared at him. "It's you. What do you want?"

"Oh, just to bring you up to date on what happened in Ulster." He lit a cigarette, took the half-bottle of wine from its bucket, and poured it into McGuire's empty glass. He sampled it. "Not bad. Yes, we missed out on Jack Barry. He managed to fly the coop. We got rid of two of his men, Daley and Bell. Do they mean anything to you?"

"Never heard of them."

"The strange thing was that Barry was expecting my American friend Blake, the man who was impersonating you. He knew everything about him, knew he worked for the President, claimed to have inside intelligence sources."

"Look, none of this has anything to do with me," McGuire said. "I told you everything I know about Barry. If you lost him, that's your problem."

"Well, a problem it certainly is, old son, but yours, not mine. You see, I think you're a terrible liar. I believe you know a lot more than you're telling."

"That's bollocks. I've told you everything I know."

"Really? All right, we'd better let you go."

"Let me go?" McGuire was astonished.

"Well, you did put us on to Barry. Bad luck he slipped us, but not your fault, and let's face it, it isn't the kind of thing we would want advertised in open court." He nodded to Fox. "Bring in the Chief Inspector."

"Certainly, sir."

Fox went and opened the door and called and Hannah entered, an official-looking document in one hand. "Collect the prisoner's things and deliver him to Heathrow Airport," she told him and turned to McGuire. "Thomas McGuire, I have here a warrant for your deportation as an unwanted alien. According to records, you entered the country on an illegal flight from Paris and you will be returned there. I have no idea how the French authorities will treat you."

"Now look here," McGuire began, and Dillon interrupted him.

"Good luck, Tommy. You're going to need it."

"What do you mean?"

"Jack Barry has a lot of friends all over Europe and the Middle East—the PLO, the Libyans, people like that. He's even done business with the Mafia over the years."

"What's that got to do with me?"

"He knows my friend Blake Johnson wasn't you, so I presume he'll want to know what you were playing at. He's going to want your balls, Tommy, so good luck."

He turned away, and McGuire said, "For God's sake, he's a sadist, that one. I mean, he killed one guy in Ireland by putting him through a cement mixer."

There was silence. Hannah said, "Is that a fact, Mr. McGuire?"

He looked at her, then Dillon, then sat down. "I'm not stirring."

"Then talk," Dillon told him.

The door opened, and Ferguson and Blake entered. "All right, man, get on with it," Ferguson said.

"Give me a cigarette, for God's sake."

Dillon offered him one from his old silver case and gave

him a light. "Let it all hang out, Tommy. You'll feel much better."

"As I told you, I'd never met Barry personally, but he dealt with Jobert in Marseilles and I worked for Jobert, so I used to meet guys Barry sent over from Ireland on arms business. There was one, a man called Doolin, who I had dealings with in Paris. Patrick Doolin."

Dillon broke in. "I know that name. Found hanging in his cell at the Maze Prison."

"That's him," McGuire said. "We went out on the town one night in Paris, ended up having supper on one of those dining boats that ply up and down the river, decent food, plenty to drink. He got pissed out of his mind. Started going on about Barry and what an animal he was."

The story had a certain fascination and they all waited. "Doolin said he used to chauffeur for Barry. I think it must have been about three years ago it happened. He was driving him somewhere at night and Barry was drunk and on something, I mean really high. He told Doolin he'd just stiffed five British Army undercover agents, four men and a woman. Said he'd put one of them through a cement mixer. I think the others were shot. I can't recall."

"My God," Hannah said.

"What else?" Dillon was relentless.

"You know he runs the Sons of Erin? He said that the coup was thanks to the New York branch, with a little help from someone he called the Connection."

"The Connection?" Ferguson asked.

"Yes, someone way on the inside. Apparently, he told Doolin it was just like in the old days, when Mick Collins had detectives at Dublin Castle working for him."

"It would seem he told Doolin a lot," Hannah said.

Ferguson nodded. "Keep him safe, Mr. Fox. We'll be in touch."

"Brigadier."

Ferguson turned to the others. "All right, let's go."

Sitting in his office an hour later with Blake, Ferguson was surprised when Hannah came in, Dillon behind her.

"I've found something, sir," Hannah told him. "Three years ago, an undercover squad in Ulster was taken out, four men and a woman. The leader, Major Peter Lang, was the subject of a car bomb so huge no remains were found. Here are the details on the other four. It has to be what Barry was referring to."

"Dear God, Peter Lang, my old friend Roger Lang's boy," Ferguson said. "You met his mother, Lady Helen Lang, at Tony Emsworth's funeral."

"The lovely lady on the terrace," Dillon said. "With that kind of proof, I'd say we're on to something. So what's the next move?"

"I think I should have words with the President," Blake said.

Ferguson shook his head. "Not yet, Blake. I know you're a free agent, but please hold back, just for now. There are things I'd like to do here." He turned to Hannah. "Was there any backup information, any connection with Barry?"

"No, sir, and I must tell you I've accessed both MI5 and MI6."

He sat there, brooding. "Phone Simon Carter at once. His ears only. Ask him what he knows about Jack Barry and the Sons of Erin and any sort of inside leak, possibly from the White House."

"Certainly, sir." She went out.

Ferguson stood up. "There's a good canteen here, Blake. Let's get a sandwich and await events."

• • •

They were sitting at a corner table half an hour later when
Hannah came in and sat down. "He was his usual irate self,
sir. Well, almost."

"What do you mean?" Ferguson asked.

"He seemed sort of shocked. In a way, I got the feeling
he knew all about it, but he couldn't have."

"That devious bugger could lie to the Almighty," Dillon
told her.

"I must say, he came back damn quick. Gave me Jack
Barry's history and that's all, everything we already know."

"And nothing about Washington or the Sons of Erin?"
Blake turned to Dillon. "Is Carter still Deputy Director of
the Security Services?"

"Absolutely."

"Then if he doesn't know anything . . ."

Ferguson said to Hannah. "Get him on your mobile."

She did so and passed it across. "Simon," Ferguson said,
"I must see you. The terrace at Westminster in thirty minutes."

"Now look here, Ferguson . . ."

"Just finalizing a report for the Prime Minister. I'd welcome your input," and Ferguson switched off and sat there
thinking about it. Finally, he said, "I'll take you, Blake, as
the President's representative. That will impress him, and
you, Dillon, because you always unbalance him."

"If ever a man hated me, it's dear old Carter."

"Yes, well, I like to have him on edge." Ferguson turned
to Hannah. "You're the computer genius, my dear. Check
everything that could possibly have a significance." He
stood up. "Let's be on our way, gentlemen."

The House of Commons, together with the House of Lords,
is a remarkable institution, and not only because of its extraordinary history as the seat of government for the United

Kingdom. Its location on the Thames is unique, but it is its facilities which are extraordinary. Twenty-six restaurants and bars provide not only excellent food but some of the cheapest in London.

Even someone with Ferguson's pull had to stand in line as the queue inched forward to be checked thoroughly by the largest policemen in London. They finally made the Central Lobby, moved in through a maze of corridors, and found the entrance to the Terrace overlooking the Thames.

It was the chilly end of March weather, but sunny enough for them to have the awnings open. There were plenty of people about, members of the House of Lords at one end, members of the Commons at the other, foreign visitors and guests of every description.

"Thank God you're wearing a jacket, Dillon. Makes a change. At least you look respectable."

Dillon waved to a waiter who had glasses of champagne on a tray. "Are you with the Japanese delegation, sir?"

"What else?" Dillon passed a glass to Blake, another to Ferguson, who accepted with reluctance, and took one himself.

They stood at the parapet and looked down at the Thames. "How good is the security?" Blake asked.

"Five-knot current down there," Dillon said. "Even a Navy SEAL would have problems."

"But not this little bastard," Ferguson told Blake. "Floated in here the other year when your President and the PM were meeting, just to show Carter the security precautions were no good. Turned up as a waiter and served them canapés."

Blake exploded into laughter. Dillon said, "Carter was not best pleased."

"Well, he wouldn't be, would he?" Blake said, and at that moment Carter appeared.

He made a face when he saw Dillon. "For God's sake, Ferguson, do we have to have this little swine here?"

"God save your honor," Dillon told him. " 'Tis a kindness for you to see me, a grand man like yourself."

"Dillon is here because I need him, so that's that. This is Blake Johnson, President Jake Cazalet's personal security man."

"Yes, I know of Mr. Johnson." Carter shook hands reluctantly.

"To business," Ferguson said. "Chief Inspector Bernstein asked you for information relevant to Jack Barry and the Sons of Erin."

"I told her everything I know. She's probably checked it out for herself on our computer. I know you do that."

"And so do you. So, you know nothing about an American connection with Barry, possibly in the White House?"

"If I had, I'd have told you."

Ferguson turned to Blake. "You do the honors. Tell him everything."

When Blake was finished, Carter was remarkably calm. "Much of this could be nonsense. Why believe McGuire? Why accept what the wretched Doolin said?"

"On the other hand, when Blake was in Barry's hands, Barry said he had excellent sources," Dillon pointed out.

"And he must have, because he was expecting me. He knew I wasn't McGuire," Blake put in.

Carter seemed to have nothing to say, and Ferguson waved to the waiter with the champagne. "Another, gentlemen. Even you might do with one, Carter."

"If you say so."

"One final point. The undercover group wiped out by Jack Barry three years ago. Major Peter Lang and company? You made no mention of that to Chief Inspector Bernstein."

"Because she didn't ask me. The facts are there on the

computer for all to see. However, there has never been any suggestion that Barry and the Sons of Erin had anything to do with that affair. Trawl all you like, Ferguson, there is no such file. Now, is there anything else? I'm a busy man."

"Not really. I'll tell the Prime Minister you've been as co-operative as usual."

Carter frowned. "You mean to involve the PM in this matter?"

"You, of all people, know my unique position in that respect. The Prime Minister's private army, isn't that what you call my department?"

"Damn you!" Carter exploded and turned on his heel.

"There you go, then," Dillon grinned. "What next?"

"I've already fixed a meet with the Prime Minister this afternoon," Ferguson said. "I'll take you in with me so that he can share your input, Blake. You, Dillon, will stay in the car as usual."

Dillon smiled at Blake. "Nothing changes and I know my place."

Back at the Ministry of Defence, they found Hannah Bernstein still at the computer. "Anything to report?" Ferguson asked.

"I did come across one interesting thing, sir. According to various sources, the Security Services have been less than generous over the past two years with sensitive information having to do with Irish operations as regards our American friends. The word was that such material did seem to end up in the hands of Sinn Fein on a regular basis."

"So what's been happening?" Ferguson asked.

"Oh, the general flow hasn't stopped, but it would seem that the quality of the material has left a great deal to be desired. Frankly, it's been the kind of stuff you could get from the political page of the better newspapers. A few tidbits thrown in occasionally . . ."

Dillon cut in. "But no more details of undercover operations."

"So it would appear."

"But if this was an official SIS attitude," Blake said, "wouldn't you have known about it?"

"I'm the last person they'd tell," Ferguson said. "They've always hated my privileged position with the Prime Minister. Placed every obstacle in my way, offered as little cooperation as they've been able to get away with."

"I know the feeling," Blake said. "I have my own problems with the CIA and the FBI."

"So what we're saying is that Carter and his people knew about what happened three years ago," Dillon said. "Maybe not straightaway, but at some stage."

"I'd say so." Ferguson nodded and turned to Hannah. "Put your fine Cambridge mind on it, Chief Inspector."

"We have two facts that are certain, sir. Something made them start treating our American friends with enough suspicion to offer innocuous material and disinformation. I'd say at an earlier stage they probably heard about what happened but decided it was simply beyond proof."

"And the second fact?"

"That there isn't a file, at least not now. If the Deputy Director says so, I believe him."

"Do you?" Blake asked Ferguson.

"Oh, yes, it fits. They play their own games, you see. With the peace process so important, they would decide they didn't want to give the Prime Minister a problem, because that would have involved the President and given *him* a problem. It would have also brought in me and involved you."

"The bastards," Blake said.

"Yes, but they weren't losing anything if they were sending your people useless information," Ferguson said. "We dealt with the Nazis during the Second World War in the same way, conned the Abwehr rotten."

"All the same, it makes you wonder who's running the country," Dillon said.

Hannah nodded. "So what do you intend?"

"To see the Prime Minister. I've no choice, just as Blake has no choice. President Cazalet will expect a report on the Barry affair, and I can't see Blake telling him less than the whole truth."

"Exactly," Blake agreed.

"And the question of the SIS involvement, sir?" Hannah asked.

"But there isn't one. No file, no knowledge of anything untoward. Astonishment at McGuire's story and delicate hints that it's all rubbish."

"So that's it?" Hannah said.

"Not at all. I'll see the Prime Minister, bring him up to date, and from now on, handle this whole business my way."

"And God help Simon Carter," Dillon said.

The Daimler was admitted through the security gates at Downing Street. Ferguson said, "I don't think we'll be long."

"Sure and I'm used to waiting when we come to this place." Dillon grinned at Blake. "I'm useful when they need a hired gun, but an embarrassment to the great man in there all the same."

"I'd read the *Times* if I were you. It's very instructive," Ferguson said, got out, followed by Blake.

The policeman saluted, the door swung open, and an aide smiled a welcome. "Brigadier, Mr. Johnson. The Prime Minister expects you."

He took them upstairs past the portraits of all the previous Prime Ministers, then along a corridor, knocked briefly at the study door, and opened it. The Prime Minister was sitting behind his desk, stood up, and came round to shake hands with Ferguson.

"Brigadier."

"Prime Minister. When you came to office, we discussed the peculiar circumstances of my position with you. Do you recall my mentioning that the President had a similar outfit working for him?"

"The Basement?"

"Yes, Prime Minister. This is Blake Johnson, who runs it."

The PM shook hands with Blake. "Be seated, gentlemen. You did indicate this was a matter of grave importance."

"Very much so," Ferguson said.

"Then tell me."

When Ferguson was finished, the Prime Minister sat there, frowning. "An incredible story. What happens next?"

"Mr. Johnson will have to report to his President. I would suggest he does that when he gets back to my office."

"I agree. As it happens, I have to speak to the President on matters concerning the peace process in Ireland later this evening. I'll discuss this affair with him and make it clear I have complete faith in you and Mr. Johnson."

"And what about the position of the Deputy Director of the Security Services?"

"What position?" The Prime Minister's face was calm. "They know nothing, Simon Carter was definite on that score. 'No file' was his phrase. Good. This would appear to be exactly the kind of thing my predecessors expected you to handle, Brigadier, so handle it."

"You have my word, Prime Minister."

He and Blake stood, the door opened as if by magic, and they were escorted out.

As it happened, Blake was unsuccessful in trying to speak to the President. He was finally routed to the chief of staff's secretary, who told him that the President was in Boston making a speech. Afterwards he was going down to his house on Nantucket for a three-day break. Next, Blake spoke to his secretary, Alice Quarmby, and because he was using the Codex Four line, he was able to speak openly.

"I was worried about you," she said.

"You should be. That bastard Barry slipped the net, but he almost got me. This Sons of Erin outfit he runs? He spoke of a New York branch. Check it out and see what you can find."

"Right away."

"I need to get back fast, so see if there's anything military leaving the UK later today."

"I'll call you back."

In Ferguson's office they had a final discussion. It was Hannah who stated the obvious. "There's nothing more we can do over here."

"Yes, it's up to you, old son," Dillon said. "New York branch of the Sons of Erin." He laughed. "Sounds like one of those Irish theme pubs."

Blake frowned. "You know something, that's not a bad idea."

"Which still leaves you with the mystery of the White House," Hannah told him. "Like one of those Agatha Christie murder mysteries."

"The thing about those mystery novels, my dear," Ferguson said, "was that they were always very simple."

"The butler did it," Dillon said.

"No, but there were usually no more than a dozen people staying at the country house for the weekend, and it had to be one of them."

The phone rang. He listened, then nodded. "Hang on." He looked at Blake. "Your secretary checked with air transport, and we have an RAF Gulfstream flying to the States this evening. They could drop in at Farley Field and pick you up there."

"Just the ticket," Blake told him.

Ferguson said, "Confirmed," and put the phone down.

"That's it, then." Dillon grinned. "It's all up to you now, old son. We'll be waiting with bated breath."

WASHINGTON
NANTUCKET
NEW YORK

SIX

IN HIS OFFICE at the White House, Blake greeted Alice with enthusiasm. He'd managed to sleep on the plane and had had one of those difficult breakfasts that took no notice of time differences, but he badly needed to shower and change, which he did the moment he got to the office—he so frequently had to sleep there overnight that he kept a change of clothes ready.

When he got to his desk, shaved, shampooed, and resplendent in a blue flannel suit, Alice handed him coffee with approval. "That's taken ten years off you."

"Look at my in-tray."

"I've done my best. Tell me what happened."

Blake ran the Basement in a most peculiar way. He had only one member of staff, which was Alice. Every time there was work to do, he pulled in members of a secret list: friends from FBI days, usually retired or invalided out; experts of every kind, from university professors to old comrades from Vietnam; whatever or whoever was necessary. He operated things like a Marxist cell system. Nobody knew what anyone else was doing. Except Alice. Who was outraged now by his story.

"It beggars belief that there is a spy in the White House."

"Why not? We've had them everywhere else. The Pentagon, the CIA, the FBI . . ."

"Okay, I take your point." She poured him another coffee. "Too much is on computers these days, that's the real problem, and in spite of every precaution, it's too easy to get at."

"Yes, life's a bitch," Blake said. "Speaking of which—did you get anywhere with the Sons of Erin?"

"Not much. Jack Barry's in the CIA and FBI files, but that's the only mention of the Sons of Erin."

Blake sat there frowning. "But he definitely mentioned them." He laughed suddenly. "I've just remembered something Dillon said. That the Sons of Erin sounded like an Irish theme pub."

She laughed. "It's a thought."

"Okay, so let's take a different route. Pubs, restaurants, dining clubs. See what you can do."

"I hear and obey, o master."

She went out and Blake got down to the paperwork.

It was no more than an hour later that she returned. "My God, it was so easy, once I looked in the right place." She had a piece of paper in her hand. "The Sons of Erin. It's listed under Irish dining clubs. Operates out of a bar and restaurant called Murphy's. It's in the Bronx."

Blake looked at the address, then checked his watch. "I can just make the shuttle to New York. Phone, get me a seat, get me a car, and book me a suite on the government. Something befitting my dignity."

She was laughing uproariously as she went out.

• • •

Murphy's was on Haley Street. It was just after three when Blake's car drew up outside. It hadn't the usual Irish theme pub look to it, all green and gold harps. This was older, more solid.

"Wait here, George," Blake said to his driver, got out, and walked to the door.

Inside it was dark and very old-fashioned, with dining booths and lots of mahogany paneling. A couple of people were finishing a late meal in one of the booths, but the lunchtime trade was through. The barman was old, seventy-five at least, his sleeves rolled up, reading spectacles on the end of his nose as he checked the sports page of the *New York Times*.

"Hi, there," Blake said. "I'll have a Bushmills whiskey and water."

"Well, you've got taste at least." The old man reached for a bottle.

Blake said, "With a name like Dooley, I should have. It was a friend told me to look in here. A guy called Barry."

The old man pushed the drink across. "I don't recall him."

"Have one yourself." The old man took a large one and downed it quickly.

"He told me he used to be in a dining club here called the Sons of Erin."

"Jesus, that was just a handful of guys, four or five of them. Nothing special about it except for the Senator."

"The Senator?"

"Sure, Senator Michael Cohan. Real nice guy."

"Hey, that's very interesting. Who were the others?"

"Oh, let's see now . . . Patrick Kelly, he ran a lot of construction work near here . . . Tom Cassidy, he had a string of Irish pubs . . . Who else?" He frowned.

"Have another?"

"Well, thank you. Don't mind if I do." He poured the drink, drank half of it, and nodded. "Brady—Martin Brady. Teamsters' Union guy. Say, I heard he got knocked off the other week."

"What do you mean?"

"Wasted. Someone made a hit when he was coming out of the union gym one night." He leaned closer. "I heard he had mob troubles. Know what I mean?"

"Yeah, sure . . . So, tell me, when do the Sons of Erin meet? I mean which night?"

"Oh, it isn't some kind of regular thing. Just now and then. They haven't had a meet here in months."

"Really?" Blake slipped a twenty over the bar. "Guess I missed my chance then. Nice talking to you. Keep the change."

"Well, thank you."

Outside, in the car, he called Alice on his mobile. "Take this down." He gave her the names of the members of the dining club. "Check the New York Police Department computer for details of the murder of Brady. I'm on my way to the Pierre now. I'll check back with you in an hour."

"Why don't I ever get the Pierre? Why you?"

"Because I'm a very important man, Alice."

"You know, it's your overwhelming ego that makes you so attractive." She put down the phone.

He was having coffee and sandwiches in his room when she phoned back. "Are you sitting down?"

"That bad?"

"You could say that. You wanted me to check out Brady's murder?"

"That's what I said."

"Well, I decided to put them all through the NYPD computer, in case this Sons of Erin thing provided a link."

"And did it?"

"You could say that. There's no mention of the group as such, but Brady, Kelly, and Cassidy are all in there."

"Go on."

"They were all shot to death, Blake. Brady first, some kind of mob street shooting. Cassidy three nights later, rumors about a protection racket, Kelly three days after, a robbery while he was out for a run at his place in Ossining."

"My God," Blake said, stunned. "And not a word."

"There were newspaper reports, but they were all separate—nothing to link them together. If you didn't know about the Sons of Erin, you'd have no reason to think they weren't what they seemed to be."

"That's true."

"Are you going to tell the police?"

"I'm not sure. What about Senator Cohan?"

"He's not on the NYPD computer, but then again, he's still alive. He was on *Larry King Live!* last night."

"What for?"

"Oh, Irish peace as usual. Everyone's into it at the moment. He's going to London to put his six cents' worth in to stay hot with his Irish-American voters. What do you want me to do?"

"Those Presidential warrants we keep in the office, the blank ones with the President's seal and signature. Fill one out in the name of Captain Harry Parker, fax me a copy here." He gave her the room fax number.

"Who is this guy?"

"A product of zero tolerance on the streets of good old New York. He runs a special homicide unit—top detectives, fancy computers. I knew him when I was in the FBI."

"So he owes you one?"

"It doesn't matter. Once I present him with that warrant, he's mine. I'll be in touch."

Next he phoned Ferguson at the Ministry of Defence in London. As it was eight o'clock in the evening there, he was rerouted to the Cavendish Square flat.

"You're not going to like this," he said to Ferguson and gave him the bad news, including the Sons of Erin background.

Ferguson said, "Someone would appear to mean business."

"You could say that. I've been thinking about Ryan's death in London. After all, he was connected with Barry as well. Could you get details from Scotland Yard? We know Dillon thought the killer was a woman, but I was wondering about the weapon that was used."

"Right away. I'll be back to you in half an hour."

He telephoned records at Scotland Yard, then phoned Dillon. "You'd better get round here fast."

Dillon was there in ten minutes, was admitted by Kim, and went upstairs as Ferguson's fax machine was pumping out two sheets.

"What's happening?" Dillon asked.

Ferguson was reading the sheets. He looked up and passed them over. "The report on Ryan when they took him out of the river. An unusual gun killed him. Look for yourself."

Dillon did, then nodded. "Colt .25. A woman's gun, but deadly when used with hollow-point cartridges." He handed the fax back. "So what?"

"I've just had Blake on from New York. He's found the Sons of Erin, Dillon—and most of them are dead. Three of them, shot to death within a seven-day period, and all within the last couple of weeks."

Dillon whistled.

"The only one left as far as we know is Senator Michael Cohan of New York . . . Jesus! And he's due over here in a few days for some Irish peace thing at the Dorchester. That's all we need, an American Senator knocked off in London. The Prime Minister is certain to give us the job of looking after him."

"So what now?"

"I'll speak to Blake and give him the facts."

In his room at the Pierre, Blake listened intently, then nodded. "I'm going over to see a top homicide specialist, tonight if possible. Here's my room fax number. Send the material, and I'll let you know what I find out. Is Dillon there?"

"I'll put him on."

"So what's your hunch on this one, my Irish friend?"

"Well, you've heard the old saying. Once is okay, twice is coincidence, three times is enemy action, and this is four."

"You really think it's the same person? A *woman*?"

"I know one thing. Someone or some group wanted the Sons of Erin stiffed, and four out of five is good going. If I were this Senator Michael Cohan, I'd be worried sick."

"So would I. I'll stay in touch."

Dillon put the phone down. "So, we wait and see," he said to Ferguson. "Will you tell the Prime Minister?"

"Not yet."

"And Carter?"

"Bugger Carter. Now have a nightcap with me and be off with you."

In his office at One Police Plaza, Harry Parker was considering going home. It had been a hard day. Three drug-related shootings, six wearying interrogations, and a mountain of paperwork. He was thinking of dropping in at his favorite bar when the phone rang.

"Harry, that you?"

"Who is this?"

"Blake Johnson."

"Why, you old dog. I haven't seen you since the Delaney investigation—what was that, two years ago, three? They tell me you've left the FBI."

"I've gone up in the world. I'll tell you when I see you."

"And when would that be?"

"Oh, I'd say around fifteen minutes."

"But I was just leaving."

"Harry, what if I told you I'm speeding toward you on Presidential business?"

"I'd say you were full of shit." There was only silence, and Parker said, "You are, aren't you? Tell me that you are, Blake." And then, every instinct acquired over twenty-five years on the street alerted him. "Jesus, what am I getting into?"

"Something fascinating, I assure you. Just put the coffee on."

Harry Parker sat there, thinking about it. He was forty-eight years of age, a 224-pound black man from Harlem who'd gone to Columbia on a scholarship and had joined the force immediately afterwards. Being a policeman was all he'd ever wanted to be and he'd never minded night shifts and seventy-hour weeks, although his wife had.

She'd left him ten years earlier, had married a Baptist preacher in Georgia, but it still left Harry with his son, a doctor, and a daughter, who was a fledgling reporter for the local CBS station, a single mother who'd borne him a granddaughter two years earlier.

He picked up the phone and called the deli across the street. "Hey, Myra, Captain Parker. I've got to work late.

Send over grilled cheese sandwiches for two, fries, and coffee."

He opened a drawer, took out a pack of cigarettes, hesitated, then lit one. He was supposed to have stopped, but what the hell, it was probably going to be a long night. He stood at the window, looking out at the rain, and the phone rang.

"Captain Parker, a Mr. Johnson to see you."

"Send him up."

A moment later, there was a knock at the door, but when it opened it was a boy from the deli.

"Put it on the table over there," Parker said, and Blake Johnson appeared in the doorway.

"Hey, that smells good. I've hardly had anything to eat all day."

"So now you want to steal mine." Parker waved the boy away. "You might as well sit down, then."

They took chairs opposite each other in the corner, the low table between them, and Blake took a sandwich. "Excellent."

Parker took the lid off one of the coffees. "Feel free. Just leave me to starve. You're looking disgustingly well, so tell me what this is about."

Blake took an envelope from his pocket. "Read that." He reached for another sandwich.

Parker opened the envelope and took out the fax. "Jesus, a Presidential warrant."

"Only the fax copy. The real article is on its way to you by Presidential messenger."

Parker was astonished. "Blake, I've never even seen one of these things, only heard of them. I know you're not FBI anymore, but what are you? CIA, Secret Service?"

"Neither, Harry. I work for the great man himself."

"Which means?"

"My department is very special, very secret, Harry. I report to the President only, which explains the warrant. In this matter, you no longer owe allegiance to the New York Police Department or the Mayor. You owe allegiance to one person only, the President of these United States. Do you accept that?"

"Do I have a choice?"

"No, this is a matter of national security I'm handling, to which your professional expertise is essential."

Suddenly, Harry Parker felt great. He reached for a sandwich and smiled. "I'm your man, Blake, I'm your man. Tell me all."

Later, sitting in front of his computer, sleeves rolled up, he said, "I'll feed in all this London stuff on Ryan." His fingers tapped the keys. "Okay, now let's start on the members of the Sons of Erin." Rain drummed against the window and Parker's fingers moved nimbly. "Number one, Martin Brady, Teamsters' Union. Came out of the union gym one night and was shot in the back of the neck as he leaned over to unlock the car. That's a typical mob execution, and we know they had it in for him."

"Yeah," Blake said. "But for that kind of hit, doesn't the Mafia emulate the CIA? They usually use a small caliber like a .22."

Parker's fingers moved over the keys. "You're right, but in this case, it was a Colt .25, with hollow-point bullets." He sat back. "Jesus, let me go back to those facts on Ryan." He tapped away. "Colt .25."

"Would that be a coincidence?" Blake asked.

"Hell, no. I'll put the images in for a match, and I smell there is one."

"Let's have a look at the other ones."

Parker went back to work. "Three days later, Cassidy

comes out of his new restaurant in the Bronx at one in the morning. Police intelligence said there was a protection racket operation and figured he was a victim." He tapped again and shook his head. "This is fucking unbelievable. The weapon involved was a Colt .25."

"One to go," Blake told him.

Parker went to work. "Patrick Kelly, construction millionaire, in the habit of rising at six A.M. and going for a five-mile run. Found shot in the heart at his country home in Ossining. Always wore a fifteen-thousand-dollar gold diver's watch and gold chain round his neck. Both missing." He turned to Blake. "Listed as an armed robbery gone bad."

"So now check the weapon used."

Parker did as he was told, waited for the result, then nodded. "Beautiful. The same weapon, from London to New York." He turned. "What do you think?"

"I think the killer was very smart, except for using the same weapon. You notice the pattern here that cleverly offers an explanation for each killing. Brady, the Mafia; Cassidy, a protection racket; Kelly, a robbery."

"As you say, smart, and as the killings had no apparent link, maybe this business of the same gun would never have come out except for you, but there's a puzzle here."

"The fact that in London, my associate said that the person who shot Ryan was a woman?"

"Hell, no, the fact that the Colt used in London was the Colt used in three murders in New York. Now that astounds me. Who in the hell gets through airport security these days with a weapon?"

Blake nodded slowly and then brightened. "Maybe people who use private planes, Harry, important people, rich people who are waved through."

"For God's sake, what is this all about?" Parker asked.

"I can't tell you, but I promise that when I can, you'll be the first to know."

"Well, thanks very much."

Blake stood up. "It's the best I can do, Harry. Now I've got to see the President," and he walked out.

In London, it was well past midnight, but he phoned Ferguson anyway and found the Brigadier in bed. "Curiouser and curiouser, Brigadier."

Ferguson, fully awake, sat up. "Tell me."

Blake did. "What do you think?" he asked when he was finished. "Some Loyalist group which had the target of taking out the Sons of Erin?"

"Blake, dear boy, I'm an old dog, long in this business, and I go by instinct. One gun in London and New York means one killer. I'd stake my life on it."

"But a woman? It's incredible."

"I'm old enough to know that *nothing* is incredible in this life. You'll be seeing the President?"

"Yes."

"Senator Michael Cohan is due in London in a few days. Point that out to the President. Maybe he should stay home."

"New York, London." Blake shrugged. "They both seem to be pretty dangerous places these days."

At the same time, in a safe house on the cliffs of County Down, Ulster, Jack Barry was having a drink in the kitchen when his coded mobile rang. It was the Connection.

"Where in the hell have you been?" Barry demanded.

"I'm a busy man, my friend. Blake Johnson turned up in Washington, so I presume you're on the run."

"You can say that again. Sean Dillon and some woman chief inspector came with him. I lost two men but managed to slip them."

"Good. No mention of our arrangement, I trust?"

"Of course not," Barry lied.

"Excellent. I'll keep you posted." The Connection rang off.

Barry cursed. He hated not knowing who he was dealing with, but then none of the Sons of Erin did. They only knew each other. He thought for a moment, then used his coded mobile to call Senator Michael Cohan. They'd met in the States several times and gotten on well. Cohan loved it all: the hair-raising stories, the action by night, the glamour.

Cohan answered at once. "Who is this?"

"Barry. Did I catch you at a bad time?"

"Yes, there's a party here. I've taken refuge in my study. I meant to phone you myself, but I've just gotten back from Mexico. Just got some bad news. Apparently, Martin Brady was murdered, some street killing. They say it's the mob."

"That's a coincidence. Tim Pat Ryan got it the same way the other day."

"Is that a fact?" the Senator said. "Mind you, he was a true gangster, that one."

"What about Kelly and Cassidy?"

"I haven't talked to them in a couple of months. Maybe I should—" A door crashed open in the background, and there was drunken laughter. "My God, here they come. I'll be in touch," and he rang off.

Blake had arranged for an Air Force plane the following morning. The brief flight was uneventful. The weather was squally, March again, but the young major in charge of transportation was all efficiency.

"The chief of staff is with the President at Nantucket, sir. He ordered us to send you on your way by helicopter."

"Beach landing?" Blake asked.

"That's it, sir."

"Hell, I did enough of those in 'Nam."

"Before my time, sir. If you'll come this way I've got sandwiches and coffee. Departure thirty minutes from now."

He held his umbrella high and Blake followed him across the tarmac.

The old clapboard house on Nantucket had been in the Cazalet family for years. It held every possible memory for the President. Childhood, school vacations, and twice, it had been a place to grow strong again after being wounded in Vietnam. Other, bitter memories were there, too: his wife's slow demise from leukemia and then the terrorist threat following his discovery of a wonderful daughter late in life— the Comtesse Marie de Brissac, now in Paris teaching art at the Sorbonne.

He had always loved the beach in any kind of weather, was walking there now with Henry Thornton and a Secret Service man, Clancy Smith, trailing them, the President's flatcoat retriever, Murchison, pounding in and out of the water. They all wore storm coats against the wind, which was blowing hard. The surf roared in, it was good to be alive, and Washington was far away.

The President stopped and waved his hand twice, and Clancy, who knew what that meant, shook a Marlboro from his pack, lit it inside his coat, and passed it across.

"I've said it before," Thornton told him. "Do that on television and you'll lose votes."

"It's a free country, Henry. It may not be healthy, but it doesn't make me a bad person." He leaned down and fondled Murchison's ears. "Now if I beat this wonderful dog, that would be different."

There was a roaring in the distance. Clancy listened via his earpiece. "Helicopter coming in, Mr. President. It's Blake Johnson."

"That's good," Jake Cazalet said. "Let's find out what happened in Ireland," and he led the way along the beach to the distant house.

In the living room, Blake sat opposite the President, and Thornton leaned by the fireplace. "The Prime Minister and I had a conversation on this matter, as you know, but the whole thing seemed so implausible. The man Barry, for example."

"Only too real, sir, and boasted about his sources, which have to be in the White House. The plain fact is Barry knew who I was, knew I worked for you."

"Knew everything, it would seem. But leaks from my White House? I can't believe it."

"It happens all the time, Mr. President. Ask any journalist about his sources," the chief of staff said. "There's no reason to think we're immune."

"And so much information is accessible," Blake said. "Everything's on the computer these days. We've got all kinds of safeguards in place, but I can access the CIA at Langley if I need to, and I'm sure that if they really try hard, they could access the Basement files. Even this conversation is being recorded."

"Oh, God, that's right—that security thing you had to install, right?" the President asked.

"Correct, sir, and it is linked by direct line to Washington."

"Coded, of course," the chief of staff said with some irony.

"Supposedly picked up by the Records Department at the White House and filed as indicated."

"On a computer," Thornton said. "And the curse of the system is that there are a lot of people around who can access any computer known to man."

"And there are a lot of people employed at the White House," Cazalet said. "Although this Connection of Barry's implies an Irish dimension or some sort of IRA sympathy."

"But, Mr. President, that covers a lot of possible ground," Thornton said. "Even my mother was Irish-born. She came from County Clare as an infant. It was my father's family, the Thorntons, who were English."

"My grandmother on my mother's side was a Dublin woman." Cazalet smiled and turned to Blake. "What about you?"

"Mr. President, Johnson is English enough, but I take the chief of staff's point. It's always been said that around forty million people in the country's population are of Irish stock. If you consider people like yourself and the chief of staff who have some sort of Irish past in their family history, then God knows how many it touches."

"A considerable proportion of the White House staff, I should say," Thornton put in.

"You can say that again. Needless to say, I'll leave no stone unturned. However, I've left the really bad news 'til last."

"You mean it gets worse?" The President shook his head. "Better get on with it, Blake."

As Blake gave his account of the lives and deaths of the Sons of Erin, the President and the chief of staff sat horrified.

When Blake was finished, Cazalet said, "This passes belief. Is the Prime Minister in possession of all these facts?"

"Not all, Mr. President. Brigadier Ferguson felt he should wait until I'd completed my investigation."

Cazalet sat there, frowning, then turned to Thornton. "A drink is very definitely indicated here. Make mine a Scotch and water, no ice. You gentlemen feel free to indulge yourselves."

He went and opened the French window and breathed deeply in the cold air. Thornton gave him his Scotch. "May I make a point?"

"Please do."

"I think we're shying away from Senator Cohan here."

"Explain."

"There's an implication of some mysterious Connection presumably passing out choice items of information on the Irish situation to the Sons of Erin, and a strong suspicion that Tim Pat Ryan was their connection in London."

"So?" Cazalet said.

"These were bad guys, Mr. President. They must have been if they were involved with Jack Barry. Which means that Senator Cohan is a bad guy."

"I'd already thought of that," the President said. "Could he be the Connection?"

"I doubt it," Blake said. "If he were, why go public by being a member of the dining club?"

"That makes sense."

Cazalet frowned, and Thornton said, "What do we do?"

"Officially, nothing," the President said. "Cohan'll deny any involvement and proof would be difficult."

"Can you forbid him to go to London?"

"What for? If he's a target, he's a target in both London or New York. Besides, despite what he says in the papers, his visit is not on my behalf. It's to make him look good to the voters."

"So what happens?" Thornton asked. "What do we do?"

The President turned to Blake. "First, tell Ferguson to inform the Prime Minister of the recent turn of events. I'll discuss it with the PM at an appropriate time."

"And Senator Cohan?"

"What's that fine old British phrase Dillon uses? Put the boot in?"

"That's it, Mr. President."

"Well, put the boot into Senator Cohan. Frighten him, send him running, watch every move. With luck, something might turn up."

"At your command, Mr. President, I'd better get back. I held the helicopter over."

"It can wait. Lunch, gentlemen, and then you can return to a troubled world, Blake."

It was some three hours later that Senator Michael Cohan received a phone call at his New York office.

"It's me," the Connection told him. "With some bad news, Senator. I'm afraid the Sons of Erin have fallen upon bad times. They're all dead. Brady, Cassidy, Kelly, Ryan. All dead. And interestingly enough—all killed by the same gun."

Cohan was aghast. "This is terrible! I can't believe it. I heard about Brady and Ryan, but Kelly and Cassidy, too. For God's sake, what's going on?"

"You've heard of the Last of the Mohicans?" The Connection laughed. "Well, you're the last of the Sons of Erin. I wonder where the ax will fall next? The President knows of your involvement, by the way."

"I'll deny it. I'll deny everything. How do you know this?"

"I've told you before. Anything that comes into the White House, I know."

"Who are you? God, I wish I'd never gotten involved."

"Well, you did, and as to who I am, that'll have to remain one of life's great mysteries. I could be using a voice distorter. I could be your best friend, I could be a woman. In fact, they think it was a woman who killed Ryan in London."

"Damn you!"

"Taken care of. Now, listen carefully. The President has

authorized Blake Johnson to speak to you, tell you something about what's going on, advise you to take to the hills."

"What shall I do? I'm due in London in three days."

"Yes, I know. In my opinion, I think you should go. I don't think it'll be any more dangerous for you there than here, and while you're away, I'll see what I can do about our problem."

"You're sure?"

"Of course. When Johnson sees you, just play dumb. You ate together once in a while and you have no idea what's going on."

"But who's doing all this? Is it the fucking Protestants?"

"More likely British Intelligence. That means you'll be safe in London."

"How do you make that out?"

"Because you're an American Senator, and whatever else, they won't want you to buy it in London."

"I'll try and believe that."

"Good. I'll be in touch. I'll handle it."

Henry Thornton put the phone down.

Panicky, and when a man panicked, he could do anything. A liability now, Cohan. With any luck, that mysterious killer out there would take care of him. If not . . . maybe he'd have to have help. As for Barry, he'd leave that for a while. See what happened to Cohan.

He went to the sideboard and poured a whiskey, Irish, of course. He'd told the President the truth. His sainted mother had been born in County Clare. What he hadn't mentioned was that she had had an illegitimate half brother by her father, a volunteer with Michael Collins in the nineteen sixteen Easter Rising in Dublin. He'd been executed by the Brits, and Thornton had grown up with the man's name in his ears.

But there was much more than that. Doing postgraduate work at Harvard in 1970, Thornton had met a lovely Irish

Catholic girl from Queen's University, Belfast, named Rosaleen Fitzgerald. She'd been the absolute love of his life. They'd spent one idyllic year together, true love way beyond sexuality, and then it had happened. She'd gone home for summer vacation and had been in the wrong Belfast street at the wrong time, a firefight between Brit paratroops and the IRA that had left her dead on the sidewalk.

His hatred of all things British had become absolute. Growing up, even with all the success, all the money, it had meant nothing, and then had come the chance to strike back.

He sipped the whiskey. "Fuck you," he said softly. "I'll have my day."

At his office in Manhattan the following day, Cohan received Blake with enthusiasm, heard him out with appropriate sounds of horror and disbelief, and walked him to the door with grave shakes of his head. He promised to be careful in London, but no, he had to go. It was for a very important cause, and he'd promised.

"Please keep me up to date," he said to Johnson, shaking his hand and staring sincerely into his eyes.

Blake promised that he would.

Afterwards, Blake spoke briefly to the President and then phoned Ferguson in London. "What will you do?" he asked.

"I'll see the Prime Minister. Place all the new facts before him, and wait to hear the outcome of his chat with the President."

"And Cohan?"

"You tell me the President won't forbid him to come, so he will come. I'll have the job of protecting him."

"And what do you think will happen?"

"As I told you, I'm an old dog, long in this business. I go by instinct, and every instinct tells me he will die in London." Ferguson hung up.

LONDON

SEVEN

AT COMPTON PLACE, it was raining. Lady Helen Lang was out riding, heavily protected by storm coat and rain hat. The wind blew in across the North Sea all the way from Holland, churning the waves into surf that pounded on the shingle beaches. She cantered through pine woods down to the sand dunes of the estuary, reined in her mare, and let the rain bring her to life.

"Come on, Dolly." She patted the mare's neck. "Let's go home."

She didn't need to dig her heels in. Dolly took off like a rocket and galloped through the pinewoods, swerving at a touch of the rein and taking a two-bar gate as if she were in the Grand National. Helen cantered into the stable yard at the house and found Wood there. The chief groom at a racing stable close by, he looked in by arrangement, not so much for the money but mainly because, like everyone else, he felt protective of Lady Helen.

He held Dolly as she dismounted. "A good run, milady?"

"Excellent."

"I'll give her a rubdown and some oats, then."

"I'm very grateful."

She moved to the kitchen door and Hedley opened it. "You've been galloping again."

"What do you want me to do, roll over and die?" She smiled. "Don't be an old fuddy-duddy. I'll go and shower and then you can take me to the village for a pub lunch."

After she'd gone, Hedley made himself a cup of coffee. He heard Wood drive off, went and opened the kitchen door, and stood looking out at the rain. It was like a dream, everything that had happened since that night in Wapping, since she had killed Ryan. And then New York. Brady, Kelly, Cassidy.

He shuddered. What could he do? As she had once said: go to Scotland Yard? And what would he say? My mistress has murdered four men who had some sort of responsibility for the butchery of her son and the assassination of four others in Ulster? On top of that, she shot two lowlifes trying to rape a girl in Manhattan? No, even thinking along those lines was a waste of time.

There was no way he could ever do anything to harm her. She simply meant too much to him. And there was another thing, too. He had killed many people in Vietnam, some for good reasons, some for bad, and he knew one thing beyond dispute. If he ever had the mysterious Connection in his sights, he would kill the man himself without compunction.

Showered and changed, Helen Lang went into her study and sat before the computer. She really was very expert now, and soon had Senator Cohan's travel arrangements on her screen, including his date of arrival, and, even, in a bit of luck, the number of his suite at the Dorchester Hotel. Apparently, he reserved the same one every time he was there.

She considered all the facts, then went down to the kitchen, where she found Hedley.

She took her sheepskin down from behind the door. "All right, Hedley, food awaits. Let's be off," and she opened the door, went out into the courtyard, and walked to the Mercedes parked in the open barn.

The pub, as usual at that time of year, was quiet. It was very old England in the saloon bar, great stone flags for a floor, a low, beamed ceiling. There was a log fire burning in the open hearth and the long bar was made of oak, with beer pumps and a range of bottles behind. There were only four locals at the bar, the usual gnarled old straw dogs. She was greeted with enthusiasm. One man even doffed his cap. Hedley was just as well received.

The barmaid was a middle-aged woman called Hetty Armsby, and the eighty-five-year-old man sitting on the end stool reading the *London Times* was her father, Tom.

"The *Times,* is it?" Helen asked.

"I like to keep up to date," he said. "Keep my brain active. The *Times* gives you the facts. For instance, all this Irish business at the moment, though why the Yanks are involved I'll never know."

"Pint for Hedley and your dad and a gin and tonic for me," she said to Hetty.

"And you'll be wanting food?"

"Shepherd's pie and that bread you bake yourself." Helen took out a cigarette and Hedley gave her a light. "Oh, I don't know, Tom. I'm a Yank, remember."

"Well, that isn't your fault, Lady Helen," and he cackled.

"You old rogue. Just look at the wall."

Hanging there was a series of framed black-and-white pictures of airplanes. Several were of German Dorniers, and two were of American B17 bombers, one in the surf off

Horseshoe Bay, the other nose down where it had crash-landed, the crew standing beside it in flying gear.

"True enough," Tom told her. "A grand bunch of lads, that. We got them in here while they were waiting for trucks from their base. Drunk out of their minds, they were, by the time those trucks came. We've had one or two back over the years. Mind you, a long time ago. Mostly passed on, I reckon."

Hetty appeared with a tray. "Over here, Lady Helen. Nice table by the fire."

She laid everything out. Lady Helen and Hedley sat down and ate. "Good, Hedley?"

"You *know* it's good," he told her. "Sometimes it's still hard for me to fathom. I was a kid in Harlem, scratching a living, on hard times, then there was 'Nam, and all those years later I live in one of the most ancient parts of England and sit in a pub like it's out of a Jane Austen novel, eating a thing called shepherd's pie."

"And you like it."

"Love it, Lady Helen, and I love these crazy people."

"Well, they love you," she said. "So that's okay."

They finished the meal and she ordered a pot of English Breakfast tea. "Much better for you than coffee, Hedley, and I want your brain clear."

"And why would that be?"

"Senator Cohan arrives at the Dorchester the day after to-morrow."

He took a deep breath. "You really mean it, don't you?"

"Of course." She took a small plastic bag from her pocket, opened it, and produced a key. "Remember when they were fitting the new stove in the kitchen in South Audley Street, and they were making such a racket, and I stayed overnight at the Dorchester?" She smiled. "I'm just a weak woman who enjoys luxury. Well, that's the key to the suite."

Hedley took it. "So?"

"You've often boasted of your wide range of rather dubious friends. When we lost those keys for the old stables, the deadlocks, you produced one that opened all of them. Said you'd got it from a friend in London. I asked you if he was a locksmith. You said not exactly."

"That's true."

"Well, we're leaving for South Audley Street tomorrow. One of the joys of the English aristocratic system, as you well know, Hedley, is that one gets invited to everything, and I'm due at the Dorchester ballroom the day after tomorrow."

He was resigned to it by now. "So what do you need?"

"This friend of yours to have a look at that key. I know it's computer-coded, and won't open a thing now, but based on something dear Roger once told me—well, I'm sure if your friend is as good as I think he is, he can produce a passkey."

Hedley sighed. "If you say so."

"Oh, but I do. Don't let me down. Now finish your beer and we'll go."

It was the following afternoon when Hedley came up from the Covent Garden tube station. It was, as always, one of the most crowded parts of London. Hedley worked his way through the crowds until he came to Crown Court, a narrow little alley with four or five shops. One of them said: "Jacko—Locksmith." The bell tinkled as Hedley went in.

A curtain at the rear parted and an old white-haired black man came through. "Damn my eyes, it's you, Hedley."

"That it is, Jacko."

"We'll have a drink on it." Jacko produced a half bottle of Scotch from under the counter, then two paper cups, and poured. "Isn't life the damnedest thing? You and my Bobby get posted on Embassy Guard here, so he sends for me to come to live in London. Then they pull him away to that stinking Gulf War and he gets wasted."

"Here's to you, Jacko." Hedley drank the whiskey. "Always thought you'd go home."

"Where's home? Hell, I still play great trombone and London's got better jazz clubs than New York. You got a purpose to this visit?"

Hedley produced the key. "You familiar with these things?"

Jacko only glanced. "Yeah, sure. It's a hotel key. What about it?"

"Could you make me a passkey, a general key, out of it? One that would open any door in the hotel?"

"My friend, I never figured you for a guy who worked the hotel racket, but yes, I can do such a thing. The hotel people think these things are foolproof, but not if you know what you're doing. I can do the job in about five minutes."

"Good. Then do it. And no, I'm not in any kind of hotel racket, but this is real important."

"Then consider it done." Jacko opened the bottle and poured. "Have another."

He went back through the curtain while Hedley finished the whiskey, and then appeared a few minutes later. "There you go."

The key looked just the same. Hedley said dubiously, "Is this kosher?"

"If I were Jewish, I'd say on my life, but I'm just an old trombone player from Harlem, Hedley. I don't know the hotel, I don't want to know, but one thing is certain. This will open any door in the fucking place."

"What do I owe you?"

"What are friends for? Use it in good health."

• • •

Michael Cohan took the Concorde from New York to London. He preferred it to the Jumbo, but then anyone would. Three and a half hours, a smooth and perfect flight, excellent food, and free champagne. The seats were smaller, but the speed made up for that. There was no movie, but that was the last thing he was concerned about, because the thoughts going around in his brain provided his own personal cinema of the mind, and it wasn't funny. He'd tried to phone Barry twice on the coded mobile but had gotten no reply, though that wasn't surprising. The Irishman was constantly on the move, and mobile phones were not something you switched on all the time, especially in Barry's case, when you were on the run.

It was a mess, though, the way things had worked out. So stupid, the whole thing. His Irish-American voters had always been crucial, and Brady had been a first-class fundraiser for him because of his power in the Teamsters' Union. It was he who had introduced him to Kelly and Cassidy.

There was a natural progression to receiving funds for the IRA. Not just for Noraid, but for other groups with Dublin links. Everybody was doing it. Most of his Irish-American voters felt strongly about the situation in Ireland. The IRA were heroes—romantic heroes.

He remembered the early days at Murphy's, the drinking, the singing of rebel songs. It was exciting, romantic, and then there had been the night Brady had introduced Jack Barry, in New York on business for the organization back there in Dublin. A real live IRA gunman.

Barry had regaled them with his stories of gun battles with British paratroopers, life on the run, and had suggested how they could help. It was Brady with his work on the New York docks for the Teamsters who was of real importance. The possibilities of smuggling arms to Ireland had been obvious. Cohan and Kelly had concentrated on the fundraising and Cassidy on the purchase of suitable weapons. Cohan remembered their first coup: fifty ArmaLite rifles smuggled in a Portuguese boat to Ireland.

They were already calling themselves the Sons of Erin at Barry's suggestion, had established the dining club at Murphy's with a plaque on their own booth, all out in the open, no reason not to. And then when Barry had come to New York again, he had mentioned his mysterious mentor, a voice on the phone the previous year when Barry had been staying in splendor at the Mayfair Hotel on IRA business. When Barry had asked who he was, he'd simply said: *Call me the Connection, because that's what I am.*

Astoundingly, he could provide information from British Intelligence by way of Washington, information crucial to the struggle in Ireland. Again, because of Brady's waterfront connections, arrangements were able to be made to smuggle IRA men on the run out of Ireland to New York. The smuggling of arms had also continued.

The really serious business had started when the Connection had passed details of British Intelligence operations in New York and Boston, including identities of operatives, all part of the shadow war being fought between the British and IRA in Ireland.

This was where Brady, because of his union work, and Cassidy with his construction business, had come into their own. They both had serious connections with mob interests. Favors were owed. The right kind of accidents took place, the Brits lost people and couldn't make a fuss. After all, they shouldn't have been there in the first place, although a lot of that kind of thing seemed to have tailed off in the past year, and Cohan had always stood well clear of any violence.

He'd always been a link man when needed, had met Tim Pat Ryan twice when on London trips. It had all worked, and then the damn roof had fallen in. Still, he was in the clear, whatever Blake Johnson implied. So he frequented Murphy's Bar, so what did that prove? How in the hell had he been so stupid, and yet there had been an inevitability about it from the beginning. Nothing to be done about it now. The Connection had promised to take care of it, and he'd taken care of everything in the past well enough.

So Brady, Kelly, Cassidy, and Ryan were dead meat. Cohan shuddered and waved for another glass of champagne and tried to comfort himself with the thought that the other guys had been one thing, but he was a United States Senator. United States Senators didn't get shot, did they?

Ferguson was with the Prime Minister again at Downing Street, on his own this time. The Prime Minister listened carefully to Ferguson's résumé of the whole business.

"Of course, as the President has pointed out to me in our conversation, there isn't a thing anyone can do legally about Senator Cohan. His membership in the Sons of Erin damns him in our eyes, but on the surface he can claim, as he apparently does, that he frequented this Murphy's Bar quite innocently."

"Agreed, Prime Minister," Ferguson nodded. "But he's here now and the thing is, what do we do with him?"

"Try and keep him alive, of course. I'm dropping the whole thing in your lap, Brigadier."

"And the Deputy Director and the Security Services?"

"You are in charge," the Prime Minister told him firmly. "I now realize the Security Services have not been as forthcoming as they could have been in the past, and I don't like that." He smiled. "You've been in this job a long time, Brigadier. I think I now know why one of my illustrious predecessors gave it to you in the first place."

"So I have full authority?"

"Absolutely. Now, do excuse me. I'm due at the House."

As Ferguson stood and the door behind him opened, the Prime Minister added, "By the way, this function at the Dorchester, the Forum for Irish Peace that Cohan is attending tomorrow night. I'm looking in at ten. You'll be there, of course."

Ferguson nodded. "I think you can take that for granted, Prime Minister," and he followed the aide out.

Hannah Bernstein and Dillon were waiting in the Daimler. Ferguson got in and it drove away. As the security gates opened, he said, "Just as I thought, it's our baby. Carter is to have no involvement."

"Which leaves us in the deep you-know-what if the Senator comes to a sticky end," Dillon pointed out.

"My dear boy, it was ever thus." Ferguson turned to Hannah Bernstein. "When is he due in?"

She checked her watch. "Only took off forty minutes ago, sir."

"Fine. Check his movements, the data at the hotel, his limousine, that sort of stuff. There's not too much we can do, as this is not really official. We can't alert the hotel or pull in extra security guards during his visit."

"There'll be plenty of security at the Forum for Irish Peace tomorrow night," Hannah said.

"Of course." Ferguson frowned. "But I'm uneasy, and why is that?"

"I'm sure you'll tell us," Dillon said.

"Well, I've never been happy since the Ryan shooting and then discovering the same gun was used in New York. I don't think it's a conspiracy, some execution squad. I have a feeling there's an executioner out there."

"The Irish woman."

"Or a woman with an Irish accent," Dillon said. "A needle in a haystack in London. Eight million Irish in the UK. A hell of a Diaspora."

"Well, I have infinite faith in you, so you can start with Kilburn," Ferguson told him.

"And Senator Cohan?" Hannah asked.

"I'll speak to him when I'm ready. Now, as this rogue here is wearing a jacket and tie for once, I'll take you to the Garrick for lunch."

But already events were happening which would change everything. Earlier that morning, Thornton had considered the situation of Cohan in London, and the longer he did, the more unhappy he became. What guarantee was there that the mysterious killer would strike in London? None at all, and yet Cohan had become a liability. The man really would have to go. It was four o'clock in the morning, American time, when he phoned Barry. The Irishman was still at the safe house in County Down.

"It's me," Thornton said. "Listen, I've got some bad news for you," and he ran through the whole story. "There's even a possibility the shooter could be a woman."

"Is that a fact? Well, I wish to Christ I could get my hands on her. She'd take a long time to die. So Cohan is the only one left?"

"That's it, and panicking. The thing is, his cover as a member of the Sons of Erin is blown. The President knows through Blake Johnson, the Prime Minister knows through Ferguson and company. He's become expendable."

"So you want him taken out?"

"He's arriving in London later today to attend some Irish peace affair at the Dorchester tomorrow. He's staying at that hotel. It would be convenient if this unknown assassin got to him, don't you think? Maybe he—or she—could use some help."

"So you want me to do it for you?"

"And for yourself. It clears the board nicely. There'd be only you and me left. I believe the Belfast flight to London only takes an hour and a half."

"There's no need for that," Barry told him. "There's an air taxi firm not forty minutes from here, based at an old World War Two feeder station. It's been a quick way to England for me for years. Run by an old RAF hand named Docherty. Cunning as a fox."

"So you'll do it?"

"Why not? It will give me something to do. It's raining and I'm bored."

Barry put the phone down, excited, and looked out of the window. No need to call in the boys. A one-man job this, in and out. He picked up the phone and rang Docherty at Doonreigh.

The place was dark and dreary in the heavy rain as he drove up there an hour later. There were two old aircraft hangars, their doors open. In one was a Cessna 310, in the other a Navajo Chieftain. Barry parked and got out. He was wearing a tweed cap, a brown tan leather bomber jacket and jeans, and carried an old-fashioned Gladstone bag in one hand.

Smoke came from the chimney of the old Nissen hut. The door opened, and Docherty appeared. He was fifty and looked older, his hair thin, his face weathered and lined. He wore RAF flying overalls and flying boots.

"Come in out of the rain."

It was warm inside from the old-fashioned stove. There was a bed in the corner, some lockers, a table and chairs, and a desk with charts open on it.

"So they still haven't caught up with you, Jack?"

"That'll be the day. Is that tea on the stove?"

"Good Irish whiskey, if you like."

"You know me. Not while I'm working. So, I want to be in London no later than six this evening."

"And out again?"

"No later than midnight. Can you do it?"

"I can do anything, you know that. I never ask questions, I mind my own business, and I've never let you down."

"True."

"All right. Five thousand, that's what it costs."

"Money's not a problem," Barry said. "As no one knows better than you."

"Fine. There's a place like this in Kent, about an hour from London. Roundhay, very lonely, out in the country. I've used it before. I've already telephoned the farmer who owns it. A grand for him, and he'll leave a car you can drive up to London. False registration, the lot."

"Just another crook," Barry said.

"Aren't we all? Except you, Jack. A gallant freedom fighter for the glorious cause, that's you."

"I'll kick your arse, Docherty."

"No, you won't, because you can't fly planes."

"So you'll get us there in spite of all this air traffic security?"

"When have I ever failed? Now let's get moving. It's got to be the Chieftain, by the way. The Cessna needs some spare parts."

He opened the Navajo's Airstair door, dropped the steps, and Barry followed him up. Docherty closed the door and locked it. "There's a following wind, Jack, so it'll take two hours with luck. It's the usual March weather, lots of rain, but that's good. Don't wet your pants when I go hedge-hopping. That's to avoid the radar. Do you want to sit with me?"

"No, I'll read the paper."

Docherty strapped himself in and started the engines, first port, then starboard. The Navajo moved out into the rain, coasted to the end of the strip, and turned into the wind. He boosted power and they surged forward, lifted off, and started to climb.

Docherty was as good as his word, for they hit Roundhay at only five minutes over two hours and came in under low cloud and heavy rain. A barn stood nearby, its doors open, an old Ford Escort car outside. Docherty taxied inside and cut the engines.

"What about you?" Barry asked as they got out.

"I'll be okay. I'll take a walk up to the farm and pay my debts."

"You mean you'll give him a thousand in cash?"

"He's the kind of man you keep happy. I never know when I might need him again."

He turned and walked away across the airstrip, and Barry got into the Escort. The keys were in the engine, but before he started it, he removed a Browning from the Gladstone bag, took out the clip, loaded the weapon, and pushed it inside his bomber jacket. Only then did he drive away.

He made good time, for as evening approached, traffic was coming out of London, not in. The car was no big deal, but nice and anonymous. He thought about things on the way. The place to make the hit, for example. Well, that was obvious, since Cohan was staying at the Dorchester. Getting in was easy. All he needed were the right kind of clothes, and he had those in plenty.

For some years Barry had had a bolt hole in London. Not an apartment, but a boat moored on the Thames close to St. James's Stairs in Wapping. He had everything there: a wardrobe and arms stashed away. He had been careful never to mention it to anyone. He'd always remembered his old Ulster grandmother's saying, when she used to come over to the States to stay with them: Always remember, Jack, a secret is no longer a secret if one other person knows about it. She'd died badly of cancer during the early days when he'd first returned to Ulster. She'd been a patient at the Royal Victoria Hospital in Belfast, the world's best on shotgun wounds, because they had to be.

He was on the most-wanted list at the time. When he said he was going to see her, the boys had told him he was crazy and implored him not to. But none of that mattered to Barry. He'd gone on his own, got into the hospital's back entrance, and stolen a doctor's white robe and plastic identity tag from the rest room.

He'd found her room and, for a while, sat there holding her hand. She couldn't talk much, except to say, "I'm glad you're here, Jack."

"It's where I should be, Gran."

And then her grip had tightened. "Take care, be a good boy," and she had slipped away.

The tears, the rage, had overwhelmed him then. He'd left and, against all advice, attended her funeral four days later, standing in the rain, a Browning in his pocket, wishing someone from the Security forces would try to take him.

And why should that be? The great Jack Barry, Lord Barry, Silver Star and bronze in 'Nam, Vietnamese Cross of Valor, a Purple Heart. How many Brit soldiers had he killed, how many Loyalists in bombings, although a Prod himself?

At the end of the day, the image that would not go away was of an old woman who had fiercely loved him. Even now, at the wheel of the Escort, his throat prickled and angry tears started to his eyes.

He was into London at five, worked his way through to Kilburn, parked and found what he was looking for: a pub called the Michael Collins. The painting on the wall—an Irish tricolor and Collins with a gun upraised—said it all. He didn't go in the bar but walked round to the courtyard at the rear, opened the kitchen door, and entered. A small gray-haired man was seated at a table in the sitting room, reading glasses on his nose, going over some accounts. His name was Liam Moran and he was a London organizer for Sinn Fein.

"Jesus, it's yourself, Jack." His eyes bulged.

"As ever was." Barry went to a sideboard, opened a bottle of whiskey, and poured one. "Is there much action at the moment?"

"Hell, no, not with the peace process. The Brits are playing it cool in London and so are the boys. What in the hell are you doing here, Jack?"

"Oh, no harm intended, just passing through. On my way to Germany," Barry lied. "Just thought I'd check in and see how the general situation was."

Moran was agitated. "Dead calm, Jack, I promise you."

"Peace, Liam." Barry swallowed his whiskey. "What a bore. I'll be in touch," and he went out.

EIGHT

LONDON'S KILBURN DISTRICT houses a mainly Irish population, both Republican and Loyalist, and sometimes you'd swear you were in Belfast. The Protestant pubs with William and Mary painted on the end wall were the spitting image of those in the Shankhill, as were the Republican pubs of those in the Falls Road.

Dillon, dressed in a black bomber jacket, scarf, and jeans faded into the drinking crowd of the latter, his Walther stuck into his waistband at the rear. That there were those who might recognize him could not be avoided, but he figured he would be all right. He was, after all, the great Sean Dillon, the living legend of the IRA, and as for anything else, it was rumors at most. But he had the Walther as insurance.

He learned nothing of any great interest, however, until he came out of the Green Tinker and paused in a doorway to light a cigarette beside the newspaper stand. The old man huddled inside was swallowing from half a bottle. His name was Tod Ahern. He wiped his mouth with the back of a hand and stared at Dillon in astonishment.

"Jesus, Sean, it's yourself."

"And who else would it be?"

Tod was well drunk now. "Are there big things doing? I saw Barry earlier. Are you and he here for some big plans?"

Dillon smiled gently. "Now then, Tod, you shouldn't talk about such things. The word is hush." He smiled. "Jack would be furious if he knew you'd seen him. Where was it, by the way?"

"Going to the back of the Michael Collins. I thought he might be seeing Liam Moran. I'd just picked up my stand. I was wheeling it round."

"Well, keep it to yourself, Tod." Dillon passed him a five-pound note. "Have a drink on me later."

Sitting at his table, still going over his accounts, Liam Moran was aware of a slight draft of air that lifted the papers, looked up, and found Dillon in the doorway, an unlit cigarette in his mouth.

"God bless all here."

Moran almost had a bowel movement. "Sean, it's you."

"As ever was." Dillon lit the cigarette with his old Zippo. "I'm told you had a visitor earlier, Jack Barry?"

Moran managed a ghastly smile. "And who's been selling you that kind of nonsense?"

Dillon sighed. "We can do this the easy way or the hard way, Liam. What did he want and where is he?"

"Sean, this is a bad joke."

Dillon's hand found the butt of the silenced Walther in his waistband, his hand swung, and the lobe of Moran's right ear disintegrated, the blood spurting as he grabbed it.

"Now, your right kneecap comes next. I'll put you on sticks, maybe forever."

"Jesus, no, Sean!" Moran was in agony. "He told me he was just checking on how hot things were in London these days. Said he was on his way to Germany."

"My arse he is," Dillon said. "He'll have a hidey-hole here in London. Where would that be?"

"And how would I be knowing that, Sean?"

"What a shame. Here goes the kneecap."

Dillon took aim and Moran cried out. "St. James's Stairs, up from Wapping. There are some houseboats. His is called *Griselda.*"

"Good man yourself." Dillon put the Walther away. "Do you want me to come back?"

"Jesus, no."

"Then keep your mouth shut. I'm sure you know someone who can fix that ear." Dillon went out.

Back in his Mini Cooper, he phoned Ferguson, and when the Brigadier answered, said, "I may have struck gold."

"Tell me."

Dillon did. When he was finished, he said, "I think it's too much of a coincidence he's here. What do you want me to do? Take him out? On the other hand, you could call in Scotland Yard's Antiterrorist Unit. They'd turn it into the Third World War."

"That's the last thing we need. Where are you?" Dillon told him. "Meet me at St. James's Stairs," Ferguson said.

"You've got to be joking."

"Dillon, when I was nineteen years old, I was in the Hook in Korea, where I shot five Chinese with a Browning pistol. I do tend to get bored polishing the seat of my desk at the Ministry of Defence."

"Oh, my, what would Bernstein say?"

"I can take political correctness so far, Dillon. I don't particularly wish to employ her on a desperate venture in rain and darkness on the Thames in an attempt to take out one of the worst specimens the IRA has on offer."

"So you think he's here for Cohan?"

"Dillon, a few days ago he was in Ulster, now he's here. What other reason could he have? Wait for me on the corner of Wapping High Street and Chalk Lane," and Ferguson put the phone down.

Barry parked the Escort at the end of Chalk Lane in a side turning and walked down toward St. James's Stairs. It was dark now, with lights on the river, more on the riverside, traffic moving in the darkness. He turned at the end and walked along the line of an old jetty, passing what looked like a couple of disused lighters.

There was a basin at the end, some old cranes standing above it, disused warehouses standing behind. Only one houseboat was on that side, the *Griselda,* with four on the other, two with a light that showed some sort of habitation. There was a connection with the shore, an electric cable and water pipe.

Barry had used the boat for three years now, had last been there six months before. He'd always expected the place to be vandalized each time he'd returned, but it had never happened. For one thing, it was remote and tucked away and then the presence of the other houseboats afforded some sort of protection.

He went across the gangplank, found the key hidden in the cabin gutter, got the steel door open, and stepped inside. There was a switch to the left. The light came on, disclosing a flight of stairs. It also brought on deck lights, one in the stern, one in the prow.

He went down and at the bottom switched on a light, revealing the cabin. It was surprisingly spacious, with portholes on each side. There were bench seats, a table, a kitchenette at one end with an electric cooker and a basin. He paused to fill the kettle, then carried on into the bedroom.

He placed the Gladstone bag on the bed, took out a toilet bag and a carton of cigarettes. He opened a pack, lit a cigarette, and checked the closet. There were clothes in there in plastic zip-up bags, shoes, new shirts in Marks & Spencer bags, underwear, socks, everything he would need. The kettle was whistling. He went in, switched it off, sat down at the table, and phoned the Dorchester with his mobile.

"Senator Cohan," he asked, when the switchboard replied.

"May I say who's calling, sir?"

"George Harrison, American Embassy."

A moment later, Cohan answered. "Mr. Harrison?"

Barry laughed. "It's me, you daft bastard, Barry."

"Jack?" Cohan laughed back. "Where are you?"

"Still in Ulster," Barry lied. "I spoke to the Connection. He told me all the bad news. Though I suppose it's good news for the undertakers."

Cohan shuddered. "You always see a joke in everything."

"As we used to say in Vietnam, if you can't see the joke, you shouldn't have joined. Look on the good side. You're in luxury at the Dorchester, your every need taken care of. You're well out of New York at the moment."

"The Connection said he'd take care of things. Can you imagine this suggestion that a woman got to Ryan? Is that crazy?"

"Well, the good news is I'm leaving for New York myself in an hour. That's why I thought I'd call you. The Connection wants me there to help clean this mess up."

"Is that a fact?"

Barry was lying smoothly now. "I'm driving down to Shannon. I'll catch the New York plane from there."

"Let's hope you can sort things out."

"I'll keep in touch. Let you know where I'm staying. What's your room number?" Cohan gave it to him. "Good. You going out tonight?"

"No, I'll take it easy. Big night tomorrow."

"Sounds right to me. Stay well."

Cohan put the phone down, aware of a feeling of considerable relief. He opened the bottle of complimentary champagne and poured a glass. If anyone could handle this whole sorry mess, it was Barry.

Barry took out an excellently tailored black suit, white shirt, and a striped tie. He laid them down on the bed, went back into the saloon, reheated the kettle, and made coffee in a mug. When it was ready, he went up the companionway and stood on the deck at the rail thinking about things.

How to do it was the thing. Access to the Dorchester was no problem. After all, he'd be dressed like a whiskey advert, and he had Cohan's room number. All he needed to do was knock on the door, drop him, and be on his way. If he left the Do Not Disturb card on the door, they wouldn't find him for hours, possibly not until the morning.

Feeling suddenly quite cheerful about it, he went back below. He took off his bomber jacket, pushed the Browning into his waistband, and put the kettle on again. He checked out the clothes, took the shirt out of its plastic envelope, and unfolded it. The kettle whistled again, and he changed his mind about more coffee. He switched it off, found a bottle of Scotch in a cupboard, poured one into a paper cup, and went back up on deck.

It was raining now, silver lances in the yellow light of the deck lights, and he stood under the slightly tattered awning, smelling the river, the damp, nostalgic for something he didn't understand. There was a sudden slight cough and he turned, his hand sliding inside the bomber jacket to feel for the butt of the Browning.

A man was standing at the end of the gangway with an umbrella over his head, smiling down at him. "We haven't met face-to-face, Mr. Barry, but the name's Ferguson."

Waiting in his Mini Cooper at the junction of Wapping High Street and Chalk Lane, Dillon had an eye out for the Daimler and had been totally astonished when a black cab had drawn up and Ferguson had got out and paid the driver. He'd carried an umbrella, which he didn't bother to put up, hurried along the pavement, and got in beside Dillon.

"Filthy night."

"You in a cab? I can't believe it. I suppose you'll claim the fare on expenses?"

"Don't be flippant, Dillon. What do you intend?"

"I haven't the slightest idea. Are you carrying?"

"What would you expect?" Ferguson asked wearily, and produced an old .38 Smith & Wesson automatic. "I also have these." He took a pair of handcuffs from his pocket.

"You are hopeful, old man."

"All right, let's get on with it," and Ferguson got out and put up his umbrella.

They walked down Chalk Lane side by side, the Brigadier's umbrella protecting them. When they reached the basin, they paused in the doorway of one of the old warehouses.

"One houseboat on this side, four on the other," Ferguson whispered. "Lights in the nearest and two of the others. Which is which?"

Dillon took a small pair of binoculars from his pocket. "Nightstalkers. Miracle of modern science." He focused them on the first houseboat and passed them to Ferguson. "Take a look."

Ferguson did so, and the houseboat emerged in every detail, although in a greenish tint, the name *Griselda* clear on the prow. "Excellent. I could have done with those in the trenches on the Hook. What's your plan?"

"I'm a simple man, and the lights being on, I presume it is Barry."

"So?"

Dillon examined the *Griselda* again. "I don't think we'll get anywhere by stepping on board and shouting down the companionway, 'Come out with your hands up.' I noticed there's a stern hatch."

"Yes, well, I'd like to point out that there could be a certain amount of noise in doing that, Dillon. Lifting the hatch, I mean, which could also be locked on the inside."

"Brigadier, you've got to travel hopefully. I'll have a go and you wait here for me."

"Oh, I see, keeping the old man safe, are we?"

Dillon didn't bother to answer, simply handed him the Nightstalker and faded into the darkness beside the warehouse wall. Ferguson focused the night sight, saw Dillon slide over the stern rail, and move to the hatch. It lifted and Dillon slipped inside.

As Ferguson lowered the Nightstalker, Jack Barry emerged from the companionway. Ferguson checked him out, the paper cup in one hand, the butt of the Browning sticking out of his waistband. Ferguson thought of Dillon down there trying to make his way through unfamiliar territory and made his decision. He put the Nightstalker in his pocket, took out the Smith & Wesson, and held it against his back in his left hand. He walked along the quay and paused at the gangway, umbrella held high.

"We haven't met face-to-face, Mr. Barry, but the name's Ferguson."

•   •   •

Ferguson started down the gangplank and his left hand emerged holding the Smith & Wesson.

Wyatt Earp, the great American marshal, once said that what had made his reputation as a gunfighter was when a young cowboy had tried to shoot him in the back in the darkness of Dodge City at fifty paces. Earp had turned and fired as a reflex, without taking aim, and shot the gun from the boy's hand, a total fluke.

Jack Barry did the same now, pulling the silenced Browning out, firing from the hip, catching the Smith & Wesson in Charles Ferguson's hand and blowing it away. Dillon, easing in through the hatch above the shower room, had heard Ferguson, took out his Walther, dashed through the kitchen and saloon, and went out headfirst into Barry as Ferguson fell back to the deck.

Dillon rammed the Walther into Barry's back. "Drop it, Jack, or I'll blow your spine in two."

Barry froze. "Why, Sean, it's you."

Ferguson got to his feet. Dillon said, "Are you okay, Brigadier?"

Ferguson was holding his wrist, which was bleeding. "Just a scratch. I'm fine."

Barry leaned over and placed the Browning on the deck, then as he straightened, he lifted his right elbow into Dillon's face, turning sideways so that Dillon's reflex shot went into the deck. Dillon dropped the Walther and they closed together, Barry staggering back as they struggled furiously. When they went over the rail, it was still together.

And it was cold, the kind of shock that numbed the brain, and the current was fierce. Dillon kicked Barry away as he surfaced, felt himself swept against the stern anchor chain, and grabbed at it. As he turned, he saw Barry being carried away.

"Fuck you, Dillon!" he called and was gone.

Dillon hung on, then hauled himself along the chain to the other side of the *Griselda* and reached for a ring bolt on the wall.

"Dillon?" Ferguson called.

"Here." Dillon pulled himself to a ladder.

He sat on the old quay, streaming water, and Ferguson said, "Do you think he's gone?"

"Only elsewhere, Brigadier. I'll confirm he's gone when I've shot him between the eyes at very close quarters, but not before."

"What now?"

"Let's go below. I'm wet through and I could do with some dry clothes."

In the shower room, Dillon stripped and toweled. In the small bedroom he helped himself to underwear and jeans and a sweater far too large, then joined Ferguson in the saloon. He nodded to the black suit, white shirt, and tie.

"Nice gear, Brigadier. I mean, if you were going to circulate at a great hotel like the Dorchester, you'd really pass dressed like that."

"You don't think he's at the bottom of the Thames?"

"No, probably on the other side by now, but he won't be turning up at the Dorchester. You see, Jack isn't a patriot, he's a very practical man, and a British prison is the last thing he needs. He came, he failed."

"I know. Strange, Dillon. When you told me he was here, I said it had to be for Cohan. I couldn't think of any reason that could bring him here from Ulster. But why? Barry runs the Sons of Erin. Why would he want to eradicate the last member of the New York branch?"

"Because that's exactly what Cohan is. He's a problem to you, he's a problem to the President. Maybe he's a problem to the Connection, too."

Ferguson was suddenly cheerful. "My dear boy, you

sometimes have a perfect facility for hitting the nail on the head. Let's go."

Dillon said, "And the boat?"

"Wherever he goes, if he's still on the planet, he won't come back here. Just turn the lights out. I'll have a recovery team check it out tomorrow."

But Ferguson was wrong. Barry surfaced at St. James's Stairs. He hauled himself up a ladder and started back to the basin. The lights were still on in the boat. He crouched there in the darkness, wet and cold. After a while, the lights went out below and Ferguson and Dillon appeared. The deck lights went out, they came up the gangway and walked away, talking.

When the sound of the voices had faded, he hurried across, went below, and stripped hurriedly. He toweled, found fresh clothes, and dressed. Then he pulled on the bomber jacket, which still had his mobile in one of the pockets. He reached under one of the benches, pulled up a plank, rummaged inside, and took out a Smith & Wesson revolver. He slipped it in a pocket and left, switching off the lights.

He walked away through the rain, not at all depressed, actually laughing out loud. What a bastard Dillon was, and it was nice to have a face to put on Ferguson's name after all these years. It was all a game, after all. He understood that, so did Dillon and Ferguson, but did the Connection? He reached the Escort, got in, and drove away.

Dillon pulled up outside Ferguson's flat in Cavendish Square. "I suppose it means we don't have to worry about Cohan for the rest of his stay."

"How can you be so sure?"

"He's no samurai, our Jack, he has no intention of committing suicide. Now that he knows we're on to him, if he was here for Cohan, he's on his way."

"You say if."

"Let's wait and see."

"And our mystery assassin—your woman?"

"Let's wait and see there also."

Ferguson nodded. "Nine o'clock. My office." He got out and Dillon leaned through the window.

"Charles? You will have that wrist seen to, won't you? None of that British stoicism, I hope."

Ferguson smiled. "Don't worry, Sean, I'm not daft. Now be off with you."

Dillon drove away.

The weather was terrible as Barry drove out of London. Heavy, heavy rain. For some reason, though, he still felt incredibly cheerful as he stopped on the motorway at a Little Chef, had an all-day English breakfast, and bought half a bottle of Scotch in the shop.

He drank a quarter of it on his way down to Roundhay, where he found the little airstrip dark and quiet, except for a light in the barn. He drove in beside the Chieftain and found Docherty sitting on a stool reading a newspaper.

"Did it go well, Jack?" he asked.

"Don't ask. Just get me out of here. Can you do it?"

"I'm your man."

Ten minutes later, the Chieftain lifted into the night, Barry sat back, opened the half bottle of whiskey again, and drank. Then he took out his mobile and rang the Connection.

"It's me, Barry."

"Where are you?"

"On my way from England to Ireland in a small plane, and lucky to be here."

"Tell me."

Which Barry did.

Thornton said, "How would they know about your houseboat, for God's sake?"

"I don't know. All I know is that they did, and I'm lucky to be getting the hell out of it."

"And Cohan?"

"He can take his chances, as far as I'm concerned," and Barry rang off.

NINE

DILLON, IN THE office at ten o'clock, woke Blake in bed at five A.M. in Washington.

"For God's sake, Sean, look at the time!"

"I'm doing you a favor, Blake. My story is better than the midnight movie. You'll come dangerously alive, go down to the kitchen in your tracksuit, drink fresh orange juice, and contemplate a five-mile run."

"Like hell I will."

"Just listen."

When Dillon was finished, Blake said, "God help us, it gets worse."

"Don't tell me. I'll keep in touch," and Dillon rang off.

Lady Helen Lang jogged through Hyde Park. It was ten-thirty the following morning. She sat on a bench by the pond and rested. She wasn't breathless, she felt fine. The prospect of the evening at the Dorchester was strangely like going into battle. She was determined on her course of action, no question of that. It was fitting that Cohan should go the same way as the rest of the club. She was realistic enough to realize that the prospect of ever facing Jack Barry or the Connection just wasn't likely. However, she would have exacted a considerable amount of justice, as she saw it. It would comfort her next time she placed flowers at her son's monument.

Her name was called and she looked up and saw Hedley walking toward her. "Thought I'd see how you were getting on."

"That was nice of you." She stood up and suddenly was struggling for breath. She clutched her chest, then sat down again, fumbled for the plastic bottle of pills in her pocket and dropped it.

He picked it up and sat beside her and opened it. "Is it bad?"

She lied, of course. "No, no, I was just a little dizzy for a moment." He passed two pills in his palm. She picked them up and swallowed them down. "That's better."

"This ain't good, Lady Helen."

She patted his knee. "A nice cup of tea and I can go on forever, Hedley. Now take me across to the café."

They stood up and she took his arm.

In his office at the Ministry of Defence, Ferguson was going over the previous night's events with Hannah Bernstein and Dillon.

"What a load of male macho nonsense," Hannah said, outraged. "And at your age, Brigadier."

Ferguson, who was wearing an elastic bandage on his gun hand, said, "I stand corrected, Chief Inspector."

"God, but you look grand when you're angry, girl," Dillon told her. "The eyes sparkle and there's a flush to the cheeks."

"Oh, go to hell," she said. "It should have been a major antiterrorist squad operation. If the place had been flooded with armed officers, we'd have had him. One of the most wanted Irish terrorists."

"We'd also have been on the front page of every tabloid newspaper, and I didn't want that," Ferguson told her. "My decision."

At that moment, the phone rang. His secretary said, "Reception has a call from Ulster. A Jack Barry?"

Ferguson pressed his audio button so that Dillon and Hannah could hear the conversation. "Jack Barry. Have them trace it."

"They can't, Brigadier, it's a coded mobile," his secretary said.

"All right, then, just put him through."

The call was surprisingly clear. "Is that you, Ferguson?"

"And who else would it be?"

"I just wanted to let you know I didn't drown in the Thames and I'm safe home. You're a lucky man. I thought I'd got you."

"Well, you didn't. You shot the gun out of my hand, mind you. That was pretty good."

"Is Dillon there?"

"Naturally."

"To our next merry meeting in hell, Sean." Barry laughed and the phone went dead.

Hannah Bernstein said, "What a fiend. What's he playing at, making stupid phone calls? Now we know for sure he's alive. We didn't before."

"It's a game to Jack, the lot of it," Dillon told her. "I could also add that some say he's as mad as a hatter, that he'll never do the sensible thing, only the crazy thing."

Hannah said, "I suppose the only good thing is that Senator Cohan won't die on us here."

"You really think so?" Ferguson shook his head. "There has never been a suggestion that Barry killed the others. The only logical reason for his presence here, if Cohan was a target, would be because the Senator had become an inconvenience. No, we've disposed of one danger, at least temporarily. The other one—our mysterious second assassin—is still out there." He picked up the phone. "Get me Senator Michael Cohan at the Dorchester."

He kept the audio button down. A moment later, Cohan said, "Michael Cohan. Who is this?"

"Charles Ferguson. I believe you know who I am."

"Yes, I do, and I don't wish to speak to you."

"Senator, believe me, I only have your best interests at heart."

"I am a US Senator on a visit on behalf of the President," Cohan lied. "If you continue to harass me, I'll complain to the Prime Minister's office," and he slammed down the phone.

"An angry man," Dillon said. "So what do we do now?"

"Why, we adjourn for lunch, of course."

Giuliano, the manager of the Dorchester Piano Bar, greeted them with enthusiasm. Ferguson had been using the place for twenty years or more, Dillon comparatively recently, but he did appear on a regular basis. Hannah Bernstein, of course, was no problem. Like any Italian male, Giuliano appreciated beauty combined with brains, and Hannah certainly had that. The fact that she was also a Detective Chief Inspector of the Special Branch at Scotland Yard was a bonus. The additional fact that she had killed in the line of duty gave an extra frisson. Giuliano remembered the newspaper story. A couple of years previously, she had been passing a street on her way to Grosvenor Square when a woman had emerged screaming that an armed holdup was taking place. As she was on American Embassy duty that day, Bernstein had been armed and had seriously embarrassed the villains by shooting one man armed with a sawed-off shotgun, dead.

Giuliano kissed her on each cheek with style, then presented his suggestions for lunch. A homemade cannelloni with mozzarella cheese and ham stuffing. Then there was a gnocchi di patate al pesto, potato dumplings in garlic and basil sauce. They made their choice, and Dillon ordered Krug non-vintage champagne.

"One thing," Ferguson said to Giuliano. "I understand that Senator Michael Cohan has a table reserved for one o'clock?"

"That's true," Giuliano said, looking startled.

"Well, then, put him at the next table, there's a good chap," Ferguson said.

Giuliano smiled. "Here we go again, Brigadier. I should write a book. All these years. The Cold War, English public school men who were communists under the skin, and then the Irish." He smiled at Dillon. "Forgive me, my friend . . ."

"I know, I'm a terrible man," Dillon told him.

Giuliano said, "So the American gets the next table. I wish you joy."

He went away, the Krug came, and Dillon insisted on pouring. He said, "How did you know Cohan would be here?"

Ferguson grunted. "The telephone, Dillon. It's a wonderful instrument. You should try it sometime."

Hannah said, "How do we handle it?"

"Head on, my dear, head on." Ferguson raised his glass. "To life and love and happiness."

"Well, if you add peace in Ulster, I'll drink to that," Dillon said, and Cohan appeared at the head of the steps.

Giuliano greeted him, brought him down to the next table, took an order for a dry martini, and went away.

Ferguson said, "Senator Michael Cohan? Brigadier Charles Ferguson."

Cohan was outraged. "This is harassment of the worst

kind. I warned you I would complain to the Prime Minister's office. I certainly will after this."

Two things happened. He started to get up and a waiter arrived with the dry martini. It was Dillon who took over.

"I don't mind you being a politician, Senator. We have them in Ireland, too, although I remember one saying, 'Don't tell my mother I'm a Senator in the Dail, she thinks I play piano in a whorehouse.' "

"How dare you!"

"Oh, shut your face," Dillon said. "Try not to be stupid, because that's what you're being. Now if you want to live, listen to the man."

Ferguson said, "Just hear me, Senator. Let's discuss the Sons of Erin and see if you can make any connection"—he emphasized the word—"with your own experience."

When he was finished, Cohan sat there, very pale. "This has nothing to do with me."

"Listen, you shite," Dillon told him. "Jack Barry was here in London last night, and why? To pick the meat off your bones."

Cohan was really worried now but tried to bluster. "I know nothing of this."

"The Sons of Erin are all dead, Senator. Now, maybe somebody just doesn't like dining clubs," Dillon said. "But our theory is that Jack Barry came over on a hasty trip to tidy things up, which meant stiffing you."

It was Hannah who put in, "But that still leaves, somewhere out there, the individual who got rid of your friends."

"Nonsense," Cohan told her. "It's all rubbish. Now I demand that you leave me alone!" He swallowed the dry martini.

Ferguson said, "So you won't cooperate. All right, Senator, have it your way. The Prime Minister and the President will be so informed. However, my instructions are to keep you alive if possible while you're in London, so we'll be there tonight at the Forum for Irish Peace doing our best to achieve that aim, whether you cooperate or not."

"Go to hell." Cohan got up and walked out.

Their pasta arrived. Hannah said, "What now, sir?"

"Why, we enjoy this delicious light luncheon, return this evening, and try to keep the bastard in one piece."

"You think there could be a problem?"

"I've never been more certain of anything in my life." Ferguson picked up a fork and turned to Dillon. "Black tie, dear boy, do try to look civilized."

With nowhere else to go, Cohan phoned the Connection on the coded mobile phone number and poured out everything, all his doubts, all his fears.

When he was finished, Thornton said, "Can't you see what they're doing to you? I had an arrangement with Barry. He flew over to protect you, so they found out he was there, and he got out by the skin of his teeth, from what you say."

"You told me I'd be safe in London."

"You will be. I was just making doubly sure by sending Barry. Everything will be fine."

"You said Barry would be taking care of whoever was behind the killings."

"There's a lot going on you don't know about. Just trust me."

"It's my hide if something goes wrong."

"Senator, Senator—nothing will go wrong. Okay? So just calm down, relax, enjoy the party. I'll be in touch."

Thornton hung up and immediately phoned Barry.

"I've had Cohan on in a hell of a state. He's had Ferguson and Dillon on his back. Why didn't you tell me how badly things went?"

"Because it only happened last night, and I was busy getting out of England in one piece."

"Let me hear your version."

So Barry did, staying reasonably close to the truth. When he was finished, he said, "It was just one of those things. How Dillon found me, I don't know."

"A considerable nuisance, that man."

"The army said that for twenty years and the IRA have been saying it ever since. Anyway, what about Cohan?"

"I'll have to leave him to do his own thing. I'll think of something when he returns to the States. I'll be in touch," and he put down his phone.

In the house in South Audley Street, Lady Helen Lang went through her wardrobe and finally selected a superb evening suit in black crepe. She held the jacket against her as she stood in front of the mirror. There was a knock on the door, and Hedley entered with a cup of tea.

"What do you think?" she asked.

"Looks good to me."

She hung the black suit inside the wardrobe. "Fine." She sipped some of her tea. "I've a hair appointment at Daniel Galvin's in forty-five minutes."

"You look okay to me, Lady Helen."

"All the world and his wife will be there tonight, Hedley."

"Including Cohan?"

She smiled. "I must look my best. Now go and get ready. I'll be with you in a quarter of an hour."

The Forum for Irish Peace in the Dorchester ballroom was a splendid black tie affair. The Prime Minister had not yet arrived, but several members of the Cabinet had. The guest list certainly included the great and the good, and Dillon, surprised as always at the people pulled in for such a thing, reached for a glass of champagne from a passing waiter. He was wearing an evening suit with raw silk lapels.

Hannah, in a dull red silk suit by Versace, said, "Take it easy, Dillon, it's a long night ahead."

"You look grand, girl," he told her. "Fit for a three-page spread in *Vogue* magazine."

"Flattery really will get you nowhere."

"I know, and isn't that the terrible shame?"

Ferguson approached. "Everything all right?"

"Jesus, Brigadier," Dillon said. "When I was a wee boy in Belfast, my grandmother would take me to the lounge in the old Grand Central for afternoon tea. The grandeur of it. She loved that. The headwaiter wore a dinner suit just like yours."

"Sticks and stones, Dillon," Ferguson said. "And my patience, as usual, is wearing dangerously thin." He frowned. "Good God, it's Lady Helen Lang," and he turned from Dillon as she came through the crowd.

They embraced. "So nice to see you, Charles." She turned and saw Dillon. "Why, it's Mr. Dillon, isn't it?"

Dillon took her hand. "A great pleasure to meet you again, Lady Helen."

"I couldn't resist coming. I live in South Audley Street just round the corner. Terribly convenient. Every time I feel like a cocktail, I walk down to the Piano Bar."

At that moment, there was a buzz over by the main door. Hannah appeared. "The Prime Minister, Brigadier."

Ferguson said, "So sorry, Helen." He nodded to Dillon. "Get Lady Helen another glass of champagne, there's a good chap. With me, Chief Inspector."

They walked away. Lady Helen said, "You sometimes appear to be on the dangerous edge of things, Mr. Dillon."

"How very astute." He grabbed two glasses from a passing tray and gave her one. "There you are." He glanced around. "A grand bunch of people."

"Whom you despise totally."

He raised his glass. "To you, Lady Helen, and me, the only two people in a world gone mad."

She smiled as she returned his toast and, for some reason, he was aware of a coldness, a terrible unease. Now why should that be?

"Forum for Irish Peace." He shook his head. "Seven hundred years coming and too late for some." He took a deep breath. "God save us, but I'm sorry."

"Ah, you're thinking of my son," she smiled, very calm. "If you work for Charles, you'll know my background, but as a great writer once said, the past is a foreign country, Mr. Dillon. No, we should never dwell on the past. We must manage with what we've got."

"A thought," Dillon said. "But not much of a comfort."

At that moment, an aging lady approached. "My dear Helen, so nice to see you."

They touched cheeks and Helen Lang said, "You two won't know each other. The Duchess of Stevely, Sean Dillon."

"A considerable pleasure." Dillon kissed her hand.

"Oh, I do like the Irish," the Duchess said. "Such rogues. Are you a rogue, Mr. Dillon?"

Helen said, "Well, he works for Charles Ferguson."

"There you are then," the Duchess said.

"I'll love you and leave you." Dillon withdrew.

He saw Ferguson talking to a Cabinet minister, Hannah waiting discreetly close at hand. She came across to him.

"Cohan just came in. He's talking to the American Ambassador in the corner over there. It's difficult to keep track in a crowd like this."

"Girl, dear, whatever else, no one is going to do anything very dramatic to him at an affair like this."

"You think he's going to be all right?" She shook her head. "The Brigadier seems so certain."

"He's older than you are, that means he's got it right more often. On the other hand, how often has he been wrong?"

"I'd rather it didn't happen on our patch if it is going to happen," she said.

At that moment, there was a flurry of movement at the entrance, and the Prime Minister came in with a small entourage.

"Come on," Hannah said and moved through the crowd to Ferguson, Dillon at her back.

The three of them stood together, watching the Prime Minister's progress as he shook the occasional hand or paused for a few words. Finally, he reached the American Ambassador, Cohan still with him. There were smiles all round. In fact, it was the first time Dillon had seen the Senator smiling.

"He seems happy enough now," Ferguson said.

"For the moment, sir," Hannah observed. "Only for the moment."

The emcee, resplendent in a scarlet coat, called, "Ladies and gentlemen, the Prime Minister."

All conversation died instantly as the Prime Minister moved to the microphone. "Your Grace, My Lords, ladies and gentlemen. We live in exciting times. Peace in Ireland is literally within our grasp, and what I want to say to you is this . . ."

He finished to considerable applause and was away in an instant, glad-handling his way to the door with his people.

"Now what, sir?" Hannah asked.

"From the look of that splendid buffet, I'd say eating time is here," Ferguson told her. "So let's get to it."

"What about Cohan, sir?"

"You two take turns dogging his footsteps."

"Although if anything was going to happen, it wouldn't happen here?" Dillon said. "Is that your drift?"

"Exactly."

Hannah said, "I'm not so hungry, so I'll take first watch."

"As you like, my dear. I see he's still with the American Ambassador."

She turned and started to push her way through the crowd.

Cohan stood with the Ambassador and a number of people in a corner, which was some sort of protection against the crowd. He was drinking too much and sweating, all due to stress, of course. He felt awful, and the truth was he was frightened.

He hadn't said a word to the Ambassador about his present situation. After all, how could he? He'd noticed Ferguson, Dillon, and Hannah Bernstein earlier, and in a sense their presence made things worse. He reached for another glass of champagne as a waiter hovered and jolted a rather pleasant-looking woman standing close by.

"I'm terribly sorry."

"That's quite all right," Helen Lang told him.

At that moment, Cohan saw Hannah Bernstein pushing her way through the crowd and was conscious of immense irritation. Why in the hell wouldn't they leave him alone?

The Ambassador put a hand on his shoulder. "Are you okay, Michael? You're sweating."

"Oh, sure," Cohan said. "I started a cold on the flight over." Suddenly, he realized that, for the moment at least, he had to get out of there. "I'll just run up to my suite and swallow some aspirin."

Helen Lang, close enough to hear, turned at once and worked her way through the crowd. She paused at the door to check in her purse for the passkey that Hedley had given her, then walked out.

Cohan finished his champagne, saw Hannah standing close by at one of the bars, a glass in her hand, and his irritation turned to anger. He started to push through the crowd, reached the ballroom entrance, paused briefly to check behind him, aware that she also was on the move, then made for the men's room and went in. It was busy enough for him to have to wait. He really was sweating now and found himself checking faces in the mirror. He dashed water on his face, took a hand towel from the attendant, and dried himself.

There were several men going out together in a rather boisterous crowd. He moved out behind them, was aware of Hannah Bernstein glancing the other way toward the ballroom. He took his chance, dashed away, and made it to the lounge. His irritation was immediately eased. It was as if he'd won a victory, small perhaps, but a victory. He reached the foyer, went to the elevators, and punched the button.

Hannah gave it ten minutes, and was still standing there against the wall when Dillon arrived. "I was looking for you. Where's our friend?"

"In there." She nodded at the door. "I saw him go in, but he hasn't come out."

Dillon smiled. "Some things are still beyond the powers of even politically correct coppers. Leave it to me."

She waited, watching the crowd, swollen now by late arrivals. Finally, Dillon emerged, pausing only to light a cigarette. "Not a sign."

"That's strange, he definitely went in." She was aware of a sudden touch of anxiety. "Let's see if he's in the ballroom," and she led the way back.

Helen Lang's passkey worked perfectly. She was into Cohan's suite instantly and closed the door. It was very luxurious. An excellent bedroom and bathroom, a shower room, and a superb paneled sitting room. The maid had drawn the curtains. Helen slipped through, slid back the French windows, and stepped onto the terrace. Hyde Park was opposite, the lights of the city beyond. Down below, Park Lane was crowded with traffic. She felt strangely nostalgic standing there. It was raining slightly and she moved under the canopy, lit a cigarette, and waited.

Cohan got out of the elevator and hurried along the corridor, his heart pounding. Christ, what's happening to me? he thought. I need a drink. He reached his suite, got the door open, and moved inside. He opened the doors of the Chinese lacquered bar unit, poured a large Scotch, his hands shaking. He took it down, then poured another. What in the hell was he going to do? He'd never felt like this ever. Everything was falling apart. It occurred to him then that the one person who could possibly tell him what to do was Barry, so he went into the bedroom, got his mobile from his traveling bag, returned to the sitting room, and phoned him.

Barry, still at the safe house in County Down, said, "Who is this?"

"Cohan. For God's sake, what's going on?"

"What do you mean?"

"Look, I spoke to the Connection. I know all about your escapade in London last night. I've had Brigadier Charles Ferguson and this Dillon guy on my back and they told me."

"And what did they say?"

Cohan told him everything he could remember. "The Connection said you were here to protect my back."

"So I was."

"Dillon said you were here to knock me off."

"Who do you believe?" Barry asked. "Your friends or that little Taig shite? We're in this together. We'll sort it together. When are you due back in New York?"

"Tomorrow."

"Excellent," Barry lied with his usual smoothness. "There are things happening that you don't know about, but all your doubts will be resolved, I promise you."

"Okay, okay," Cohan nodded. "I'll stay in touch."

"You do that."

Barry thought about it, then phoned the Connection. "I've just had Cohan on the line from London."

"And?"

"He's coming apart. You've got to do something."

"Such as?"

"Couldn't you arrange for him to be hit by a truck when he gets back to New York?"

"I'll give it my consideration," Thornton told him and rang off.

Cohan put the mobile phone down and picked up his glass. "Why in the hell did I ever get mixed up in all this?" he whispered.

He put the glass to his lips, the curtains opened, and Lady Helen Lang entered, the Colt .25 in her right hand, the silencer in place.

TEN

"WHAT IN THE hell is this?" Cohan demanded, shocked at the appearance of this grandmother-looking person with a gun. And she looked familiar somehow.

"Nemesis, Senator, that just about sums it up."

"Now look here." He was blustering now. "If it's money you want . . ."

She laughed. "No, that's not it. Remember those old movies with the highwayman demanding your money or your life? In this case, I'd prefer your life. I have money."

Cohan was horrified. "Who *are* you?"

"Sit down and I'll tell you."

He subsided into one of the sofas, shaking like a leaf. "What is this?"

"I think it's what they call in those old gangster movies on television, payback time."

"But what have I done?"

"Oh, nothing personally. I'm sure you have clean hands,

you're a typical politician, but you did connive, along with the rest of the Sons of Erin."

Cohan had never been so terrified. "Oh, my God, it *is* you! But why? Why?"

She took out her silver cigarette case one-handed, got one in her mouth, and lit it. "I had a son, Senator, a brave and gallant young man. Let me tell you what his ending was because of the stupid fantasy games you and your friends got up to."

When she was finished, Cohan was ashen-faced. He sat there, huddled in the corner of the sofa. She poured another whiskey and passed it to him.

"It's unbelievable," he said.

"But true, Senator, your worst nightmare. I shot Tim Pat Ryan here in London, went to New York and got your friends Brady, Kelly, and Cassidy."

He swallowed the whiskey. "What do you want?"

"Let's start with some questions. The Connection. Who is he?"

"A voice on the phone, I swear it."

"But surely you have some clue?"

"No! He knows things, but I don't know *how* he knows them! He never says!"

"And Jack Barry? Where would he be?"

"Somewhere in Northern Ireland, that's all I know."

"But you were talking to him, I heard you."

"A special phone, a coded mobile. It has a number, but it can't be traced."

"Really?" She picked the mobile up. "What's the number?" He hesitated and she raised the Colt.

He gave it to her.

Barry was having supper when his mobile rang. "Who is this?"

Helen Lang said, "Nobody special, Mr. Barry, but I *will* be in touch."

She put the mobile in her purse, moved to the desk, quickly noted the number on a notepad, and put that in her purse also. She had switched the Colt to her left hand so that she could write, and Cohan, seizing his chance, threw his glass at her and plunged through the curtains to the terrace.

It was stupid, really. He had nowhere to go. There was a small fountain, a fish spouting water, and a step beyond, the terrace wall. He peered over, looked at the ribbon of light moving along Park Lane, and below the ledge spotted an iron ladder going down, obviously for maintenance purposes. He quickly sat astride the coping, one foot feeling for the ladder, just as Helen Lang came through the curtains, the Colt ready.

"No, for God's sake, no!" he screamed, and then his foot slipped and he was falling.

Helen looked down, saw a sudden stoppage of traffic, horns honking, the sound drifting up. She turned at once, went through the suite to the door, opened it, and went out. A few moments later, she was descending to the foyer. She walked through to the ballroom, took a glass of champagne from a tray held by one of the waiters by the door, and mingled.

Nemesis was the right word. It hadn't needed her on this occasion. Cohan had paid an inevitable price. Everything came around, a law of life. She hadn't needed to do it herself, only that it should be done. It was enough. She saw a great deal of movement down at the main door, caught a glimpse of Ferguson and Dillon, and then was aware of a pain in her chest. She found her pillbox, swallowed two with a gulp of champagne, and walked toward the ballroom entrance.

• • •

"Perhaps he's gone up to his suite," Dillon said as they finished their search of the ballroom, and then there was the sound of horns from outside the ballroom, a considerable disturbance.

Hannah said to Ferguson, "I'd better see what the trouble is, sir."

The traffic had slowed considerably, and Hannah immediately saw the cause of it. There were people on the pavement surrounding a body, and a single motorcycle cop was standing beside his machine and calling it in. Hannah flashed her ID.

"Chief Inspector Bernstein, Special Branch. What happened?"

"I was just passing, guv. He fell from up the top, nearly hit a passing couple. The woman is in shock over there. I've called an ambulance and backup."

Hannah leaned down and recognized Cohan at once. She straightened. "I know this man, Constable, he's a guest at the hotel. You stay shtum, no answers to any questions, not to the press, not to anyone. This is a red alert. You know what that means?"

"Of course I do, guv."

"I'm going inside, but I'll be back."

They checked out Cohan's suite, the three of them, with a decidedly shaken duty manager. Hannah said, "Not a thing, no sign of a struggle."

"I agree, Chief Inspector," Ferguson said. "But did he fall or was he pushed?" He turned to Dillon. "What do you think?"

"Oh, come on, Brigadier, who believes in coincidence in our business?"

"Yes, I agree." Ferguson nodded. "She must be one hell of a woman."

"I'm inclined to agree," Dillon nodded.

Ferguson said to the duty manager, "Keep this suite locked and secure. You'll have police here to do forensic tests quite soon."

"Of course, Brigadier."

Ferguson turned to Dillon. "You break the bad news to Blake and, obviously through him, to the President. I'll handle the Prime Minister."

"The great pity it is, your knighthood going down the drain like this," Dillon said.

Ferguson smiled. "I always knew you were on my side, Dillon."

In spite of the close proximity of the house in South Audley Street, Lady Helen had arranged for Hedley to wait for her in Park Lane in the Mercedes. She pushed her way out through the curious onlookers, passing what was left of Senator Michael Cohan. Hedley saw her coming, jumped out, and got the rear door open. She got in, he climbed behind the wheel and drove away.

"Just drive around, Hedley, it's been a heavy night." She lit a cigarette.

"What happened?"

She told him everything. "So, Cohan's gone and I'm actually left with a link with Jack Barry." She held up the mobile. "I'll try him again, shall I?"

Barry grabbed at the phone when it rang. "Who is this?"

"Nemesis," she said. "But first, some hot news. Senator Michael Cohan took a fall from the seventh floor of the Dorchester in Park Lane. I'm using his mobile."

More than at any time before in his life, Jack Barry was shaken rigid. "What are you telling me?"

"That Senator Michael Cohan is lying on the pavement in Park Lane outside the Dorchester Hotel. It's like a bad Saturday night in Belfast. Police, ambulances, onlookers, but then you know about this kind of thing."

Strangely enough, Barry wasn't angry. He actually knew a kind of fear. "Who in the hell are you?"

"Brady, Kelly, Cassidy in New York, Tim Pat Ryan in London, and now Senator Michael Cohan. That's who I am." She laughed. "That just leaves you and the Connection."

Barry took a deep breath. "Okay, so who are you? Loyalist freedom fighters? Red Hand of Ulster? Protestant scum?"

"Actually, it may surprise you to know that I'm a Roman Catholic, Mr. Barry. Religion doesn't come into it, and I'm surprised you say Protestant scum. You're a Protestant yourself. So was Wolfe Tone, who invented Irish Republicanism; so was Parnell, who came close to achieving a United Ireland." She was enjoying herself now. "Then there was Oscar Wilde, George Bernard Shaw, Sean O'Casey, all Prods."

He cut in, angry now. "What kind of shite is this? I don't need a fugging history lesson. What's it about? Who are you?"

"The woman who is going to execute you, just like I executed the others. Justice, Mr. Barry, is what it's about, a rare commodity these days, but I intend to have it."

He listened to her soft, measured voice, entirely the wrong kind of voice for what he was hearing. His anger increased. "You're mad."

"Not really. You butchered my son in Ulster three years ago, and executed his friends, four of them, including a woman. You wouldn't remember, Mr. Barry, I'm sure. You've got so much blood on your hands, it's hard to remember which corpse is which." She was giving him too much information, but it was all right. A plan was forming in her mind.

Barry had never felt so frustrated. "Look, Cohan's mobile is no use to you. It's coded. Any calls are untraceable."

"Yes, but I can at least speak to you."

"Okay, so what is it you want?"

"It's quite simple. As I said, you butchered my son in Ulster three years ago. I'm going to butcher you."

He felt a sudden touch of fear again. "No way. You're crazy, lady!"

"At least I can talk to you when I want on this very useful phone. We could even arrange a meeting. I'll be in touch."

"Any time, you bitch. You got a time and place, just name it," but she had already rung off.

Lady Helen said, "Pass me the flask, Hedley." He did so. She took a swallow and passed it back. "Excellent. I feel great." She got out her silver case, lit a cigarette, and inhaled deeply. "Marvelous. Drive round for a while. The Palace, Pall Mall."

The rain had increased again, the wipers clicked backwards and forwards. Hedley cruised the traffic carefully.

"I like driving in the rain," she said. "It's a safe, enclosed feeling. It's as if the rest of the world doesn't exist. Do you like the rain, Hedley?"

"Rain?" He laughed out loud. "Lady Helen, I saw too much of it in 'Nam. Patrolling in the swamps of the Mekong Delta, leeches applying themselves to your more important bits and those monsoon rains sluicing down."

"Just hearing about it makes me shiver. Find a pub. I feel like a drink."

Which he did, a very respectable place called The Grenadier close to St. James's Place. They'd used it before. The landlord, Sam Hardaker, was an old Grenadier Guards sergeant and knew Hedley from his days at the Embassy.

"A real pleasure, Lady Helen."

"Nice to see you, Sam. I don't expect you have such a thing as a bottle of champagne?"

"One in the fridge. Nonvintage, but Bollinger. Promised to a Grenadier Guard's officer at the Palace, but he'll have to do without."

She and Hedley sat in a corner booth, Sam brought the Bollinger in a bucket and produced two glasses. He uncorked and poured. Lady Helen tasted it.

"Heavenly." She smiled as Sam filled the glasses. "They say that if you're tired of champagne, you're tired of life."

"I wouldn't know," Sam said. "Being a beer man myself."

He retired and she lit another cigarette. "All right, Hedley?"

He nodded. "Just fine, Lady Helen."

She raised a glass. "To us, then. To love and life and the pursuit of happiness." He raised his glass and they touched. "And damnation to Jack Barry and the Connection."

Hedley drank some of his champagne and put the glass down. "You wouldn't really try to meet that bastard?"

She lit another cigarette, frowning, considering the point. "The only way to see him, Hedley, would be in some way to bring him to me."

Hedley nodded. "Okay, so let's say you brought him down just like the others. What then? That still leaves the Connection, and you'll never know who he is—none of them did."

"Pour me another glass of champagne and let's take a philosophical viewpoint to all this." She leaned back. "Politics, Hedley, are responsible for so many ills. Take the situation we are so involved with. Forget about the Sons of Erin and the Connection. The whole thing starts with governments having a dialogue. Events couldn't have proceeded without dialogue between the British and American governments, the Prime Minister and the President and their cozy chats on the telephone."

"So?" Hedley said.

"If they hadn't agreed to pool information, there wouldn't have been all that juicy stuff from the Intelligence Services for the Connection to poach." She reached for the bottle and poured him another glass. "So, where does ultimate responsibility lie?"

"I don't know what you mean."

"Ultimate power, Hedley, holds the final responsibility in this case. If the White House was involved, ultimate power lies with the President himself." She glanced at her watch. "Oh, it's late. Let's go."

Hedley handed her into the Mercedes, went round, and got behind the wheel. As he drove away he said, "For God's sake, what are you saying?"

"I've secured an invitation to Chad Luther's party at his Long Island estate next week. The President is the guest of honor, I understand."

Hedley swerved. "My God, you wouldn't!"

She frowned and then laughed. "Oh, good heavens, Hedley, do you think I mean to assassinate him? Oh dear, oh dear, what must you think of me?" She shook her head. "I haven't gone over the *edge,* Hedley. No, I meant that I could always discuss it with him."

"Discuss it? You mean, lay the whole thing on the table, everything you've done? The killings? Hell, he'd have you arrested."

"You don't see it, do you?" She lit a cigarette. "It's his White House, so it's his mess. He doesn't want it out in the open any more than I do. This whole White House Connection business would be an enormous scandal. It could imperil his presidency. It would certainly damage the peace process in Ireland that he's worked so hard for. He *has* to unmask the Connection." She gazed at Hedley. "Or who knows what might leak to the press?"

Hedley was aghast. "You mean, you'd *blackmail* the President? You'd be willing to go that far?" He shook his head. "You've got the bad guys, Lady Helen. Let it go. Just let it be."

"I can't," she said. "I'm on borrowed time, Hedley, much more so than you realize, and this is too important. So Long Island it is. If you're not happy with that, then don't come."

"Hey, I don't deserve that."

"I know you don't. You've been solid as a rock. My truest friend."

"I don't need a snow job, that's all I'm saying."

"So you'll come?"

He sighed. "Where else would I go?" He changed gears. "You're not still going to carry that Colt in your purse, are you?"

"Of course I am," she said. "Who knows." She smiled. "I might meet the Connection."

Blake listened to what Dillon had to say. When the Irishman was finished, Blake said, "Takes me back to my FBI days and the most-wanted list. The kind of killers who are obsessive."

"So, you think the same person got Cohan as got the others?"

"Of course I do. I believe in coincidence as much as you do."

"So that means the woman?" Dillon said.

"I suppose it does."

"How does that fit in with FBI or CIA statistics? I mean, we know of women involved in terrorist movements in the past—the Baader–Meinhof gang in Germany, the IRA, the Palestinians—but it's still a minority classification."

"So?"

"*If* we accept the idea, it means that a single woman is responsible for the total demise of the Sons of Erin. She's killed five people."

"Sean, my friend," Blake said, "have you got a better suggestion?"

"Actually, no, but I think it would be useful if you put some more work in with your police friend, Captain Parker."

"Such as?"

"I haven't the slightest idea, but cops are cops. They smell things other people don't. If he sniffs around what's left of the good Senator, there might be some useful information."

"Okay, leave it with me."

Blake rang off, sat there thinking about it, and phoned the President. "You've heard about Cohan?"

"I could hardly avoid it," Cazalet said. "It's all over CNN."

"Can I see you?"

"Come straight up."

The President sat at his desk in the Oval Office in shirtsleeves signing papers passed to him by the chief of staff. Thornton, also in shirtsleeves, looked up and grinned lopsidedly.

"You look glum, Blake, and no wonder."

Cazalet leaned back. "We'll finish these later. So, what now, Blake?"

"God knows," Blake told him.

"You think he was pushed?" Thornton asked.

"Of course he was pushed, or else he panicked and jumped." Blake was exasperated. "Come on, gentlemen, you know the background, you know the score. Do you really believe this was an accident, Cohan simply leaning too far out over his balcony?"

Cazalet said, "So let's simplify it. There's somebody out there who's killed the five American members of this Sons of Erin."

"Closed it down, I'd say," Thornton put in.

"So what's left?" Cazalet asked.

"Jack Barry hiding out in Ulster, and the Connection here in Washington."

Thornton said, "But is this of any importance in view of what's happened?"

"Let's put it this way," Blake said. "The Connection's power didn't derive solely from the classified information which came his way. That information was only of use because he had people to act on it."

"And they're all dead," Cazalet said.

"Not Barry. He's still alive and kicking and more dangerous than any of them. With the Connection still in place and Barry out there as his gun hand, we've still got a big problem."

"What do you suggest?" the President said.

"I thought I'd check Cohan's New York background. My friend, Captain Parker, might be able to come up with something." Blake looked at Cazalet. "And I think it's time for a full-bore investigation right here in the White House, Mr. President."

"Good. I agree," Cazalet told him. "You check on Cohan." He turned to Thornton. "And you see what you can come up with here, Henry. If there's a White House leak, then I think that's a matter for my chief of staff."

"I'll get right on to it, Mr. President," Thornton said, and he and Blake walked out together.

As they moved along the corridor, Blake said, "What do you intend?"

"God knows. We need to keep the lid on this. It's political dynamite. You do your thing, Blake. I'll start doing background checks on everyone in this place. I'll put the Secret Service on it."

"Will you tell them why?"

"Good God, no, not at the moment. We'll just do a discreet check. If nothing shows up, we'll think again. Stay in touch."

Blake moved on and Thornton watched him go, smiling, no fear in him at all. It was strange how excited he felt.

Blake reported the interview to Ferguson, and Ferguson spoke briefly to the Prime Minister on the phone.

"It really does seem to be getting out of hand, Brigadier."

"I obviously take full responsibility for what happened last night," Ferguson told him.

"I don't need that, Brigadier," the Prime Minister said. "Not your fault, not my fault, but let's get it sorted," and he put the phone down.

Ferguson, at his desk, said to Hannah Bernstein and Dillon, "At least he isn't asking for a scapegoat."

"What now, sir?" Hannah asked.

It was Dillon who provided the answer. "It's all up to Blake, I'd say."

"Yes, I think you could be right," Ferguson said.

Thornton phoned through to Barry. "Cazalet, Thornton, and Blake Johnson just had a little talk in the Oval Office."

"Should I get excited?" Barry asked. "Just tell me."

Thornton did. When he was finished, Barry said, "Ah, that's tame stuff. What is there for them to find out about

Cohan in New York? Was he into girls, did he use men's toilets too much? Come on!"

"I agree. It's a negative exercise. I don't think we have anything to worry about."

"We?" Barry said. "They know exactly where I am. They don't know a damn thing about you."

"And it will stay that way as far as I'm concerned. So don't go getting any ideas in your head, Barry. Remember, even if they get to you, it won't help them get to me."

"Bastard," Barry told him, and Thornton rang off.

Barry lit a cigarette and moved to the window. The rain drove against it. One thing he hadn't told the Connection, of course, was the matter of Cohan's mobile and the fact that the mystery woman was linked to him. It was a bizarre kind of psychological umbilical cord. He turned and looked at his own mobile on the table. Strange how he almost wanted it to ring. To hear her voice.

She was at that precise moment driving back to Norfolk, sitting in the rear seat of the Mercedes for once, the only light the one from the dashboard and the headlights cutting into the dark. She felt very calm, very comfortable. It was that safe, enclosed feeling again.

Music was playing softly, just loud enough to hear. She'd told Hedley to put the tape on, one of her husband's favorites, Al Bowlly, the most popular British crooner of his day, more popular in England in the nineteen thirties than Bing Crosby. Killed in the Blitz.

"I like this one," she said. " 'Moonlight on the Highway.' Rather appropriate, but not your cup of tea."

Hedley said, "You know my tastes, Lady Helen. I'm strictly an Ella Fitzgerald and Count Basie man."

"A strange man, Al Bowlly." She lit a cigarette. "Apparently he was from South Africa, but some people said from the Middle East. In England, he took ten years off his age. Became a big band singer. Women adored him. He dined at the Savoy with the aristocracy, was friends with the most notorious gangsters in London."

"Some guy," Hedley said.

"He believed in his personal destiny, especially during the Blitz in London in nineteen forty, when the Nazis tried to bomb us out of the war. One evening, he was walking up a London street when a bomb fell. The blast went the other way. He was unharmed."

"Hell, that happened to me more than once in 'Nam."

"Bowlly interpreted it as a sort of sign from heaven. He believed it meant he was invincible."

"And what happened?"

"Oh, a few weeks later, there was an air-raid warning. Everybody at the apartment block was supposed to go down to the cellars. He stayed in bed. Nothing to fear, you see."

"And?"

"They found him dead in bed. The blast from a falling bomb had blown his door off its hinges."

"Which hit Bowlly?"

"Exactly."

Hedley drove in silence for a while and finally said, "Look, what was the point of that story?"

"Fate, I suppose, and how it can't be avoided. You think you've avoided Death in one place and he finds you in another."

"Sure, I can see that, but I don't see how it affects you."

"Oh, I do, Hedley." She leaned back. "The story illustrates the inevitability of things."

"Like you taking on the President of the United States? I can't buy that, Lady Helen, I surely can't."

"Remember the sign another President had on his desk? The buck stops here? Well, he was right." She peered out at the dark. "Oh, look where we are. I need tea and a sandwich. Let's stop."

They were at an old-fashioned truck stand at the side of the road, one they'd stopped at before, the flap up against the rain. It was almost two in the morning, two roadliner trucks parked nearby, the drivers eating in their cabs. Hedley ordered steak sandwiches on white toast and tea, hot and strong. She joined him, watching the woman who ran the place frying the steaks.

"Smells good, Hedley."

"It always does, Lady Helen."

She bit into the sandwich, juice running down her chin, and the woman leaned over and offered a paper napkin. "There you go, love."

Rain poured off the canopy, she finished the sandwich and drank the strong bitter tea, and when she was finished, said, "Let's go."

She sat in the passenger seat beside him. "You think I'm crazy, Hedley." It was a statement.

"I think you're going too far, Lady Helen."

She lit another cigarette. "Most people take the other way in life, let things go, all good manners and politeness. I remember once sitting in the corner of a London restaurant with a man who'd been my accountant. Next to us were four women, all smoking, one of them in a wheelchair. My friend whispered that he couldn't take the smoke, would have to leave. The woman in the wheelchair said loudly that it was a pity some people couldn't learn a little tolerance."

"What happened?"

"I put him in a taxi, then went back and told the woman in the wheelchair that at least she was alive, whereas my friend with lung cancer had three weeks to live." She frowned. "Why am I telling you this? Probably because it was the first time I really stood up, in a public sense, to be counted. I couldn't stand by."

"Just like you couldn't stand by over the Sons of Erin. Okay, I see that. Only, the President?" He shook his head.

"You don't see anything, Hedley. You're a lovely man, but like most people, you see only what you think you do. You look at me and think I'm the woman I've always been. It's not true. I'm a woman in a hurry, Hedley, because I have no time to lose."

"Hey, don't say things like that."

"It's the truth, Hedley, I'm going to die. Not tonight and not tomorrow, but soon, too soon, and I've got things to do, and by God, I'm going to do them. I'm going to Long Island to face the President, and I've got Barry on the end of that coded mobile any time I want him. All I have to do is reel him in." She took out her pill bottle and shook two into her palm. "So pass that whiskey flask and put your foot down. We could be home by three."

But the weather became even worse, the rain torrential, and when they drove down the hill overlooking the village, it was a scene of chaos, the water overflowing a foot deep in the street, and men struggling at the lock gate.

Hedley pulled in at the pub. Old Tom Armsby was putting sandbags at the door and Hetty was helping him. She looked up as the Mercedes stopped and Lady Helen opened the door.

"Looks bad."

"It is bad, and all down to the Parish Council. The mean bastards wouldn't find the money to fix that lock gate after the last time, when Hedley saved us. Much more of this and every cottage in the village will be flooded."

Lady Helen turned to Hedley. "They're ordinary folk, most of them pensioners. It would ruin them."

"I know." He got out into the rain, took off his chauffeur's tunic, and rolled up his sleeves, standing there in a pool of water. "What's that phrase where you have a sense that you've been here before?"

"Déjà vu. It's French."

"Yes, it would be."

He turned and went toward the men struggling at the lock gate, and she got out and waded after him. There was a young man in the turbulent waters below. He was obviously half-dead, but he tried to go under again and was thrown back up, retching.

"Get him out of there," Hedley ordered. The boy was plucked from the water and dragged up the bank. "Where's a crowbar?"

Someone held one out. Hedley took it and, without hesitation, plunged in. He surfaced, took a deep breath, went down, and felt for the iron clasps on the gate that had been temporarily repaired after the previous occasion. He forced the crowbar in, worked at it, then had to surface, gasping for breath.

He went down again, twice, three times, always more difficult, and then the clasp gave, the gates started to open, and then the force of the water forced them wide. Hedley surfaced to a ragged cheer, for already the flood waters were subsiding.

Willing hands pulled him from the water. He got to his feet and stood there in the rain, and Hetty Armsby ran over with a blanket and put it round him.

"Oh, you wonderful bastard. Come on in the pub, and the rest of you as well. To hell with the law tonight."

Everyone moved forward, and Lady Helen joined Hedley. "Don't let it go to your head. I wouldn't be as blasphemous as to say you walk on water, but they just might change the name of the church to St. Hedley."

• • •

The following morning at Compton Place, the weather was still dreadful, an east wind driving in the rain, waves breaking across the long flat sands of Horseshoe Bay.

Helen, wrapped up in storm coat and hood, cantered her mare through pine woods that broke the worst excesses of the storm, paused in the shelter of the wall of an old ruined chapel, and lit a cigarette with difficulty in her cupped hands.

She looked out at the churning sea and remembered a visit to friends in Long Island some years before, not in the fashionable summer, but late winter, just like this. She'd been shown Chad Luther's mansion, a palace of a place, lawns running into the waters of the Sound, no one in residence, so she didn't enjoy a conducted tour. Chad had invited her many times, mainly because he liked money and she had more than he did. She had never accepted, for a simple reason. She didn't like him. Vulgar, vain, conceited.

She pulled herself up and said softly, "Come on, my dear, who are you to make such judgments? Somebody must love him. Though God alone knows who."

Which still left Long Island in her mind. She shook the reins and galloped away.

Hedley had driven down to the village to see the state of the game. It was still raining hard and the water in the slot was high, but there were no problems. He called at the village shop, filled out a grocery order, and drove back to the house. There was no sign of Lady Helen. He left the groceries in the kitchen, went out into the yard, and heard the sound of pistol fire coming from the barn. When he went in, she was standing shooting at the targets with the Colt .25.

He said, "So I take it we are still going to Long Island and the Colt will still be in your purse?"

"Day after tomorrow," she said, and reloaded. "I'll use one of the company Gulfstreams. We can land at West-hampton Airport in Long Island. Very convenient."

"I still wish you weren't taking the gun, though."

"As I told you, I want to be ready for anything. For whatever opportunity arises. You don't need to come if you aren't happy."

"Oh, but I do need to come." He picked up a Browning from the selection of weapons on the table and fired very rapidly at the targets, shooting four of them through the head.

"Showing off again, Hedley?"

"No," he said. "Just checking I'm on form so I can make sure you're on form. After all, what if you meet the Connection?"

"So you'll come? You're with me?"

"Oh, I'll come all right. *Someone's* got to watch out for you." He took the Colt from her, checked it, and handed it back. "Okay, take your stance and remember what I told you."

NEW YORK
WASHINGTON

ELEVEN

BLAKE SAT IN Parker's office the following morning, drank coffee, and ate a ham sandwich. He was quite alone. Outside, the end of March weather was as lousy as it could be. Powdery flakes of wet snow drifted against the window. The door opened and Parker came in in shirtsleeves.

"They said you were here. Hey, feel free with my coffee break."

"I just flew in from Washington. The weather was so bad they couldn't serve breakfast."

"Serves you right for joining the jet set." Parker sat down, picked up the phone, and ordered another sandwich and more coffee. He shook his head. "You are in deep shit, my friend."

"I beg your pardon?"

"Come on—Cohan? All the newspapers indicated an unfortunate accident, but you and I know better."

At that moment, his assistant, an older woman police sergeant, came in without knocking and put more coffee and sandwiches on the desk.

"Have mine. I've already ordered more. I figured Mr. White House here would clean you out."

She went. Blake said, "What a treasure—and what a healthy appetite. Too much for you, with your weight to consider."

He took another sandwich and Parker said, "Screw you, Blake." He took a sandwich himself. "So what's the score?"

"Simple. The Sons of Erin, all gone to the great diner's club in the sky. Cohan, Ryan, Kelly, Brady, Cassidy. That's five." Blake opened one of the coffee containers. "Come on, you bastard, all those years on the street, how many murders have you investigated?"

"A hundred and forty-seven. I kept count."

"So what's your verdict? You don't accept this sectarian nonsense, do you?"

"Crap." Parker finished his sandwich. "The pattern is clear. The motive is revenge."

"Revenge for something the Sons of Erin were responsible for."

"I'd say so."

Blake sat there thinking about it. "I agree. But it still doesn't get us very far. I've been thinking about Cohan. Why wasn't he attacked in New York, like the others? You don't happen to have any attempted burglaries on his house, do you? That sort of thing?"

"Let's have a look."

The last sandwich in his left hand, Parker went to his computer, sat down, and tapped the keys. "No, no such reports." He paused. "Just a minute. That's interesting."

"What is?"

"Last week there were a couple of murders in an alley next to Cohan's house. Typical street bad guys. Shot dead. Autopsy showed lots of alcohol and traces of cocaine. Both of them were in police hands many times. Street dealers, one of them ran whores."

The screen kept changing. Blake, trying to suppress a rising excitement, said, "What kind of gun was it?"

Parker tapped, then leaned back. "Dear God, a Colt .25." He turned. "Let me cross-reference." He attacked the keys in a kind of frenzy and finally stopped. "There you go, Blake. You thought you had four members of the Sons of Erin shot by the same weapon. I've got you two more."

Blake was stunned. "But why these guys?"

Parker sat there thinking about it. "Look, the obvious link is Cohan's house. That's in an exclusive area. These guys were lowlifes, probably just passing through."

"You mean in the wrong place at the wrong time?"

"How in the hell would I know? I'm clutching at straws, man. Maybe someone was waiting for Cohan and these two turned up."

Blake nodded. "Yeah. Oh, man!"

"So what are you going to do?"

"I'm going to take a look at the scene of the crime." He stood up. "Thanks, Harry, I'm sure I'll be back," and he left.

Lady Helen went for a walk, holding a golfing umbrella against the rain. She stopped in the pine trees, looked out at the turbulent sea, took out the mobile, and phoned Barry.

"Ah, there you are," she said.

"What do you want?"

"Nothing special. I just thought I'd make a connection. It's a terrible day here. Raining like hell."

Barry felt surprisingly calm, that link again. "Where are you?"

"Ah, progress, it's the first time you've asked. I'll tantalize you. The east coast of England."

"Yorkshire—Norfolk?"

"That would be telling."

He was surprised at how reasonable she sounded. "Look, what do you want?"

"You, Mr. Barry, that's what I want. Dead, of course."

She rang off. Barry went to the cupboard, got a bottle of Paddy whiskey, and poured one. It scalded the back of his mouth. When he lit another cigarette, his hand was shaking. She wasn't going to go away, that was obvious, so he phoned the Connection.

"Look, I didn't tell you everything about the Cohan business."

Thornton said, "Well, you'd better do it now." Which Barry did. When he was finished, Thornton said, "Tell me again what she said about her son."

Barry thought for a moment. "She said I butchered her son in Ulster three years ago and executed his friends, four others, including a woman."

"Does that strike a chord with you?"

"For God's sake, I've been at war for years. You want to know how many people I've killed?"

"Okay, okay. Just leave it with me. There may be a link here. I'll check it out."

Blake had his car drop him in front of Cohan's house on Park Avenue, but on the other side of the street. He sat there reading the scene-of-crime reports. It was all pretty straightforward. It had been after midnight, heavy rain clearing the streets.

He tried to imagine the scene, as he looked across at Cohan's place: dark, wet, not much of a struggle because the pathologist's report indicated instant death in both cases, and then he frowned. There was an anomaly here. He turned to the pathology report and examined it quickly. Victim One, blood group O. Victim Two, blood group A. The only trouble was that there were traces of another blood group on Victim Two's shirt, this time B.

So, there was a third-party involvement, some sort of a struggle. Could that have been the killer? Blake frowned. For some reason, he didn't buy that. The way the two guys had been shot had been so instantly effective, so ruthless. Why would there have been a struggle? He frowned again. Unless there had been another person. Four persons, not three.

He decided to try and get the perspective from the pavement, a different viewpoint. "Go back to police headquarters and wait for me there," he told his driver. "I'll get a cab. Just hand me the umbrella."

The driver did as he was told and drove away as Blake opened the umbrella. So, it was night and she was waiting for Cohan to return home from some function or other. Where would you wait? This side of the street, not the other, because from here you got a clear view, from here a halfway decent shot was possible.

He turned and looked behind. Plenty of doorways to stand in concealed by the shadows. So what happened? What went wrong? To hell with it, Blake thought, took out a pack of Marlboros, and lit one. This wasn't a time to give up smoking. He inhaled deeply and that damn March rain dripped from the umbrella.

The two victims were in the alley, probably sheltering from the rain. They shouldn't have been there, not at such a time and in such an area. So, I'm the killer, Blake thought, and I'm waiting here for Cohan, so what went wrong? He looked across at Cohan's house, and at that moment, a young couple came around the corner farther along Park Avenue, huddled under an umbrella. Blake watched them go, move past the alley, walk to the next corner, and disappear.

"That's it," he said softly, "just as I thought. Someone walked into something. The wrong place at the wrong time."

So, the individual with the B blood group had left the scene, God knows in what condition, and to where?

Blake crossed the street and paused at the alley. So, say someone was running, which way would they go? Right or left? What the hell, he would go to the left first, for no better reason than that's the way the young couple had gone.

He lit another cigarette and walked steadily along the sidewalk in the rain, turned the corner, and carried on for another block, passing offices, the occasional boutique, all of which would have been closed after midnight.

"But not that place," he said softly, looking across the intersection. "They never close."

The sign said St. Mary's Hospital. It was private, and a large painted board offered a range of services including ambulance, accident, and emergency.

"So here we are," Blake said. "It's the early hours of the morning, it's raining and you're bleeding. Now where would you go?"

He moved into a doorway, got his mobile phone out, and called Harry Parker. "Harry, I need you."

"Have you got something?"

"Let's say my nose is twitching, and if I'm right, I need a police presence."

"So where are you?" Blake told him. "Fine, I'll see you soon."

When Parker and Blake went into the emergency room of St. Mary's, they found it surprisingly luxurious: fitted carpets, comfortable chairs, calming music. The duty nurse at reception wore a uniform which could have been designed by Armani, and probably had been.

"Gentlemen?" She was slightly wary. "Can I help you?"

Harry flashed his gold badge. "Captain Parker, NYPD. I need some information. It's tied to a murder investigation."

"Then I'd better get our Chief Administrator, Mr. Schofield."

"You do that, honey," Harry said.

Schofield wore a blue chalk-striped suit, and looked tanned and fit. They sat in his rather sumptuous office and Blake told him all he needed to know. That there had been a double shooting not too far away, and that there was a possibility of a third person injured to some degree or another.

"Sounds important," Schofield said.

"Yes, well, my friend here is FBI, that's how important it is," Harry Parker told him.

"So what do you want from me?"

Blake reached for a memo pad and scribbled a date. "The early morning of that day. Did you get anyone coming into the ER sometime after midnight, bleeding?"

"There's a question of patient confidentiality here, gentlemen."

"And there's the question of a Presidential warrant here." Blake produced the document and presented it.

Schofield said, "Jesus. Okay, let's take a look."

At the desk, he looked through the admissions book, then nodded. "There was a patient noted here. Name of Jean Wiley. Booked in at one-fifteen A.M. on the indicated date. Her face was cut. The night intern handled it, Dr. Bryant."

The lady receptionist said, "Dr. Bryant is on duty today, Mr. Schofield. I saw him going down to the cafeteria."

"Fine," Parker said. "Just point the way, Mr. Schofield."

Bryant was around thirty, slightly overweight, with glasses, dark curling hair, and a beard. He was sitting at a corner table eating French bread and soup.

He looked up. "Schofield, my man, what are you trying to sell me?"

"These gentlemen would like a word with you." He turned to them. "Dr. Bryant graduated top of his class from Harvard Medical School. We're lucky to have him. Do bear that in mind, won't you?"

"Oh, Clarence," Bryant said. "Stop stroking me. Now what is this?"

So Parker introduced himself and Blake, got rid of Schofield, and told him. Parker said to Bryant, "You know something about this, I know you do."

"Okay, I'm thinking about it."

Blake said, "I'll get you some coffee."

"Tea, man, tea. I spent three years at Guy's Hospital in London, got a taste for it. English Breakfast."

Blake got the tea and returned to find Bryant crumpling an empty cigarette pack. Blake took out his Marlboros. "I thought you doctors were against tobacco?"

"Are you denying me my rights?"

"So let's get to those really lousy early morning shifts and someone called Jean Wiley coming in off the street. What was that problem?"

"Her face had been cut, not too badly, but by a knife unmistakably."

"Did you ask for details?" Parker said.

"Of course. She said she'd slipped and cut her face in the kitchen."

"Balls, would you say?" Blake asked.

"No, bollocks they would say in London. Her face had been cut by a knife. I did some excellent embroidery work, she gave us her insurance information and left."

"Okay," Parker said. "If she gave her insurance details, they'll have it on the computer. We can get her blood group that way."

"No need for that," Bryant said. "I remember it." They looked at him, and he seemed to blush slightly. "I've seen her around a few times, in the same coffee shop for lunch. Nick's Place around the corner. She's . . . well, she's attractive." He shrugged and grinned. "Anyway, she's a B."

Parker checked his watch. "Lunch just coming up."

Bryant hesitated and repeated what Schofield had said earlier. "Hey, there's such a thing as the doctor-patient relationship here."

"There's also such a thing as a double killing up the street just before she came in here. This is important, doc. The NYPD doesn't put police captains out on shit cases, and neither does the FBI."

"She's not much more than a kid. You're not saying *she* killed anybody?"

"No, I'm not," Blake said. "But to use a fine old police phrase, in pursuance of our inquiries, we need to cross her off the list."

"Okay," Bryant said wearily. "I'll show you who she is. But take it easy on her, huh?"

"This is the new police department," Parker told him. "We're trained for sensitivity. Now let's get going."

Nick's Place was small, tucked away in a side street, three guys behind the counter rattling away at each other in Greek as they handled short orders and one of them made fresh sandwiches. It was warm and muggy and, because of the rain, the windows were partially steamed up. Bryant peered inside.

"I can't see any sight of her."

"Okay, so let's stand over here and wait," Parker said.

"I've got patients," Bryant said as they stepped into a shop doorway, and then he stiffened. "Hey, there she is, crossing the road. The small, dark girl in the blue raincoat. Black umbrella."

Jean Wiley put the umbrella down and went into Nick's Place. "Nice legs," Bryant observed.

"Yes, well, remember your concern over the doctor-patient relationship," Parker told him. "Thank you very much, Dr. Bryant. You can go now."

"If you need me, you know where to find me." Bryant walked away, pulling up his collar.

Blake and Parker moved to the window of Nick's Place and peered in. The girl had taken coffee and a sandwich on a tray and moved to the back of the room to a booth. It was still early and there were few customers.

"How do we play this?" Harry Parker asked.

"Good guy/bad guy shouldn't really be necessary. Let's say you're a nice big avuncular cop doing your duty with deep regret, and I'm Mr. Nice Guy Fed. But remember one thing, old buddy," Blake said, "I'm in charge. I'm the one who decides what happens to her."

"The more I find out about this business, the more I'm happy to know it isn't my responsibility," Parker said. "In we go."

Jean Wiley was eating a chicken sandwich with salad and reading a paperback novel at the same time. Blake noticed it was Jane Austen's *Emma*. She glanced up, a slight frown on her face.

"May we join you?" Parker said.

"I'd have thought there was plenty of room elsewhere."

"I think you'd better," Blake told her gently.

Parker flashed his gold badge. "NYPD, Captain Harry Parker. My friend here, Mr. Johnson, is with the FBI."

"We think you might be able to help us," Blake said. "It relates to a double shooting last week."

Her face said it all. It seemed to crumple, went very pale.

'Oh, my God." She aged right there in front of them. "I need the bathroom."

"Sure you do," Harry Parker said. "Only don't go trying the back door. I know who you are, so I'd have to send a squad car, and I'm sure your boss wouldn't like that."

She gave a dry sob as she got up, knocking over her coffee cup. She ran to the back of the coffee shop, and one of the men came from behind the counter, a cloth in his hand, all belligerence.

"Hey, what gives? She's a nice kid. You can't come in and interfere with my customers."

"I can close you down if I want." Harry's gold badge appeared again. "Police business."

"The young lady witnessed a crime," Blake said. "We just need a few questions answered."

The man's attitude changed completely. "Hey, I'm Nick, this is my place. You want some coffee?"

"Great," Parker told him. "That's what I like—cooperation."

The girl returned in a few minutes, still pale but composed. There was a hint of steel there. This was no bimbo, Blake was certain of it. She sat down and sipped some of the coffee Nick had brought.

"Right, what do you want?"

"A few details. Jean Wiley, am I right?" Parker said. "Twenty-four?"

"So?"

"That's a neat scar on your left cheek. It'll fade with time, but it could make you look interestingly different."

She was angry, her eyes dark. Blake said, "What do you do?"

"I'm an associate at Weingarten, Moore just round the corner. I got my law degree from Columbia two years ago, so I know my rights, gentlemen."

"Hey, why are we being nice here?" Parker appealed to Blake and turned to the girl. "You want to tell us how your blood got onto the shirt of a murdered man?"

That really jolted her. She turned to Blake, startled, inquiring, and he said, "Look, why fool around? Last week, two lowlifes were shot dead in an alley a few blocks from here, sometime after midnight."

"The thing is, one guy was blood group A and the other O," said Parker.

"Except there were traces of blood group B on his shirt," Blake said.

"Which obviously got there when he cut your cheek," Parker told her. "Probably as he held you and you struggled. I'm right, aren't I? Those two grabbed you as you walked past."

Her face was wild now, her voice low. "Bastards. Dirty rotten bastards." She took a deep breath and sipped some coffee, her hand shaking. "It's a nice story, Captain, but I know my rights and I'm saying nothing."

"Hell, a DNA check would say everything."

Blake saw it all now, saw it as it must have been. It all came together. Dillon at Wapping in the Thames staring up at Tim Pat Ryan and certain death, and saved by the woman, the unknown executioner who had taken out the Sons of Erin one by one.

"They intended to rape you, perhaps murder you," Blake said softly. "You struggled, you were threatened with a knife, your face was cut, and then a woman walked out of all that darkness and rain and shot them dead."

Parker turned to him, frowning. "What is this?"

But it was the girl who was most affected, total shock on her face. "How did you know that?"

There was total stillness between them. Blake said, "Sometimes these things are like a jigsaw. You keep getting nowhere and then all the pieces fall into place and there it is, the complete picture."

Even Parker was gentle now. "Tell us about her, honey."

"I can't," she said. "I'd rather die than see anything happen to that woman."

She was shaking. Blake turned and called to Nick. "Can we have a brandy here? You carry that? Good. And fresh coffee, some of that black Turkish stuff?"

She got her purse open, fumbled out a pack of cigarettes, and dropped them. "Damn!" she said. "I'm supposed to have stopped."

"You, me, and everyone else I know." Blake got out his Marlboros, lit one, and passed it to her.

"Just like *Now Voyager.*" She laughed nervously.

"Yeah, he's really a very romantic guy." Parker took the brandy from Nick and passed it to her. "Get that down." She did as she was told, coughed once, then reached for the coffee. "Best fix in the world," Parker added. "And it's legal."

"And here's something else that's legal," Blake told her. "Something they probably only whispered about in your law courses." He passed her the Presidential warrant.

She read it quickly and looked up at him in awe. "My God."

"Which means that you could tell Captain Parker here that you killed those two guys and he couldn't do a thing about it."

She glanced at Parker. "He's right, honey," he said.

She nodded and it was as if she was looking back into the past. "You've no idea what it's like, you men, when you're a woman in a really bad situation. It's the worst thing in the world." She shuddered. "So dirty, so foul. It's like the end of everything."

"And then a guardian angel descends?" Blake suggested. "Tell us about it."

"I was on a date that went wrong, a guy who lied, didn't tell me he was married. We were having supper at this Italian place a few blocks away, late supper after a show. He got drunk, let slip the fact that he had a little woman at home and a couple of kids. I ended up walking out."

"And you couldn't find a cab?" Parker said.

"It was after midnight, but more than that, it was raining like hell, and when can you get a cab in Manhattan when it's raining?"

"So you started walking?" Blake said.

"In all my finery. I had a small umbrella, but I still got soaked. I was so angry, just storming along in a kind of rage, and then I passed this alley and there were voices shouting and then I was grabbed, hustled inside. One guy held me, the other cut my cheek with one of those spring blade knives." She shuddered deeply. "They kept saying what they were going to do. The language was foul."

"And then she appeared?" Blake asked.

It was as if they weren't there, as if she was talking to herself. "It was unbelievable. Her voice was so gentle. She told them to let me go. I could see her standing there in the entrance to the alley. One of them was holding me from behind and the other shouted at her, all threats, I can't recall the exact words, and he made a move, I think, and her hand came up with a hat on it and she shot him through the hat."

"A big explosion?" Parker asked.

"No, sort of a muted sound."

"A silencer." He nodded. "And the other?"

"He tried to use me as a shield, he had a knife, but she shot him in the head over my shoulder."

Parker turned to Blake. "I'll tell you one thing, she must be good to risk a shot like that. And then there's the silencer. You were right, Blake. A pro in a way I hadn't realized."

Blake said, "Tell me about her."

"That was the strange thing. She was a real lady. Could have been late sixties. She wore a rain hat, a trench coat, carried an umbrella. Her hair, what I could see of it, was white."

"Her face?"

"Don't ask me to go through the photos. It would be a waste of time. I didn't see enough of her to make a positive identification, and I wouldn't."

"That's okay," Blake said. "I wouldn't ask you to. There's a lot to this that you'll never know, matters of national security. This is not a case that ever comes to court. The two guys she shot are just two more on a list of New York street killings never solved."

"So I won't be pulled in or anything?"

"Absolutely not." He turned to Parker. "Please confirm that."

The police captain said, "He's in charge, I'm only here to help in any way I can. I'm as much at the mercy of that Presidential warrant as you are."

"I guarantee that your identity will be mentioned to no one," Blake said. "I will tell only the facts of this affair, even to the President, but you have my solemn oath that your name will never be mentioned."

"How about him?" She nodded to Parker.

"Tell her, Harry," Blake said.

"Don't know what you're talking about, honey," Harry Parker told her. "Never seen you before."

The two men got up. "With luck, I won't need to speak to you again, Miss Wiley." He turned and hesitated. "Just one thing. What did she sound like?"

"Oh, a lady, a real lady, like I said. You know the kind of person? Almost English."

"Are you saying she could be English?" Parker said.

"Oh, no, just blue-blooded American, that kind of accent."

"You mean you could have bumped into her going round the designer rooms at Bergdorf Goodman?" Parker asked.

"Or Harrods in London." She shrugged. "She was an upper-class lady, what more can I say?"

"Good." Parker nodded. "Don't forget to get the restaurant to book you a cab next time," and he led the way out.

They stood there in the rain. Blake said, "What do you think?"

"It's the damnedest thing I ever heard of, Blake. You've got some angelic elderly lady out there like the President's mother, knocking off two lowlife rapists like she's an aging Dirty Harry."

"Just like she did Tim Pat Ryan in London."

"And Brady, Kelly, and Cassidy in New York, and probably Cohan in London. I told you, Blake, every policeman's instinct tells me this whole thing is very personal."

"I agree."

"I think there's more there to do with the Sons of Erin than you realize, but that isn't my problem, it's yours. According to your Presidential warrant our lunch with the Wiley girl never happened." He glanced at his watch. "Got to go. I've got a meeting with the Commissioner and you know what's so frustrating? I can't tell him what great work I've done on this case."

He went off like a strong wind, hailing a cab. Blake watched him go, then turned and walked away.

He caught the shuttle back to Washington, thought about things, then called Alice Quarmby and told her to set up a meeting with the President.

"Did you get anywhere?" She was guarded, as usual.

"It's a highly unusual story, Alice," he said. "But I'll tell you later."

As luck would have it, he was alone, the next seat vacant.

He lay back, tilted his seat, closed his eyes, and started right at the beginning, allowing one event to flow into another, trying to make sense of it all. The only trouble was that he became so relaxed he fell asleep and was only aroused by the touch of a hand on his shoulder as they landed at Washington.

Alice had coffee waiting, hot and strong, and he sat behind his desk, sipped it, and looked at the in-tray. "Looks like a lot to me, Alice."

"I can handle most of it. Just needs a signature. What happened?"

He told her, everything that had taken place, everything Jean Wiley had said, though he didn't disclose her name.

"I think Captain Parker is right," she said when he was finished. "It's something personal we're missing, something to do with those Sons of Erin bastards."

"Why, Alice, bad language at your age."

"Don't be funny." She looked at her watch. "If you're interested, you've got six minutes to get up to see the President. Try the pool first."

"Thanks very much." He pushed his chair back and jumped up. "I'll do you a favor sometime, Alice," and he hurried out.

TWELVE

JAKE CAZALET WAS in the White House swimming pool, flailing up and down, one length after another, watched by two Marine sergeants, immaculate in white tracksuits, who acted as lifeguards. He swam to the side and looked up at Blake.

"Anything productive?"

"You could say that, Mr. President."

"Okay, we can't talk now. I'll shower and change and see you upstairs, but I don't have long. Got a pile of work to do."

When Blake went into the Oval Office, Henry Thornton was arranging a stack of papers on the desk.

"How did it go?"

"Well, let's say I learned a lot, but not enough."

Thornton raised a hand. "Don't tell me. Let's wait for the great man himself. I always prefer to share bad news with others. It detracts from any feeling of personal responsibility."

"Are you getting anywhere with your background checks?" Blake asked.

"Not so far," Thornton said.

The President breezed in, his hair still damp and tousled. "Okay, Blake, let's hear the worst."

When Blake was finished, both his listeners looked serious. Thornton said, "Well, there's one thing, Mr. President. At least we know this mystery woman Dillon mentioned exists."

"More than that. It would appear she's been responsible for all the killings, and that really is incredible," Cazalet said. "But why?"

"Some sort of vendetta," Blake told him. "It's the only explanation."

"And this girl, whose name you won't give us," Thornton said, "she wasn't able to help in any other way?"

"As I've told you, she described the woman, for what it's worth."

"And what a description," Thornton said. "Sixties, white-haired, blue-blood accent. We seem to be talking *High Society* here. Come on, Blake, this girl, can't she come up with more?"

Cazalet raised a hand. "No, what Blake got is all there is. I accept that just as I accept Blake's integrity in holding to his word, both to that young woman and to Captain Parker for backing him to the hilt in this matter."

"Fine, Mr. President," Thornton said. "But where does it leave us? No further forward."

"Have you got anywhere with your own investigation?"

Thornton said, "I'm afraid not."

Cazalet nodded, frowning. "I suggest you speak to Brigadier Ferguson, Blake. Bring him up to date. Is there anything else you can do?"

"I've been wondering whether any of the premises near

the alley where the two shootings took place might have anything on their security videos for the time in question."

"That would show the woman?"

"Perhaps. A long shot."

"Okay, pursue that, and as I say, bring Ferguson up to date." Cazalet nodded. "Perhaps it might even be an idea to have Dillon over."

"But how would that help, Mr. President?" Thornton asked.

"Well, he did catch sight of the mystery woman in Wapping after the Tim Pat Ryan shooting."

"A glimpse only," Blake pointed out.

"Yes, but the same glimpse on a security video could match up. What else have we got?"

"Not very much, Mr. President."

"So, to other matters. This party of Chad Luther's day after tomorrow in Quogue." He turned to Thornton. "Any special problems, Henry?"

"None, Mr. President." He turned to Blake. "Good old Chad is our biggest fund-raiser, and he'll have all the world and his wife there."

"Will you use Air Force One, sir?" Blake asked.

"No. I'll go down in one of the Gulfstreams." The President nodded. "Pursue your inquiries, but I want you to join up with the security arrangements, too, and come to Long Island. Take the helicopter."

"Forgive me, Mr. President, but I'll have Sean Dillon here by then."

"Bring him with you, by all means. I'd appreciate seeing him again." Cazalet smiled. "But now, I really must get on. Good old Henry here will be breathing fire and smoke before I know where I am."

Thornton laughed appreciatively, and Blake withdrew.

• • •

Back in his office, he spoke to Harry Parker and raised the question of security videos. Parker said, "That's a good point. Thinking about things after you left, it occurred to me, too. I'll check."

"That's that, then," Blake said. "I saw the President, told him everything about our talk with the girl. He said he appreciated your help, Harry."

"Hey, don't fuck with me."

"It's the truth, Harry. I'll keep you posted."

Harry Parker sat there at his desk, frowning, thinking about what Blake had said. Then his phone rang again, and a woman's voice said, "Captain Parker?"

"Who is this?"

"I have the President for you."

Parker sat there in total astonishment, gripping the phone, and the President said, "Harry Parker? Jake Cazalet."

Parker managed to mumble, "Mr. President?"

"Just wanted to thank you for your efforts. Blake Johnson has filled me in. I know the fact of a Presidential warrant must have given you a problem. It goes against the grain of all your service experience. But I'm personally immensely grateful for the help you've given without hesitation in a most serious and confidential matter."

"Mr. President, I am yours to command."

"Blake handles a very special unit on my behalf, Captain, and frankly, there are more demands on its services all the time. I know it would be asking a lot to ask a long-serving NYPD captain to make a move at this time in his career, but I wonder if you'd be interested?"

Parker managed to stay calm. "I said yours to command, Mr. President, and I meant that."

"Excellent. Not right away, but you'll be hearing from Blake in the future."

The phone clicked off. Harry Parker sat staring at his own and then replaced it. He got up, went to the window, and looked out at New York in the rain. A whole new life beckoned at a time when other guys were thinking about retirement.

He went back to his desk, opened the second drawer, and took out a highly illegal Romeo y Julietta Cuban cigar, bit off the end, lit it, and sat down.

"Well, now." He was grinning all over his face. "Well, now."

It was evening in London when Blake spoke to Ferguson. He gave the Brigadier a total résumé of what had happened, the interview with the Wiley girl, what the President had said.

Ferguson listened, then said, "So, as regards hunting down our mystery woman, we're left with the slim chance that some Park Avenue security video might feature her?"

"I'm waiting to hear. The President feels it might be worth having Dillon here. He's the only other one who's ever glimpsed this woman. Perhaps he could match it to a glimpse on video."

"I doubt it, but I'll have him on his way on the next available flight."

"I appreciate that, sir."

"Good, stay in touch."

Ferguson put the phone down, thought about it, then rang transportation at the Ministry of Defence. "Brigadier Ferguson here. What's the quickest flight to Washington?"

"Concorde in the morning, sir."

"Well, Her Majesty's government will just have to spring for it, I suppose. Book Dillon on it. If it's full, throw someone off."

Next he phoned Stable Mews. There was no reply. He

tried Dillon's mobile and did better. The Irishman's voice was clear against a background of voices and music.

"And who is this disturbing my early evening?" Dillon demanded.

"Me, you silly bastard. Where are you?"

"Mulligan's."

Ferguson hesitated, then gave in. "Well, the oysters are appealing, even if you aren't, Dillon. I'll be there in twenty minutes."

Dillon sat in the upstairs bar of Mulligan's Irish restaurant in Cork Street, not too far from the Ritz Hotel, and devoured a dozen oysters and a bottle of Cristal champagne to help things along. Ferguson came up the stairs and pushed through the crowd.

"So there you are." He picked up the Cristal bottle. "What happened to the Krug?"

A young Irish girl appeared. "Is there a problem?" she asked Dillon in Irish.

"A decent girl from Cork who understands me," Dillon told him and smiled at the girl as he replied in Irish, "Don't be put off, my love. He looks like the kind of English Lord who'd put his boot to you, but his sainted mother was from Cork. Give him a dozen oysters and a pint of Guinness."

She gave him a smile and vanished to the kitchen. Ferguson said, "I didn't understand a word, but you're going to feed me?"

"Of course. Now what's up?"

"You, at dawn, then it's Heathrow for the Concorde to Washington."

Dillon still smiled, but the gray eyes didn't. "Tell me."

Forty minutes later, the Brigadier swallowed his last oyster, an expression of ecstasy on his face. "Superb! Only an Irish bar could do oysters like this. So, Dillon, what do you think?"

"About Blake and where we are? God knows. I knew we were dealing with a woman, because I'd seen her. Now this girl's story confirms what any kind of sense always indicated, that it wasn't some organization after the Sons of Erin, but some individual seeking revenge. But for what?"

"Perhaps you'll come up with something over there," Ferguson said.

"I always believe in traveling hopefully." Dillon poured him a glass of Cristal. "Mind you, one thing does intrigue me."

"What would that be?"

"We know all these facts about the whole Sons of Erin business, and yet the Secret Intelligence Service knows nothing. Just the usual stuff on Barry, but nothing more. A great big blank. It smells to me of one of those it-didn't-happen jobs as far as Simon Carter and company are concerned."

"You could be right."

"I always am," Dillon said.

In his office in the Basement, Blake sat thinking. Finally, he pressed a buzzer for Alice. She came in and sat down.

"You look as if you've got a problem."

"The leak. The White House leak. There has to be more we can do on it."

"So you don't have much faith in the chief of staff's efforts?"

"It's not that. I just feel we're missing something. Look, Alice, say you're the Connection. The Sons of Erin are all gone. You're left with one person to talk to—Jack Barry."

"So?"

"So remember when we tracked down that Pentagon spy a couple of years ago? Patterson?"

Comprehension dawned. "You mean Synod?"

"Exactly. Why not set the Synod Computer to tracking some calls. Insert the name Jack Barry. See what crops up."

"We're tracking Northern Ireland?"

"No, I would suspect coded mobiles at that end, so that's no good. Stick with Barry and see what comes up. The White House first, then Washington."

"Millions of calls, Blake. That's what Synod covers."

"But it will tell us where any calls to someone called Barry originate from. Let's try it, Alice. What have we got to lose?"

In Washington, Thornton phoned Barry. "I have more intelligence for you. Blake Johnson managed to track down a young woman in New York with quite a story."

"Well, tell me." Which Thornton did.

When he was finished, Barry said, "The old bitch, just let me get my hands on her."

"Don't get so worked up. You don't even know who she is."

"Neither do you."

"And neither does Johnson or the President or your old pal Dillon in London. By the way, Dillon is due here soon, to see if he can recognize the woman from security videos."

"I keep wondering how you know all this."

"I've told you before, I have my sources. You let me worry about my end. Just you worry about your own."

"All right. So what about the woman?"

"Leave it with me. Maybe I can come up with something."

That evening, Thornton started to trawl his computer. He had the ability to access most things, probably anything when he had the time. To start with, he went into CIA records of Protestant Loyalist paramilitary groups in Northern Ireland. He ran Jack Barry through, as well as every IRA and Sinn Fein activist from Gerry Adams to Martin McGuinness.

Jack Barry had spent a lot of time in the Middle East, was known to have visited the States under three false names during the same period. This still left what had happened to the Sons of Erin, from Tim Pat Ryan to Senator Cohan. There was no way of denying a deliberate campaign to wipe them out.

Why would that be? He nodded to himself. Vengeance, but for what reason? What could they have been responsible for? He thought about it, and the one thing that made sense was what the woman had said to Barry: You butchered my son in Ulster three years ago, executed his friends, four of them, including a woman.

He went back three years earlier on the computer, looking for information to the White House from Brit Intelligence, and then he remembered. His first big coup. The undercover group in Ulster. In those halcyon days, the Brits had been encouraged by their own government to give the fullest information to the White House. The information had streamed in and was only one of many things he had passed on to Barry. He returned to the computer, tapped the keys, and brought it all back.

Jason, a lieutenant in the Marine Commandos, shot in Londonderry. Archer, a lieutenant in the Military Police, a car bomb in Omagh. There was a woman lieutenant, also Royal Military Police, shot in the street in Belfast. A young acting captain of infantry, chosen apparently because his mother was from Ulster.

Which left one. Thornton sat there thinking about it, then tried the fifth member of the group and its commander. Major Peter Lang, Scots Guards and SAS, killed in South Armagh by a car bomb of such devastating power that nobody had ever been discovered. He sat there thinking about it and knew he was on to something, reached for the phone, and rang Barry's coded mobile.

Barry, asleep, came awake churlishly. "Who is this?"

"Tell me," Thornton said. "The undercover group of Brit officers you took out three years ago."

"What is this?"

"The woman said you butchered her son and executed four more, including a woman. I've just remembered myself. I sent you the information in the good old days when the Brits trusted us."

Barry sat up. "I remember now."

"And the Commander, a Major Peter Lang? According to the records, he was killed by a car bomb so big that even his bits and pieces were never recovered."

Barry reached for a cigarette. "He didn't die in a car bomb. We blew his car up with a big charge to confuse the opposition."

"What did you do?"

"What do you want to know for? You never asked for details then."

"It's important. Tell me."

"He was very English upper-class, a hard bastard. Got him coming out of a pub. One of the lads had served in the Scots Guards and recognized him."

"What did you do?"

"Put the screws on him. It's all coming back. He had a great South Armagh accent. I mean, it all stank to high heaven."

"So you tortured him?"

"Something like that." Barry snapped. "What's so special with this guy?"

"And why did you blow up his car and pretend?"

Barry laughed. "The boys left him in such a mess, we put

him through this big concrete mixer we found on a motorway bypass they were building in the area."

The thought of it was so nauseating that even Thornton
had to catch his breath.

"What's so important?" Barry asked.

"I might be on to something. I'll phone you back."
Thornton rang off.

He went back to Peter Lang, Scots Guards, SAS, Military
Cross for unspecified reasons, the father Sir Roger Lang, a
colonel in the Scots Guards. Then came the information that
took his breath away. The mother was Lady Helen Lang, an
American citizen, born in Boston. The rest of the details
flowed across the computer screen. Her companies, her immense wealth. Her addresses in London and Norfolk. There
was even an end piece on her chauffeur, a Vietnam vet.

Thornton sat there, staring at the screen, then went to a
cupboard, found a bottle of Southern Comfort, and poured a
large one. He went to the window, savoring the drink, and
looked out at what had turned into an evening of rain and
sleet. One thing was certain. He had found the mystery
woman.

Barry had got out of bed at the safe house in County Down,
found a robe, and made tea in the kitchen. He was working
his way through the previous day's *Belfast Telegraph* when
the phone went again.

"Just shut up and listen," Thornton said. "You killed
Major Peter Lang of the Scots Guards and SAS. His father
was Sir Roger Lang, Scots Guards, and his wife—and this is
the good bit—was Lady Helen Lang. I think she's the
woman who's spoken to you, the one who said you
butchered her son. It all fits: the timing, the identity of the
other four."

Barry exploded. "The bitch. She's dead meat. What I did to her son is nothing to what she gets."

"Okay, don't go through the roof. What will you do?"

"Where does she hang out?"

"London and Norfolk." Thornton gave him the addresses.

Barry said, "I'll check out where she's going to be. I've friends in London who'll handle that."

"And?"

"My private flying system. I'll go over with some of the boys and take care of her."

"That's good to know. Clear the decks, that's what I like."

"You can depend on it. Leave it to me."

Thornton put the phone down and sat there, thinking about it. For some reason, he still felt uneasy. Now why should that be?

The following morning, the Concorde lifted off at Heathrow for Washington, and Dillon accepted a glass of champagne and sat there, thinking about it himself. In a strange way, he felt a connection with the mystery woman. It was still an incredibly intriguing situation. Why all those deaths? What was the reason? They were no further forward, really. All the Wiley girl had done was confirm the existence of the woman, confirmed her ability to kill.

But why, why, why? That was what really fascinated him, and there was no answer.

It was the following morning, round about the time Dillon was reaching Washington, that Thornton, trawling on Helen Lang's whereabouts, was stunned to note that she was booked to land at Westhampton Airport at Long Island in her private Gulfstream the following afternoon. He sat there, thinking about it. The question was why, and the obvious an-

swer was Chad Luther's party. He accessed the right side of
the computer again, looked for Luther's guest list, and there
she was. He thought about it, then phoned Barry again.

"Lady Helen Lang. She's attending a big fat-cat party tomorrow night on Long Island, so don't look for her at
home."

"I can wait," Barry said. "Don't worry. She's history."

Lady Helen, at the South Audley Street house, went into the
kitchen and put the kettle on, as Hedley took the bags upstairs. He appeared as the kettle boiled and she made tea.

"Anything you want me to do?"

"Not really. We'll leave from Gatwick in the morning,
land in Long Island in the afternoon, and carry on to Chad
Luther's place."

"Are we staying over?"

"I'd have thought I might need to leave in a hurry."

Hedley refused to be drawn. "Whatever you say, Lady
Helen," and he turned and went out.

Ferguson, at his desk, rang through to Hannah Bernstein,
and called her into his office. "How are you getting on with
your fresh computer investigation?"

"I'm still looking, sir. The thing I can't understand is that
we know a great deal about the Sons of Erin and what they
got up to, but we don't have any information on the specific
act that would explain a personal vendetta on the part of this
woman."

"So you agree with Johnson and Parker about that."

"Oh, yes, sir. You spend years on the street, sir, you in-
vestigate one rotten crime after another . . ."

"And you get a nose for it, a copper's nose?"

"Exactly, sir. Unlike in an Agatha Christie novel, when I
visit the scene of the crime and take a look at who is in-

volved, in most cases I can pick out who it is almost straightaway."

Ferguson smiled. "I'm with you on that, Chief Inspector, so what does it leave us? What does that fine Cambridge-educated mind tell you?"

"That central to all this is Jack Barry, but all the computer tells us is his background of offenses. No mention of his connection with the Sons of Erin, or indeed any mention of the Sons of Erin, and that doesn't make sense, sir."

"And your conclusion?"

"It's not there because somebody didn't want it there."

"The Secret Intelligence Services?"

"I'm afraid so."

Ferguson smiled. "You know, you really are very good, my dear. It's time Special Branch elevated you to Detective Superintendent. I must speak to the Commissioner at Scotland Yard."

"I'm not too worried about elevation, Brigadier. There's a black hole that needs filling. What do we do?"

"What would you suggest?"

"I think you should see the Deputy Director of the Security Services, sir, and, as our American colleagues would say, I think you should kick ass."

"Oh dear, Simon Carter wouldn't like that, but I think you're absolutely right. Phone him and tell him to meet us at the Gray Fox in St. James's in exactly one hour."

"Us, sir?"

"I wouldn't dream of depriving you of the pleasure of putting one of those Manolo Blahnik high heels in him, Chief Inspector."

Hannah smiled. "A pleasure, sir."

The Gray Fox was one of several upper-class pubs in the vicinity of St. James's Palace. It was two-thirty, most of the lunch trade running out, the place almost empty. Ferguson and Hannah took a secluded booth.

"Gin and tonic, Chief Inspector?"

"Mineral water, sir."

"What a pity. Personally, I'll have a large one."

The barmaid brought their drinks, and almost immediately Simon Carter came in. His raincoat was wet and he shook his umbrella, obviously not in the best of moods.

"Now what in the hell is this, Ferguson? The Chief Inspector here actually *threatened* me, the Deputy Director of the Security Services."

"Only when you said you were too busy to come, sir," Hannah told him.

He took his coat off, called for a whiskey and soda, and sat down. "I mean, threatening me with Prime Ministerial privilege. Not on, Ferguson."

"My dear Carter, you don't like me, and if I thought about you at all, I probably wouldn't like you, but we're into serious business here, so listen to the Chief Inspector."

He drank his gin and tonic, waved for another, and sat back.

She went through everything, the Tim Pat Ryan shooting, the extermination of the Sons of Erin, Jack Barry, Jean Wiley's statement. It left Carter stunned.

"I've never heard such nonsense," he said weakly.

Ferguson shrugged. "Good, that clears the decks." He turned to Hannah. "What time was our appointment with the Prime Minister?"

She lied cheerfully. "Five o'clock, sir, though he can't give you long. He's due at the House this evening."

Ferguson started to rise, and Carter said, "No, just a moment."

Ferguson subsided. "What for?"

It was Hannah Bernstein, the copper as always, who said, "Are you able to assist us in our inquiries, sir?"

"Oh, don't give me all that police procedural nonsense." He called for another Scotch and turned to Ferguson. "I haven't said a word about this. I'll always deny it."

"Naturally."

"And I want your Chief Inspector's word that this stays with the three of us. If she can't guarantee that, out she goes."

Ferguson glanced at Hannah, who nodded. "My word on it, Brigadier."

"Good, let's get to it," Ferguson said.

"We've never got on, my organization and yours, Ferguson. Too damned independent." He shook his head. "Prime Minister's private army. Never liked that. People should be accountable, and you do what you damn well like."

"And you don't, sir?" Hannah said gently.

Carter sipped his Scotch. "There are things we never told you, Ferguson, because we didn't trust you, just like there are things you've never told us."

Ferguson nodded to Hannah, who said, "You know the facts, sir. I'm a police officer, I'm trained to look for answers, and what I see here is that one individual has taken care of all the victims, and there has to be a reason for it. Something very bad happened, and I think you know what it was, and I think you had it erased from the computer memory and expunged the records."

"Damn you!" Carter told her.

"Barry," Ferguson said. "It has to be him behind all this. Tell us now."

Carter took a deep breath. "All right. When the peace process began, we were told to be nice to our American cousins, pass them any useful information about what was happening in Ireland."

"I know," Ferguson said.

"Then we began to realize that stuff we'd passed to the White House was ending up in IRA hands. The culmination was a shocking atrocity, which we found later was committed by Jack Barry and his gang. An entire undercover group, some of our best officers, was taken out."

"Who were they?"

"A team of five, headed by a Major Peter Lang, a former Scots Guard and SAS man. There were three other men and a woman."

"Yes, I recall the facts of Peter Lang's death," Ferguson said. "His parents were great friends of mine. He was in a car bomb of such proportions that no trace of his body was ever found."

"Not true. We found out through an informer later that Peter Lang was tortured, murdered, and then put through a cement mixer used in building the local motorway."

"My God!" Hannah said.

"We also heard via this informer of the Sons of Erin and Jack Barry and this Connection thing."

"And how did you handle it?"

"The peace process was at a delicate stage, we didn't want to unbalance it."

"So you didn't tell the Prime Minister?"

"If we had, you'd have known, Ferguson, as well as Blake Johnson and the Basement and the President and God knows who else. We decided there was a better way to handle it."

"Let me speculate, sir," Hannah said. "You went the road of disinformation mixed in with the usual not very important rubbish available in any of the better newspapers."

"Something like that," Carter said lamely.

"Well, there you go." Ferguson stood up. "Thanks for your help."

"I haven't given you any." Carter struggled with his rain-coat and picked up his umbrella. "Is that it, then?"

"I think so."

Carter went out. Hannah said, "What do you think, sir?"

Ferguson said, "Let me ask you a question, Chief Inspector. Say you lost a beloved son in Ulster, blown away as if he'd never existed, so that the shock finished off your husband. And say you then found out the truth, which was that your son had been tortured, murdered, and put through a cement mixer."

"But how would you know that, sir?"

"I haven't the slightest idea. This is all speculation. But the drive, the energy necessary to kill all those men, would need a hugely positive reason, and I think that of the five undercover agents, what happened to Peter Lang was the most terrible."

"But the vigilante would need to know, sir."

"Exactly. But note one thing: a three-year delay. That argues to me that by whatever means, the real truth has only come out recently."

Hannah said, "What are you suggesting, Brigadier?"

"Why, it's simple. The woman who killed Tim Pat Ryan, who killed Brady, Kelly, Cassidy, and the less-than-illustrious Senator Cohan, is my old and dear friend, Lady Helen Lang."

LONG ISLAND
NORFOLK

THIRTEEN

IN BLAKE'S OFFICE in the Basement, Dillon drank tea and ate a cheese sandwich Alice Quarmby had provided.

"You're looking good, my Irish friend," Blake told him.

"Oh, the Concorde is no handicap. I like traveling like the rich."

"Sean, you *are* rich, we all know that."

"You don't understand," Dillon said. "What I like about the Concorde is that someone else is paying for it. Anyway, what did you want me for?"

"Harry Parker is checking the security videos on the other side of the street from Cohan's house and the alley where the Wiley killings took place. We thought there was a chance the woman might be on them and, if so, you might be the one to recognize her."

"I might recognize her from Wapping, but that doesn't mean I'd know who she is."

"I know, but what else do we have to go on?"

Alice Quarmby looked in. "I've got Harry Parker on the line. Can you speak?"

"Of course."

Blake picked up the phone. "Harry? How goes it?"

"All bad, Blake. I checked out the security videos. There were only three cameras that viewed the area. All of them have been recorded over. No help there at all."

"Too bad," Blake said. "Well, thanks, Harry. If you can think of anything else, please let me know. I'll speak to you soon."

Blake hung up. Dillon said, "Another dead end?"

"I'm afraid so."

"So I've had a free flight on the Concorde for no good reason."

"Looks like it. Sorry, Sean. At least we can entertain you while you're here. A very important supporter of the President's, one Chad Luther, is giving the mother of all parties on Long Island this evening. You know Fitzgerald's novel *The Great Gatsby*? Luther loves it. He has a mansion like Gatsby, lawns down to the sea. If you're anybody at all, you're on the guest list."

"Let me guess," Dillon said. "And if you're nobody at all, you're on the guest list. If you have a ring through your nose and play the guitar indifferently, you're on the guest list."

"You are, as usual, uncomfortably close to the truth, my friend, and it gives the Secret Service a serious headache." Blake picked up a file of papers. "I've had to go through the guest list myself."

"Looking for what? Arabs in white sheets?"

"Don't laugh. The President is flying down in one of the Gulfstreams. There's a helicopter shuttle service for security people. That includes you and me."

"I'm honored."

There was a knock at the door and Alice looked in. "Fresh coffee? Tea?"

"No, we're fine. What about . . . what we talked about before?"

"We're still trawling."

She went out. Dillon said, "Trawling?"

Johnson hesitated for a moment, and then said, "Oh, hell, I'm sure Hannah knows all about it. It's a special computer program, called Synod. Thousands of conversations pass through, millions of words. Insert a name, for example, and instead of going through it all, painstakingly, the computer tags it for you. Then you go back and listen to the relevant conversation."

"Jesus," Dillon said. "And it works?"

"Remember Patterson? That's how we caught him."

"So what's the name you're inserting?"

"Jack Barry."

"You're after the Connection."

"That's it."

"Science and technology," Dillon said. "People like you and me are going to be obsolete."

The phone rang and Blake picked it up. "Brigadier, how are you?" He frowned. "Of course, he's right here." He held the phone out. "Ferguson. For you."

"Brigadier?" Dillon said.

"I've got some rather astonishing news for you. Listen well."

A few minutes later, Dillon put the phone down slowly. Blake said, "Bad news?"

"He's just told me who he thinks the mystery woman is."

Blake sat up. "Tell me, for Christ's sake," which Dillon did. Afterwards, he shook his head. "I've met that woman. A great lady. But the facts are plain. I mean, this horror story from Ulster did take place?"

"So it would appear." Dillon slammed a clenched fist on the desk. "Damn Jack Barry—damn him to hell."

"Lady Helen Lang." Blake frowned. "Just a minute." He picked up the guest list for Luther's party and leafed through it. "I thought so. Here she is, a guest at Chad Luther's party tonight."

"So?" Dillon said.

"Well, we were going anyway." Blake frowned.

"And tell the President?"

Blake was strangely reluctant. "What do I do? If the Brigadier's right, she's killed several people."

"And I've just remembered something," Dillon said. "That function Cohan attended at the Dorchester that night he took the big fall, the Forum for Irish Peace?"

"What about it?"

"Helen Lang was there. I had a chat with her. A wonderful woman, Blake. I knew her son had died in Ulster, but not the manner of his going."

"It would seem likely that she does."

"It would explain a great deal." Dillon got up, lit a cigarette, and paced across the room. "There was always something about her, from that first day at the funeral. Don't get me wrong, I liked her from the first, but I always felt uneasy."

Blake nodded. "I'd better have a word with the President." He picked up the phone and rang upstairs to the Oval Office. "Blake Johnson for the President." He nodded. "I see." He put the phone down. "He's already left for Long Island." He thought for a moment. "We've got time. I'll tell him then. I'd rather this be in person."

The door opened and Alice appeared and she was excited. "Synod's come up trumps, but my God, you aren't going to like it. It's thrown up conversations to Jack Barry as recently as the last few days. You'd better come down to the audio room."

They sat in the small enclosed room, the huge spools of tape turning, and listened to the final conversation between the Connection and Barry. "Lady Helen Lang. She's attending a fat-cat party tomorrow night on Long Island, so don't look for her at home."

"I can wait," Barry said. "Don't worry. She's history."

The computer whirred and switched off. Alice said, "Who would have believed it?"

Dillon said, "You mean you know who it is?"

"Oh, yes," Blake said. "I'd know that voice anywhere." He turned to Dillon. "That's the President's chief of staff. That's Henry Thornton."

Dillon took a moment to digest it, then said, "It's going to knock the President for six when he knows what that bastard's been up to."

"You can say that again." Blake turned to Alice. "Check his background, see if you can find a reason." He glanced at his watch. "I've got a few things to check myself, then book Dillon and me on the helicopter to Long Island in two hours."

"I'll get right on it."

She went out. Dillon said, "A hard one, Blake, a hard one."

"I'm an angry man, my Irish friend, I despise treachery."

"And Ferguson?"

Blake thought about it and nodded. "I trust you, Sean, and I trust Ferguson. But this is for his ears only, not the Prime Minister's. It's up to the President to deal with that."

At his office at the Ministry of Defence, Ferguson listened, his face grave.

"It's really in Blake's hands and the President's," he said. "I'm glad you're there. I'm horrified at the identity of the traitor, of course. I'd like to take the bastard outside and shoot him myself. On the other hand, I'll be frank, Sean. We've known each other for some time." He paused. "Lady Helen Lang is a dear friend."

"You don't need to go on, Brigadier. I'll do what I can."

"Thank you, Sean."

The Gulfstream landed at Westhampton, and Lady Helen and Hedley were escorted through with a minimum of fuss. She had changed on the plane and wore an evening outfit in black silk, a close-fitting dress and jacket. Hedley was in a gray uniform. It was just after five.

"Cocktails at six," she said. "Is the limousine ready?"

"Of course."

"Tell Captain Frank I want a slot out of here back to the UK no later than ten."

"You're sure about that?"

"Absolutely. See to it now."

Hedley went off, leaving her in the private arrival lounge, and she got the mobile out and phoned Barry.

When he answered, she said, "Hello, Mr. Barry, it's me."

"Yes, and I know who you are, bitch. I even know where you are, on Long Island."

"My goodness, you are well informed."

"It's all catching up, Lady Helen Lang. I know your London address, your house in Norfolk. What I did to your son is nothing to what I'm going to do to you."

"Why, Mr. Barry, you're quite worked up. It's not good for your heart," she said and rang off.

Chad Luther had started life in Charlesville, Texas, the third of six children to a farmer who was a failure from the day he was born. Five of the children had died, and the father had sunk into drink and apathy. Chad, caught in the draft, had spent two years in Vietnam and had discovered he was a survivor. He'd returned home to find his father dead and his mother dying, and had inherited the four hundred and twenty-eight acres of farmland, bare and useless as they were—until someone discovered oil next door. The companies had descended and Chad had held out for ten million. It was the start of an empire. The ten was now eight hundred in oil, construction, and leisure parks, and Luther was in the company of the great and the good, including the President.

His house on Quogue was his special pride, a magnificent mansion. There were lawns down to the sea, an inlet with a pier for his yacht and various motorboats. All life was there, as the velvet darkness descended. Lights blazed from the windows, music drifted out. Everyone who was anyone was here—and as Dillon had noted wryly, even if you weren't anyone, you were there anyway.

Luther, resplendent in a blue velvet evening jacket and ruffled shirt, greeted the President and Henry Thornton. "A real pleasure, Mr. President."

"Glad to be here, Chad."

"We've prepared an apartment on the ground floor." Luther led the way, the President and Thornton following, Clancy Smith bringing up the rear. The sitting room was pleasant, with a log fire, wood-paneled walls, French windows open to the sea. The President moved out to the terrace. The water was close.

"Very nice."

"I look forward to seeing you later at dinner, Mr. President."

"A pleasure." Luther went out and Jake Cazalet said to his chief of staff, "The things I do for America."

• • •

The helicopter landed at Westhampton, where a limousine waited for Blake and Dillon. At the same time, Helen Lang was arriving at the mansion in a Lincoln driven by Hedley. She got out, straightened her skirt, and stood there, her purse in one hand.

"Will I do?"

"As always." He was wearing a plastic disc which had been sent to them to identify him.

"I'll see you later."

She went up the steps to the open door and faced a pair of Secret Service men. "Invitation, Madam?"

She unsnapped her purse to get it out, and felt her blood run cold as her fingers brushed the pistol. God, how stupid could she have been! How had she expected to get the gun by the security people? Any moment now, they were going to inspect her purse, and then what was she going to do? She froze, her hand in her purse, for what seemed an eternity, but must have only been a couple of seconds, when Chad Luther burst through the crowd. "Don't be silly. This woman doesn't need to show her invitation. My darling girl." He kissed her on the right cheek. "You look marvelous, as usual. I've put you on the top table with me and the President for dinner."

"You always were a sweetie, Chad."

"It's easy with someone like you. Now, come on, come on, there's someone I'd like you to meet." The Secret Service men started to object, but before they could say anything, Luther had swept her inside.

She smiled, took a glass of champagne from a waiter, and moved into the crowd.

Dillon and Blake arrived a little later, walked through the crowd, and discovered the President besieged.

"There's no way you're going to get to him just yet," Dillon said.

"There's time."

There was a table plan to the dining room by the door, and Dillon checked it out. "What a shame, we're not eating."

"Well, that's life," Blake said. "I've got arrangements to make. Keep an eye on our principal players." He went off.

Dillon lit a cigarette and reached for a glass of champagne, then he walked through the crowd and out into the garden. It was cold and a little raw, a few people walking about. He stood at the balustrade and Helen Lang came up the steps.

She smiled. "Why, it's you, Mr. Dillon."

"We do have a habit of bumping into each other. Can I get you anything?"

"A cigarette would be nice."

He got his old silver case out and gave her one. "There you go."

"And what brings you here, Mr. Dillon?"

He took a chance then. "Oh, maybe the same thing as you, Lady Helen. We have something in common, I think. A certain White House connection?"

He gave her a light from his old Zippo. Her expression didn't change. She simply said, "How interesting."

"It's over," he said urgently. "I don't know what you intend, but it's all over—"

Before he could continue, she smiled, the kind of smile that turned over the heart in him. "Nonsense, my friend, nothing is over until I decide it is." She smiled again. "My poor Mr. Dillon, you kill at the drop of a hat, and yet you're such a good man," and she turned and walked away.

• • •

Chad Luther managed to pull Cazalet away from the crowd surrounding him. "The President needs a breather before dinner, ladies and gentlemen. Please."

"Good for you, Chad," Cazalet said as they walked away, Clancy Smith following.

Luther took them back to the sitting room. "Bathroom through there, Mr. President, and if you need a drink I think you'll find everything you need in here." He opened a panel in the wall and disclosed a superb mirrored bar.

"Chad, as always, you're the perfect host."

"I'll leave you now."

Luther went out and Clancy Smith moved into the study and did a quick inspection. He checked the bathroom, then opened the French windows to the terrace. He closed them again.

"Clancy, you're like a hound dog, you never stop sniffing," Cazalet said.

"That's what I'm paid for, Mr. President. There are Secret Service men in the garden. I'll be right outside." He went into the corridor and closed the door.

Cazalet went to the bar and debated whether to indulge. He took a bottle of Scotch from a shelf, then changed his mind and replaced it. Better not. After all, it was going to be a long night. Instead, he took out a pack of Marlboros and selected one. Damn it, a man was entitled to one vice. He lit the cigarette and went and opened the French windows.

There was a half-moon and the rain had stopped. That part of the house was very close to the water. There was a lawn, pine trees, and a bay almost encircled by two prongs of land. By the water was a boathouse and a wooden jetty, a rather magnificent speedboat moored beside it. He could see the odd couple walking about.

It was really very lovely. He took a deep breath, and a

calm and pleasant voice said, "I wonder if you could oblige me with a light?"

He turned, and Helen Lang moved out of the shrubbery at the bottom of the steps.

She had walked through the garden, strangely sad, as if at the final end of things. Another of her breathless attacks had led her to sit down on a convenient bench. She'd taken two of her pills and stayed there for a while until she felt better.

It was Cazalet she thought about. It had to be now, before the evening got too late. For a moment, she hesitated, unexpectedly uncertain. Cazalet was a good man, a hero from a rich and powerful family, who could have avoided Vietnam and yet had chosen to serve and been decorated a number of times. Who had become a solid, progressive President, untainted by the arrogance of power. Who had for many years supported a wife dying by inches from leukemia. A good man. But Peter had been a good man, too. And time was so very short.

She got up, followed the path back to the house, was aware of French windows opening, looked up, and saw Cazalet on the terrace. She hesitated, then opened her purse, her fingers brushing the Colt as she produced her silver cigarette case.

"I wonder if you could oblige me with a light?"

"Why, of course." He came down the steps, his lighter flared.

She held his wrist. "That's unusual. An old Lee Enfield cartridge."

"A souvenir from Vietnam, but how did you know it's a Lee Enfield?"

"My husband was a colonel in the British Army. He had a similar one. You won't remember me. We've only touched hands once, at a function in Boston. I'm Lady Helen Lang."

He smiled warmly. "But of course. My father and yours did business together back in Boston in the old days. You married an English baronet, as I recall."

"Sir Roger Lang."

"Is he here with you?"

"Oh, no, he died two years ago. Our only son was killed serving in Northern Ireland, and my husband was old and frail. The shock was too great for him."

"I'm truly sorry."

"Yes, I believe that."

For some reason he took her hand, and she opened her mouth to speak, and then there came a knocking at the study door. "Excuse me," he said and went up the steps. On the terrace he hesitated and glanced back, but she had faded away as if she had never been there.

Dillon and Blake were standing in a corner of the crowded ballroom when Blake's mobile rang. It was Alice Quarmby.

"I checked Thornton's background, boss, like you asked. Boy, did I come up with a lulu. Listen to this."

She went on for several minutes, as Blake's face betrayed no expression. Finally, he said, "Thanks, Alice, you're an angel."

"Anything important?" Dillon asked.

"You could say that. Thornton's our man, all right, and now I know why. I'll explain later. Right now, we'd better find the President."

"He doesn't seem to be here."

"There's Luther over there. He'll know where he is," Blake said.

But when they got there, they found Luther in conversation with Henry Thornton. The two men were laughing, each holding a glass of champagne, as Dillon and Blake approached. "Hey, you two, you're not drinking," Luther told them.

"Duty calls, Chad," Blake said lightly. "This is a colleague of mine from London, Mr. Dillon. The President asked to see him when he arrived."

"He's taking a rest right now."

The chief of staff held out his hand. "Mr. Dillon, a real pleasure. Your reputation precedes you, sir."

"That's nice to know."

Thornton put down his glass and said to Luther, "I know where the sitting room is, so I'll take them down. This way, gentlemen."

He pushed through the crowd and led the way to the back corridor, where Clancy Smith sat on a chair beside the door.

"Everything okay, Clancy?"

"Apple-pie order, Mr. Thornton."

The chief of staff knocked, opened the door, and led the way in.

Cazalet was still on the terrace as they crossed to the open French windows.

"Anything wrong, Mr. President?" Thornton asked.

"No, I was just talking to a very unusual woman, but I seem to have lost her," and then he smiled. "Why, Mr. Dillon." He clasped his hand warmly. "A pleasure to see you."

"Not this time, Mr. President. I think you really would rather kill the messenger than listen to what Blake and I have to say."

"That bad?" Cazalet leaned against the balustrade. "Then I'd better have a cigarette on it." He took out a Marlboro and Dillon gave him a light from his Zippo. "Okay, gentlemen, let's hear the worst."

And below, concealed in the shrubbery, Helen Lang listened.

Blake said, "You know all about the Sons of Erin, Mr.

President, just as we do. We always felt the killings to be the work of one person. We also felt there had to be a strong reason."

Cazalet nodded. "Acts of revenge for some kind of terrible act."

"Yes, well, now we know just how terrible." He turned to Dillon. "Sean?"

"For years, information from British Intelligence was passed on by our White House connection to the Sons of Erin and Jack Barry. Because of such information, three years ago the members of a British Army undercover unit were all killed by Jack Barry and his boys. The commander was a Major Peter Lang. He was tortured, murdered, and disposed of in a cement mixer."

"A truly appalling crime," Blake said.

"Let me get this straight," Cazalet said. "Major Peter Lang?"

"That's right."

"But I've just been talking to a Lady Helen Lang out here. She told me her son was killed in Ireland."

"Yes, sir," Dillon said. "She's his mother."

"And she's the person responsible for the destruction of the Sons of Erin," Blake said.

The President looked stunned, and Thornton jumped in. "Come on, that's past belief. One woman? An old lady? I can't believe it."

"I'm afraid there's little doubt," Blake told him.

"Yes, she did rather well, when you think of it," Dillon said. "Only Jack Barry and the Connection are left now."

Thornton said, "What happens now? I mean, if this story is true, why isn't this woman under arrest?"

The President said, "Blake?"

"I said there's little doubt. I'm also afraid there's no hard proof, Mr. President. For obvious reasons, it would be better to handle this thing quietly. And there is something else, sir."

"What would that be?"

"Well, inextricably involved with the whole mess is the question of the Connection himself—the traitor in the White House."

The chief of staff said, "Yes, but nobody knows who it is."

"Oh, we do," Dillon said. "We knew your investigation wasn't getting anywhere, Mr. Thornton, so Blake mounted his own."

Blake took a small tape recorder from his pocket. "I had the Synod Computer monitor telephone calls from the White House first, then Washington, to anyone named Jack Barry. The computer picks the name out, then we can retrieve the call."

"And it worked?" said Cazalet.

"We have recordings of a number of calls, Mr. President, but just one will do."

He put the tape recorder on the balustrade and switched it on. The voice came through clearly. "Lady Helen Lang. She's attending a big fat-cat party in Long Island, so don't look for her at home."

"I can wait," Barry said. "Don't worry. She's history."

Blake switched off the recorder, and Cazalet turned in horror to his chief of staff. "My God, Henry, that's your voice."

Thornton seemed to sag and leaned back against the balustrade, head down. He stayed that way, breathing deeply, and yet, when he looked up, his eyes were glittering.

"Why, Henry, why?" Jake Cazalet demanded.

"Let me answer that. Let's see if I can get it right," Blake said to Thornton. "Your mother had an illegitimate half-brother born in Dublin. He was a volunteer with Michael Collins in the Easter Rising in nineteen sixteen. Executed by the Brits."

"Shot down without mercy," Thornton replied. "Hunted down like a dog. Seven bullets in him. My mother never forgot and I never forgot."

"And when you were a postgrad at Harvard, there was a girl named Rosaleen Fitzgerald from Northern Ireland, killed in a firefight in Belfast," Blake said. "You loved her."

"Murdered," Thornton told him. "By British soldiers. The bastards!"

Dillon jumped in. "And years later, there you were, chief of staff at the White House, and all that juicy information started to roll in from British Intelligence, and it was your chance for revenge," he said. "Up the rebels and Ireland must be free."

"How did you get mixed up with the Sons of Erin and Jack Barry?" Blake asked.

"Oh, that was Cohan. I was invited to a Sinn Fein fundraiser in New York, just as a guest. He was drunk. Rambled on about the diner's club and how they all helped the glorious cause."

"And Barry?"

"He was in New York on business to do with arms for the IRA. Brady, the Teamsters' Union guy, knew him and introduced him to the group. That's when they started calling themselves the Sons of Erin. Cohan boasted about it. A real-life gunman."

"And how did you connect with Barry?"

"He was in New York during the early days of the peace process under his own name, all legitimate, staying at the Mayfair. His presence was mentioned in the *New York Times*. It was simple. I offered him information, nice and anonymous. Just a voice on the phone."

"And then retribution struck."

Thornton actually smiled. "Isn't that the craziest thing you ever heard? I mean, a woman like her? Who would believe it?"

Cazalet turned to Blake. "This is one hell of a mess. What are we going to do?"

At that moment, Thornton put a hand on the balustrade and vaulted over.

He landed on his hands and knees and was up and running, unaware that Helen Lang stood in the shelter of the shrubbery nearby and had heard everything.

"You've got nowhere to go, Henry," Cazalet shouted and followed Blake and Dillon down the steps.

Clancy Smith, alarmed by the shouting, flung open the study door and hurried through. "Mr. President?"

"Stay close, Clancy," Cazalet called. "This way," and he ran after Dillon and Blake.

Clancy immediately called in a general alert to the rest of the Secret Service men on duty and went after them.

Helen Lang waited until they were well ahead, then followed cautiously.

There were many guests in the garden, those who'd come out with a glass in their hand to sample the view in the evening, and the sea beyond. One of them was Hedley. Concerned about Lady Helen, he'd taken off his chauffeur's cap and worked his way round to the garden at the rear of the house. Checked there by Secret Service men, his identification badge had sufficed and, of course, there were the other guests in the garden. It was simple chance that he'd seen Lady Helen by the terrace, had also seen the President outside the French windows, and had watched her go up the steps to speak to Cazalet.

He had no idea what was happening up there when Thornton, Blake, and Dillon appeared, and he saw Lady Helen fade into the bushes. There was only the sound of the voices, and then Thornton jumped over the balustrade. The President and the others went after him. Of Lady Helen, there was no sign. Hedley followed in the direction she must have gone.

Thornton weaved his way through the shrubbery, dropped to one knee, and paused. He felt at his waist for the pistol he'd stuck there earlier. He'd planned to use it on Helen Lang that evening, but now it would have other uses. There was a certain panic now. The Secret Service men, alerted by Clancy, trawled the garden, alarming the guests already disturbed by the shouts they had heard. Helen was close on his heels. She had followed him from that first moment when he had vaulted the balustrade and ducked into the shrubbery so that the others didn't know where he'd gone.

What she didn't realize was that Hedley was close behind her. The sounds of pursuit faded and she saw Thornton come out of the shrubbery in front of her and run, crouching, down to the water. He reached the wooden jetty by the boathouse, his running steps booming. He stopped at the speedboat and started to cast off the moorings as Helen arrived.

"Mr. Thornton," she called.

Thornton paused, then turned, a Smith & Wesson in his hand. The image, the woman, standing in the diffused light, was enough.

"It's you, you bitch."

"Yes, Mr. Thornton, I'm afraid it is. Everything comes around. I believe you know what happened to my son. This is what you might call payback time."

"Well, fuck you." Thornton arced and aimed his Smith & Wesson.

Helen Lang reached in her bag to find the Colt.

Hedley, close on her heels, slid in the darkness, over the stern rail of the speedboat, moved in behind Thornton, and slipped on the wet deck. Thornton turned, raised his weapon to fire, and Helen shot him in the back of the head. Thornton went down on his knees and then fell forward. Hedley stood up.

"Wait for me in the parking area. I can handle this. Just go."

She turned and ran.

Hedley had examined the description of Chad Luther's estate supplied by her corporation's London office and knew that there was a reef at the entrance of the bay that was only negotiable at high tide. Now it was low. He shoved Thornton's body over onto the stern deck, went into the wheelhouse, and turned on the engine. When it was going well, he jumped to the jetty, cast off, and let the speedboat go. When it hit the reef at the entrance of the bay, the force was so great that the speedboat bounced into the air and fireballed.

There were cries of alarm from guests in the garden, shouts as Secret Service men called to each other. Hedley stood in the bushes as the President arrived with Blake and Dillon.

"Oh, my God," Cazalet called, staring out at the fire.

Hedley faded into the shrubbery and started back, and a moment later was aware of a sudden cry, a woman's voice. Helen's voice.

"Let me go!"

"I need to look in your purse, ma'am."

It was Clancy Smith, holding her by the right wrist in the diffused light of a garden lamp.

Hedley moved in, grabbed Clancy by the arm, and pulled him away. "You leave her be, boy."

Clancy said, "Secret Service, Presidential bodyguard. I'm doing my job."

"Not with this lady, you're not."

And Clancy, a Gulf War veteran, knew trouble when he saw it. He pulled a Beretta from his shoulder holster very fast indeed. To Hedley it was like grass blowing in the wind. His left arm moved with incredible speed, knocking the silenced Beretta to one side. It discharged with a muted cough. Clancy had never known such strength.

Hedley twisted the arm. "You were Special Forces, right?"

"Hey, fuck you."

"You couldn't fuck your grandmother, boy. Now, me, I had three tours in 'Nam in the Marines. I made sergeant major. The Gulf War was a joyride. Now drop it."

Clancy Smith was a brave man, but the strength was terrible. The Beretta fell and Hedley turned him around, felt for the handcuffs Clancy carried, forced up the wrists, and cuffed him. Clancy fell on his face.

Hedley said, "Don't take it personal. I've killed more people than you could ever imagine." He turned to Helen. "Let's go, ma'am."

They hurried away along the path. Clancy scrambled to his feet awkwardly. A moment later, two of his colleagues found him.

Hedley handed her into the limousine, got behind the wheel, and drove away.

"You okay?"

She was catching her breath. "Fine, Hedley. Back to the airport. Phone ahead. Tell them to be ready for instant departure to London."

He reached for the phone. "You saw the President?"

"Yes. A good man, Hedley. And a lucky one."

He said nothing, just made the call and replaced the phone. "So what was all the fuss back there? Who was that guy?"

"That was the Connection making a very bad end. He was one Henry Thornton, chief of staff at the White House."

"Good God!" He shook his head. "That's unbelievable."

"There's one more thing I should tell you. They know, Hedley, about me. The President, Blake Johnson, Dillon, Ferguson. It's all over."

He was horrified. "But what are you going to do?"

"We'll go back to Compton Place and review the situation." She lit a cigarette. "Drive on, Hedley, drive on."

She pulled out the coded mobile, phoned Barry, and found him still in bed. "It's me again," she said. "Just keeping you up to date."

He sat up, reached for a cigarette, and managed to stay surprisingly calm. "Good news or bad news?"

"All bad, I'm afraid. Your Connection turned out to be a man called Thornton, the White House chief of staff. He enjoyed playing up-the-rebels because he had an uncle shot by the British after the Easter Rising, plus a girlfriend killed in a firefight in Belfast by British troops. Wrong place, wrong time."

"And how would you be knowing all this?"

"Oh, he was run to earth by Sean Dillon and Blake Johnson. There was a confrontation at the party the President was attending. I happened to be in the garden at the right moment. I overheard everything."

"And Thornton?"

"I shot him in the back of the head. Afterwards, he was blown to pieces in a rather large explosion. Does that sound familiar?"

There was a long silence. "Well now," Barry said, "I

guess that just leaves you and me. Where would you be now?"

"Still in Long Island. I'm flying out almost at once to Gatwick, then home to Norfolk."

"Compton Place. I know about that."

"So I can look forward to a visit?"

"You can depend on it. I'll come flying in."

"I'm so glad."

She put the mobile away and Hedley said, "You're just asking for it, Lady Helen, and others could be coming looking for you, like Brigadier Ferguson."

"I couldn't care less, Hedley, as long as Barry finds me first. Just pass the flask." He did so reluctantly. She shook a couple of pills into her palm and washed them down with whiskey.

"Good. Now get me to the airport."

On the terrace with the President, Blake, and Dillon, Clancy told them what had happened.

"Okay," Blake said. "He was big and black and he said he served in Vietnam?"

"That's it," Clancy said.

Dillon turned to the President. "It has to be Hedley Jackson. The final proof, I'd say."

Blake said to Clancy, "You and the boys go looking."

"There's more than five hundred people here," Clancy said.

"Just do it."

Clancy went out. Cazalet said, "What happened to Thornton—a convenient accident, wasn't it?"

"If you say so, Mr. President," Dillon told him.

"Except that you don't believe in accidents?"

"Never did, Mr. President." Dillon smiled softly: "And certainly not with this lady."

FOURTEEN

NOT LONG AFTER Helen Lang had called Barry, Dillon spoke to Ferguson at Cavendish Square. "I always seem to be phoning you at ridiculous hours in the morning to give you bad news."

"Tell me."

Which Dillon did.

"What a mess," Ferguson said. "The chief of staff? Who'd have believed it?"

"Doesn't matter now," Dillon said callously. "Cooked to a turn and I'm not sorry. He was responsible for many deaths, and in the case of Peter Lang, an atrocity of the first order. Heinrich Himmler would have been proud of him."

"Where is Helen Lang now?"

"Blake's checking. I'll keep you posted. She certainly isn't here."

Ferguson put the phone down, thought about it, then called Hannah Bernstein. She answered astonishingly brightly, but then that was fourteen years of police work.

"Bernstein? It's me," Ferguson said. "And what a tale I have to tell. Long Island has turned out to be the modern equivalent of a Greek tragedy. Sorry, Chief Inspector, but I'm going to have to ask you to make an early start."

"Of course, sir."

"There is one thing. The Commissioner phoned me late last night from Scotland Yard."

"Trouble, sir?"

"Only for some. You are now a Detective Superintendent, Special Branch."

"Oh, dear," Hannah said. "The boys won't like that in the canteen."

"Let me be brutal," Ferguson told her. "Forget your Cambridge M.A. in psychology. To my knowledge, you've killed four times in the line of duty."

"Something I'm not proud of, sir."

"If I may stir your Hasidic conscience, Superintendent, Sword of the Lord and Gideon, those people were all worth killing. You took a bullet yourself, and I'm damn proud to have had you work for me. Anyway, Kim can get scrambled eggs going, and we'll wait together to hear further bad news from Dillon. I'll fill you in when you get here."

Blake came into the study where Dillon was talking to the President by the fire. Cazalet turned. "Any news?"

"On Lady Helen Lang, Mr. President? Yes. She flew over here from Gatwick in one of her firm's Gulfstreams and landed at Westhampton."

"And?"

"By the time I'd chased all this up, she'd taken off again just before ten."

"Destination?"

"Gatwick.'" Blake hesitated. "What do you want done, Mr. President?"

"About Lady Helen?" Cazalet frowned, the tough, experienced politician in charge. "If this comes out, the whole peace process can come toppling over. Let's be practical about this mess. Thornton's death can be dismissed as an unfortunate accident. A man tried to attack me, Thornton chased him, and they both died. Brady, Kelly, and Cassidy already have explanations for their deaths. Tim Pat Ryan in London?"

"A gangster," Dillon said. "And every other gangster in London wanted his crown."

"Exactly. As for Cohan"—Cazalet shrugged—"I'm not going to shed tears over that bastard. So he'd had too much to drink and fell from the terrace of his suite."

Blake said, "You mean it never happened, Mr. President?"

"Blake, it stinks, not only for the White House, but for Downing Street. We're all for peace and yet a thing like this . . ."

"Sinks the ship," Blake said.

"And there's always Jack Barry." Dillon lit a cigarette. "The last man standing. Now, if he went down?"

"It would be as if the whole thing really had never happened," Blake put in.

There was a pause before Cazalet said, "That still leaves Lady Helen. She killed six men that we know of."

"I see," Dillon said. "You mean she must pay for sending out of this vale of tears a bunch of absolute bastards, directly responsible for many deaths and the appalling circumstances of her son's death."

"She broke the law and about as badly as it could be broken," Cazalet pointed out.

"I've killed many more in my time and sometimes for worse reasons," Dillon told him. "Come to think of it, you earned a few medals in 'Nam, Mr. President, and Blake, too. What was the body count?"

"Damn you, Dillon," Cazalet said. "Right. But it still leaves us with the problem: What do we do about her?"

"She's out of your jurisdiction now," Blake reminded him.

"But she's still partly my responsibility." Cazalet hesitated. "Okay, get me Brigadier Ferguson."

A moment later, Ferguson was taking his call. "Mr. President."

"Dillon tells me you know the worst. The thing you don't know is that Lady Helen Lang has left Long Island in a Gulfstream for Gatwick. This is a mess, Brigadier. Let me tell you of my conversation just now with Dillon and Blake Johnson."

"So, it never happened, Mr. President," Ferguson said, his voice clear over the speaker. "All right, I think I can work with that over here. But what about Lady Helen?"

"I'm hoping you can think of something for that. You can speak to the Prime Minister, if you want. I'll talk to him later, but what we need is a solution from you. Tell you what. I'll send Dillon and Blake posthaste to London. I've got a plane here they can use."

"Leave it with me," Ferguson told him. "God knows what, but I'll come up with something."

Cazalet turned to Blake and Dillon. "You heard. In view of what we've said, I think we can keep the lid on what happened here."

"I'll stay in touch," Blake told him.

"Minute by minute, preferably." The President smiled. "On your way, gentlemen."

•　•　•

The Gulfstream rose to fifty thousand feet and turned out over the Atlantic. Lady Helen Lang, an old Foreign Office hand, phoned the Ministry of Defence and asked for Brigadier Charles Ferguson, most immediate. She also remembered a code number from her husband's day. It all worked surprisingly well, and she was patched through to Ferguson at Cavendish Square.

"Who is it?" Hannah Bernstein asked.

"Lady Helen Lang." Helen smiled. "Ah, I know you. That very nice lady policeman." Hannah pressed the audio button and waved frantically to Ferguson. "Are you there, Charles?"

Ferguson said, "This is not good, my love."

"Charles, insufferable as you are, I've always liked you, but for once, just listen. They've all paid the price. The chief of staff was a bonus. I didn't know he was the Connection. He tried to shoot me and I shot him. Not that it matters. He was blown to pieces in the end, in a rather large explosion. Your Mr. Dillon was very kind. Told me it was all over. Tried to help. Such a nice man."

"In between killing people."

"My dear Charles, that's what you've been doing for years."

"Helen, tell me one thing: How did you know?"

"Oh, that was poor Tony Emsworth. Riddled with guilt and dying of cancer. He had an illegal copy of the file from the SIS that told the whole story. Gave it to me just before he died. Everyone was in it. You, Mr. Dillon, that nice police lady. Barry. The Sons of Erin."

"I see," Ferguson said. "So what now?"

"Back to Compton Place. I've guests to receive, Mr. Jack Barry and friends. He couldn't resist the invitation. I've spoken to him again. He's promised to come flying in to see me. I shouldn't think that means by scheduled airline."

Ferguson was stunned. "You can't do this, Helen."

"Oh, yes, I can. He's the last one, the one who really did butcher my son. If you want to join us, Charles, you're very welcome, but if it's the last thing I do on earth, I want to face him."

Ferguson felt a chill. "Why do you say that?"

"My heart, Charles, it's not good. Amazing how whiskey and pills keep you going. Anyway, if I can't get him, I'm sure your Mr. Dillon will."

"For God's sake, Helen."

"For my own sake, Charles."

She switched off, and Hannah said, "What do you think, sir?"

"Well, what do you think I should do? There isn't one fact, including the shooting of Tim Pat Ryan, which would allow us to arrest her even on suspicion."

"So?"

"I'll be at Gatwick to greet her. We'll see then."

At Doonreigh, Docherty was having breakfast when his phone rang. Barry said, "I've got a big payday, I want to fly to the North Norfolk coast. A village called Compton, a house called Compton Place. An in-and-out."

"How many?"

"Four, maybe five. This afternoon."

Docherty hesitated. "I don't know. There's military traffic in North Norfolk."

"Listen, you shite. There's ten thousand pounds cash in a supermarket bag for you in this. Make up your mind."

"Just give me time, Jack," Docherty said. "Let me check the charts. I'll be back."

"How long?"

"An hour."

Barry slammed the phone down, and instead of reaching

for a drink, poured a cup of tea. He lit a cigarette and stood at the window, staring out at the rain, but he wasn't angry, he was actually excited. What a woman.

The President's plane lifted off at Westhampton. As always, Dillon was surprised at the luxury. The enormous club chairs, the maplewood tables. The flight attendant was Air Force, a Sergeant Paul. He brought coffee for Blake, a Bushmills for Dillon, and then the portable phone.

"For you, Mr. Dillon. A Brigadier Ferguson."

"Early breakfast, Brigadier?"

"Shut up and listen," Ferguson told him. "I've had her on the phone."

"And?"

"She found out about the whole thing from Tony Emsworth before he died. He had an illegal file. Had all of us in it, including you. The whole rotten details of her son's death, kept under wraps by the Secret Intelligence Services. Told me she shot Thornton before the explosion. She's told Barry she's going to Compton Place. She's pulling him in."

Dillon nodded. "Yes, she would do that. He's the last, you see. Thornton was a bonus. Is she serious?"

"She's told me she's got a bad heart," Ferguson said. "Pills and whiskey keeping her going, she said. She's hanging in there, Dillon. A marvelous woman like her taking on that swine."

"Hey, take it easy."

"You know what she said? 'If I can't get him, I'm sure your Mr. Dillon will.' "

"Really?" Dillon said, ice cold.

"God knows what I'll do at Gatwick."

"I can tell you now," Dillon said. "Nothing, because she won't be there. Put the Chief Inspector on."

"All right, Superintendent now."

Dillon said to Hannah, "You finally made it. If I said good for you, you'd say I was being patronizing."

"Get on with it, Dillon."

"I checked with the weather people at Westhampton before we left. Weather for the UK was poor. Big front, fog, Gatwick not too good. That's why I just told the boss she won't be there, but then I don't think she intended to. I think she'll land elsewhere."

"Right, I'll check on that."

"You do. We'll speak later."

Docherty, on the phone to Barry, said, "Okay, I can do it. The Chieftain again. Just like the guy we used last time. I've a connection in North Norfolk called Clarke. Ran a flying school at a place called Shankley Down, an old World War Two feeder station. The flying school went kaput. He's been doing illegal flights to Holland in a Cessna 310."

"I don't give a stuff if he flies to Mars. Is it on?"

"Yes, I've spoken to him. Shankley Down is an hour at the most to Compton Place."

"Good. You're on. I'll be there in two hours."

Barry slammed the phone down, picked it up again, and dialed a number. A voice said, "Quinn here."

"Barry. I've got a hot one on, private flight into Norfolk and out again."

"For God's sake, Jack, Norfolk?"

"What are you doing? Lying there like a gorilla in your own shite because the great days are gone? A two-hour flight to a very deserted airfield and two hours back."

"And in between?"

"We do what we do best."

Quinn was excited now. "How many?"

"You, me, Dolan, Mullen, McGee. Are you with me?"

"By Christ, I am."

"Meet me at Docherty's place in Doonreigh in two hours. If the boys can't make it, we'll do it together. ArmaLites and handguns."

"We'll be there, Jack, all of us, I swear. Up with the Sons of Erin."

He rang off and Barry said morosely, "Right up," and this time, he did pour a whiskey instead of a cup of tea.

On the Gulfstream, Helen Lang listened to the second pilot's account of weather conditions in the UK. "So, not good," she said.

"Oh, we can scrape into Gatwick, Lady Helen. Rather a lot of fog creeping across the country, but we can make it."

"What about East Midlands Airport, is it clearer there?"

He nodded. "It would certainly be better than Gatwick."

It had been her intended destination all along, but she smiled. "Then let's land there. I'm going to Norfolk anyway. It would be quite convenient."

"Whatever you say."

"Radio ahead and order a limousine. We won't need a driver. Hedley can take care of things."

The pilot departed. Hedley said, "You had it all worked out."

"Of course." She took out a cigarette. "Light, please." He gave her one. She sat back. "I've only one regret. I'm not giving you a choice."

"Haven't had a choice since the day I met you." He smiled. "Let me get you a cup of tea."

At Doonreigh, Barry arrived to find Quinn and the others already there. They were crowded into Docherty's office, checking ArmaLites and handguns, and Docherty looked distinctly unhappy. There was a stir of excitement as Barry appeared, much backslapping and laughter.

"What's it about, Jack?" Quinn demanded.

Barry, as always, knew exactly how to handle the situation. What he was faced with was a group of men who would not have disgraced the Mafia, but as with so many terrorists in Ireland on both sides of the coin, they needed to believe they were gallant freedom fighters.

"Comrades, we've fought shoulder-to-shoulder for an ideal of Irish freedom, and many of us have fallen by the wayside, and often it's been due to treachery and dishonesty. You never knew this, but I had a branch of the Sons of Erin in New York, a member in London. Four of them shot dead." They were silent now. "The person responsible was a woman. It's that woman we're visiting in Norfolk. Retribution, that's what it's about. We take care of her and fly straight back. Anyone wants out, say so."

It was Quinn who spoke. "We're with you, Jack, you know that."

Barry slapped him on the shoulder. "Good man yourself. Now let's get to it," and he led the way out.

The front advanced across England like a plague, fog drifting everywhere. At Gatwick, Ferguson and Hannah waited in a special security lounge.

Ferguson looked out of the window. "It's gone rather silent."

Hannah said, "I'll check." She went out, returned a few minutes later, and made a face. "All traffic canceled at the moment, sir."

"Damnation. Is anywhere open?"

"Oh, yes. Manchester and East Midlands."

"Check them out. See if she's diverted."

Hannah left, and a moment later, the phone rang. The switchboard operator said, "Call for you, Brigadier."

Helen Lang sounded good. "Dear Charles, sorry I missed

you. Filthy weather. I just landed at East Midlands. Lucky to get in. On our way to Norfolk. Scattered fog but not too bad. Hedley is such a good driver."

"This is madness, Helen. Look, Dillon and Blake Johnson are hard after you. Leave it to us, Helen."

"God bless you, Charles." She rang off.

Hedley said, "What happens now?"

"That depends on Mr. Barry."

"He won't get anywhere near Norfolk, not in weather like this."

"I wouldn't depend on that, Hedley. He's a man of infinite resources and guilt." She shook out a couple of pills. "The flask, please."

He passed it across. "You'll kill yourself."

"As long as I kill Barry first, I'll be happy."

It was late afternoon as the Chieftain crossed the English coast over Morecambe. It was raining hard, fog swirling, but Docherty kept below the overcast. Barry sat beside him.

"Are we going to make it?"

"It isn't good, but I think so. We can always turn back."

"You do and you're a dead man when we land." Barry's smile was terrible. "You see, this meeting I'm going to is the most important in my life."

Docherty was terrified. "Jesus, Jack, it'll be fine. Just give me a chance," and he concentrated on the flying.

Sergeant Paul came in with the portable phone. "Brigadier Ferguson, Mr. Dillon."

Dillon said, "Here I am."

"Bad weather, fog. She's landed at East Midlands. On her way to Norfolk by road."

"So?"

"Listen. She told me Barry said he'd be flying in. Now

that would mean by some highly illegal means, presumably direct to Norfolk."

"You mean you think she could be on her own at Compton Place when he arrived?"

"Something like that."

"You could always ring the Chief Constable of Norfolk and . . ."

"Don't be stupid, Dillon. For once forget that Irish propensity for gallows humor and be serious."

"Well, she needs backup," Dillon said. "She's got good old Hedley with a great record in 'Nam, but that was years ago. If Barry arrives, he won't come alone. I've known him long enough to know that."

"Dillon, North Norfolk is one of the last truly rural parts of England. It would take us hours to get there by road and she's determined to do this thing. I mean, what can we do?"

"First of all, you check whether we can land at Farley Field. Then you call in Flight Lieutenants Lacey and Parry and tell them we're going to war."

"What in the hell do you mean?"

"I know something of the North Norfolk coast. It's got broad beaches, especially when the tide's out. They can take me in and drop me by parachute. We've done it before. Leave it to Lacey to work out."

"For God's sake, Dillon."

"He's got nothing to do with it. I'll have Blake order our pilot to divert to Farley. I'll call you back."

Blake said, "Farley?"

"Come on, Blake, you remember Farley, the RAF proving ground outside London. The department has a regular Lear jet operating out of there, piloted by Flight Lieutenants Lacey and Parry. We've had some interesting moments together. Now, we have another problem."

"And that would be?"

"Lady Helen Lang wants the last man standing in this whole rotten mess, Jack Barry. So she's drawn him out. He can't resist, so he's told her he would fly in. She could be in a bad situation at Compton Place. It's miles from anywhere in the depths of the English countryside. So, we land at Farley. They have an armorer there, full facilities. Just listen and learn."

He phoned Ferguson again. "Tell Lacey to find me a suitable beach near Compton Place. As I said, I'll drop in by parachute. At least she'll have backup. Just have the necessary equipment and weaponry ready."

Blake reached over. "Excuse me. Make that for two."

Dillon laughed and said to Ferguson, "Hey, I've got this crazy middle-aged American who's decided to come along for the drop. He's a kind of war reporter for the President."

"You're mad, the both of you," Ferguson said.

"Of course we are, so get on with it," and Dillon rang off.

The Chieftain landed on the old decaying bomber runway at Shankley Down and rolled to a halt by the decrepit hangars and the Nissen hut with the chimney smoking. There was a Cessna 310 parked on the apron, an old Ford Transit beside it, a man standing there in a flying jacket.

They all got out. Docherty said, "Hey, Clarke, you look good."

"Where's my money?" Clarke said.

Docherty produced a fat envelope. "Two grand in cash."

Clarke fingered it and Barry punched him in the shoulder. "Okay?"

Clarke looked at the Irishman and his friends, and discretion, as always, was the better part.

"Sure, fine, anything you want. Key's in the Transit."

Barry patted his face. "Good boy. We'll be back."

He nodded to his men. They got in the Transit, Quinn at the wheel, and drove away.

The Gulfstream landed at Farley, rolled to a halt, and Dillon and Blake got out. Ferguson and Hannah were standing there, Lacey and Parry behind them.

"Everything organized?" Dillon asked.

"Let's go in and discuss it," Ferguson told him.

Inside, they had a room to themselves. There was a trestle table with parachutes, two AK47 assault rifles, and two Brownings with silencers.

Dillon said, "I see you remember my preference." He turned to Lacey. "What's the score?"

"Let me show you on the chart, sir." Lacey led the way to the table. "Ordnance Survey map, large scale. Compton Place, so close to the sea it makes no difference. Here is Horseshoe Bay. Very wide when the tide's out and it's turning tonight. We could wait until it's really out, but . . ."

"No way. If we leave now, how long?"

"Forty minutes."

"I should say we're coming with you," Ferguson said. "We can drop you, then there's an RAF feeder station at Bramley twenty minutes flying time away. We'll come by on road."

"Terribly good of you." Dillon looked at the chart again and turned to Blake. "That's it, then, Horseshoe Bay."

He and Blake put themselves in the hands of the armorer, an aging sergeant major, who went over the equipment with professional competence. They took only one parachute, no reserve, an AK each, a Browning plus magazines.

Dillon said, "Look, Blake, Vietnam was a long time ago."

"Stuff you, Dillon, okay?" Blake told him.

"Hey, I'm with you."

They dressed in jumpsuits, shoulder holsters for the

Brownings, and checked the AKs. Ferguson and Hannah came in. "Lacey says still sporadic fog, but worse for you at Horseshoe Bay. Not too bad at Bramley for our landing."

"Well, good for you, Brigadier." Dillon grinned at Blake. "Let's do it."

"Why not?" Blake said, picked up his parachute, and walked out.

NORFOLK
ULSTER

FIFTEEN

IN THE TRANSIT, the mood was euphoric. Barry, sitting beside Quinn at the wheel, brought them up to date.

"The woman we're visiting is called Lady Helen Lang, originally American, but don't be fooled by appearances. She's killed several times. There's one wild card. She has a very big black chauffeur called Hedley."

"Just another nigger," Dolan said and patted his Arma-Lite. "I'll take care of him."

"You've already made a mistake that could cost you your life," Barry told him. "As you all know, I'm an old Vietnam hand and so is Hedley Jackson. Marines, Special Forces, medals. This man could be bad news."

"So he's a bad nigger," Dolan sniggered.

"Your funeral, old son." Barry produced a large-scale Ordnance Survey map and passed it back to them in the rear of the Transit. "You'll find Compton Place there. Right on the edge of the sea. There's a village called Compton, but it's five miles away. One of those no-no places you find in the countryside, with a dying population of about fifty. No problem."

Mullen, a large, evil-looking specimen with a shaved head, said, "This is a walkover, Jack, why bring us all along? You could do it yourself."

"Because she's invited me. I killed her son three years ago, a Brit officer working undercover. That's why she stiffed Tim Pat Ryan in London and my friends in New York. Now she wants me. It's a bit like one of those old Westerns on television where the hero says meet me on the street at dawn."

"She must be puddled," Mullen said.

"Five dead men, all killed with the same gun. That says she knows her business. She even stiffed two lowlifes on Park Avenue one night who were trying to rape some girl."

"We'll blow her away," Quinn said. "Her and the black."

"I sure as hell hope we do," Barry said. "I don't want her on my case for the rest of my life, and that's where she'll be if she isn't wasted."

There was a kind of regret in his voice as he said that, a regret he couldn't explain even to himself, and Quinn said, "An easy one, Jack. We'll be on our way back before you know it."

"Let's hope so," Barry said. "Study that map. Just make sure you know where we're going."

It was late afternoon, with fog, and rain falling, and the Mercedes passed through Compton, followed the winding roads through that ancient countryside. Hedley pulled into the courtyard and switched off. Lady Helen was already out of the car and unlocking the kitchen door. Hedley carried the bags in.

"Now what?"

"I'm going to change, then we'll get ready."

"Ready for what, Lady Helen?"

"Jack Barry." She raised a hand. "Oh, he'll come, Hedley, he won't be able to resist. On the other hand, Charles Ferguson, Mr. Dillon, Blake Johnson . . ."

"Could arrive first and I hope they do."

She looked out at the fog. "Don't be silly, Hedley. If they have to drive from Gatwick in this pea-souper, it will take hours. I'll see you in fifteen minutes."

In her bedroom, she undressed, took a one-piece jumpsuit from the wardrobe, and put it on. She found some elastic-sided ankle boots, then opened her purse and took out the Colt .25. She unloaded it, screwed the silencer on the end, then inserted the magazine again. She opened a drawer, took out four magazines, and put two in each pocket.

She was breathing heavily now, found her pill bottle, shook two into her hand, hesitated, then shook out two more. She went into the bathroom, filled a glass with water, and swallowed them down.

"What the hell," she murmured. "What's an overdose matter at this stage? It's all the same in the end."

She went downstairs and found Hedley in the kitchen, making tea. He was wearing a tracksuit. He handed her a cup. "Ready for war, Hedley?"

"It's been a long time."

"I suppose some things you don't forget." She smiled. "You've been a good friend."

"It's easy where you're concerned." He swallowed his tea. "Hell, I even drink this stuff instead of coffee to please you." He put the cup down. "Still, if you're intent on seeing this thing through, I suggest we adjourn to the barn."

There, she didn't use the Colt, although she had it in a small holster at her waist. Hedley gave her a .9mm Browning pistol with a silencer on the muzzle and slammed in a twenty-round magazine which protruded from the butt.

"I really feel I'm going to war with this," she said.

"Believe me, you are. Legs apart, both hands."

She worked her way across the target figures, shredding them. "Oh, my word. Now what, Hedley?"

He said, "It's simple. We wait to see who gets here first."

The Transit pulled in by a pine wood overlooking the estate at Compton Place. The fog swirled, touched by the wind, giving occasional glimpses of the countryside below, and there was the house and grounds and the sea beyond, and then the fog descended again.

"Leave the Transit here," Barry told them. "Keys under the mat. We'll go on foot."

"We're with you, Jack," Quinn said.

"That's good to know. You can take point, as we used to say in Vietnam."

It started to rain as they went down the hill and approached the outbuildings. Hedley, on top of steps leading to the upper floor of the barn, had an AK47 with a silencer and a night sight. He focused on Quinn and pressed the trigger. By chance, Quinn turned at the precise moment to speak to Barry, and the bullet missed his heart and hit the stock of his ArmaLite. He staggered back.

"Christ, Jesus."

"Down!" Barry called, and they all obeyed him.

He crawled to Quinn. "You okay?"

"I think so."

"I recognized the sound. A silenced AK. I heard enough of those in Vietnam." He spoke to the others in low tones. "She's there and she's waiting. Take care. Now fan out and move forward."

•　•　•

The Lear jet went down and down, passed through fog at one thousand feet, then broke clear, Horseshoe Bay below, surf creaming in, a touch of early evening gray.

Flight Lieutenant Lacey said over the intercom, "It's not good. Half tide at the moment. Better to abort."

Dillon and Blake in parachutes, jumpsuits, shoulder holsters, AKs suspended across their chests, glanced at Ferguson and Bernstein.

The Brigadier said, "Your call, gentlemen."

"What the hell." Dillon reached for the lever and dropped the Airstair door. "Who wants to live forever?" He grinned at Blake. "Hell, you're an older guy. You can go first."

"You're so kind," Blake said and, as Lacey made a pass at eight hundred, dived out headfirst and Dillon went after him.

The sky was turbulent, fog swirling to the horizon, the evening light fading. Dillon, aware of Blake in front of him, went down the Airstair door and allowed himself to fall, turning over in the Lear's slipstream. He pulled the ring of his rip cord, looked up, and saw the plane climb steeply.

Below him, Blake landed on the sand just in front of the surf. Dillon, farther behind, plunged into six feet of very salty water, surfaced, and plowed forward with difficulty because of the parachute trailing behind. He punched the quick-release clip, let the harness slip away, and waded to the beach.

Blake came to meet him. "You okay?"

Dillon nodded. "Let's do it."

They went up the beach, paused in the pine trees, then started toward the house. They stood together, looking down, and there was a sudden explosion and smoke drifted up.

"I'd say that was a smoke grenade," Dillon said. "Let's go," and they charged down the hill.

• • •

Barry stayed back, some instinct telling him to. Quinn led the others down toward the barn, and Hedley focused on Mullen and shot him through the head. Then he tossed a smoke grenade. The others flung themselves down and sprayed the first floor of the barn with fire. Hedley lay there at the top of the steps, head down, a round creasing his right shoulder.

Lady Helen crouched behind him. "Are you all right?"

"Slightly damaged. Don't worry."

Barry said, "Get on with it, Quinn."

Quinn stood up. "Let's get to it," he urged, and they all stood and followed him. Lady Helen, behind Hedley, raised the Browning and fired it repeatedly, blowing Quinn away. They retreated, she reached down for Hedley.

"Come on, inside."

Dolan and McGee crawled back. Barry said, "Right, lads, into the barn. They've nowhere to go."

"Christ, Jack, it's a bad scene," Dolan said. "Walk in the door and get your head blown off."

Barry took out a Beretta. "Well, you fucking will get in or I'll blow your head off myself. Go on, up those steps."

Dolan, terrified, started up, and Blake, arriving in the courtyard at the same moment, sprayed him with his AK, sending him headfirst to the cobbles below.

Blake crouched, and Barry moved closer to McGee. "Don't worry, we'll manage."

Dillon appeared on the other side of the courtyard and fired his AK. "You there, Jack?"

Barry called, "So it's you, Sean. You always arrive too late."

Blake fired in the general direction of Barry's voice, and there was return fire. He felt a red-hot poker in his left arm and fell back. Dillon fired in reply, three rounds, catching McGee in the face.

There was silence now, only the rain and the fog. Barry crawled forward, eased open the bottom door, and passed inside. He saw her, up there on the barn platform, pulling Hedley back to safety, hay drifting down.

"I'm here," he called.

She turned, dropping Hedley. Barry had his gun hand raised as she pulled out the Colt without hesitation.

His Beretta jammed. He worked the slider desperately, and she took deliberate aim. And then something strange happened. She seemed to struggle for breath, staggered back, and fell to her knees. Barry ejected one magazine, rammed another in, and took aim, and Dillon burst in through the barn door.

"No!" Dillon cried and fired, and his bullet creased Barry's face, sending him lurching back with a cry.

Barry recovered and fired back repeatedly, sending Dillon down, then vanished through the back door. There was silence. Dillon stood and went up the stairs.

Hedley lay there, blood on his shoulder, Lady Helen beside him, face gray. Dillon kneeled beside her. "What is it?"

"My heart, Mr. Dillon. I've been on borrowed time for a while. Did we get them?" Dillon hesitated. "The truth now."

"From the looks of it, his gang, but not Barry."

"What a shame." She closed her eyes.

A moment later, an RAF Land Rover drove into the courtyard with Charles Ferguson and Hannah Bernstein.

Dillon worked his way from one body to another. Quinn, shot several times, was only just alive. Dillon said, "Jesus, Quinn, I haven't seen you in years."

"Dillon?"

"All down, your mates finished."

"And Jack?"

"Oh, the Devil always looks after his own. He's away out of it as usual."

"Bastard."

"Where would he be going?"

Quinn managed a ghastly smile. "It'll cost you a cigarette."

Dillon got his silver case out. The cigarettes inside were still dry in spite of his dunking. He gave Quinn one and a light from his Zippo.

Quinn said, "We flew from Doonreigh in a Chieftain with Docherty. Remember him from the old days?"

"Surely."

"Landed on an old airstrip not far from here. Shankley Down, run by a man called Clarke. Docherty was to wait." His voice was tired. "A bastard, Jack, he always thought of number one. Flying back to Ulster and to hell with the rest of us." He was wandering now. "Back to Spanish Head. Always his bolt hole."

He was going fast. Dillon said, "Hang on, Quinn, I could still get him. Remember that special thing about me? I can fly anything with wings. This Shankley Down. Was there another plane there?"

Quinn nodded. "Small plane, but two engines. The kind where you walk over the wing to get in."

"Cessna 310," Dillon said.

"Get him, Dillon, fuck the bastard." The cigarette fell from Quinn's fingers and his head lolled to one side.

Dillon went to Ferguson, who was speaking into his mobile. He switched off. "I've sent for a disposal unit. I shouldn't think they'll make it in this weather in less than four hours. What about him?"

He nodded to Quinn and Dillon said, "Dead, all four dead."

"Anyone I should know?"

"Oh, you'll be delighted. Four to cross off your most-wanted list."

Hannah Bernstein had got the medical kit from the RAF Land Rover. She had wrapped a field service bandage round Blake's arm. Hedley was holding another to his shoulder as he crouched beside Lady Helen. Dillon dropped to one knee and she smiled.

"So he got away, Mr. Dillon, what a pity."

Dillon took her hand, never so cold, never so calm. "He only thinks he has. I'll get him for you, my love, I swear it." He stood up and helped her to her feet. "Take her inside," he said to Ferguson.

They stood there, Hedley and Blake, Ferguson and Lady Helen, Hannah with an arm around her. Blake was obviously in considerable pain and Hedley didn't look good.

"Terrible mess, all this, Charles," Lady Helen said. "I won't look good in the papers."

"It won't be in the papers," Ferguson said. "My disposal unit will take this trash back to London, where they will be processed in a certain crematorium. They'll be several pounds of gray ash each by the morning, and they can dump it in the Thames as far as I'm concerned."

"And you have the power to do that, Charles?"

He took her from Hannah and put an arm around her. "I can do anything."

Dillon said, "I'll leave you to it. I'll be away. I'll take the Land Rover."

Ferguson said, "What is this?"

"Quinn told me they flew into a place called Shankley Down in a Chieftain piloted by an old acquaintance of mine called Docherty. I should imagine Jack's taking off about now, if he hasn't already."

"But what can you do?"

"The place is run by a man called Clarke and there's a Cessna 310 there. I'm going to chase Jack Barry to the hob of hell. Oh, the 310 is a bit slower than a Chieftain, but I think I can take care of that. You see, I know his ultimate destination."

And it was Blake who saw it. "Spanish Head?"

"Got it in one."

"But it would be crazy for him to go there."

"He is crazy."

"But where can you land, Sean?"

"I know the place well from the old days. Great beaches off the Head with the tide out."

"In weather like this?" Ferguson said. "You're mad."

"I always was, Brigadier."

Hannah Bernstein said, "In the circumstances, I'd better go with him, sir."

"Like hell you will," Dillon told her.

"Let me tell you something, Dillon. To leave here in the Land Rover, you need the keys and I have them. Secondly, you have no authority to proceed without a police presence, which as a Detective Superintendent of Special Branch I will provide, Northern Ireland being part of the United Kingdom."

"Jesus, but you're a hard woman."

"I'd have thought you'd have realized that before now," Ferguson said. "All I can say is stay in touch."

When Barry arrived at Shankley Down, Docherty and Clarke were standing inside one of the two hangars, smoking. The Transit braked to a halt and Barry got out, face bleeding where Dillon's bullet had creased him.

"Right, let's be moving," he said.

"What about the others?" Docherty asked.

"They won't be coming," Barry said. "All dead."

Clarke said, "Just a minute. What are we into here?"

Barry took out his Beretta and shot him between the eyes, then he leaned over him, searched in his bomber jacket, and found the envelope with the two thousand pounds. When he looked up, Docherty's face was haggard.

"Jack?"

"It went wrong. Load of shite. Now let's get moving," and he pushed Docherty toward the Chieftain.

A moment later, they roared down the runway and took off into the fading light.

It was forty minutes later that Dillon and Hannah arrived in the Land Rover, Dillon driving. They pulled up beside Clarke's body and got out.

"He certainly passed this way," Dillon told her. "Call Ferguson on your mobile and tell him you've got another candidate for his disposal unit."

He went into the second hangar, mounted the wing of the Cessna, climbed over to the left-hand seat, and checked the instruments. She joined him a few moments later and followed him in.

"Everything okay?"

"The tanks are full, if that's what you mean. Look, he's on his way and the Chieftain is a lot faster than we are. Docherty's place at Doonreigh is about forty miles from Spanish Head, and Quinn thought that's where the bastard will go. I'll catch up with him by making that beach landing below the cliffs I spoke about."

"Is the tide out or in?"

"We'll check on the way." He switched on. "If you're not happy, leave me to it."

"Go to hell, Dillon." She closed the cabin door and buckled her seat belt and reached for the spare headphones.

"Just turn the dial to five," he said. "That's UK weather, then trawl through it for Ulster."

He put his own headphones on, started first the port engine, then starboard, and taxied out into the rain, moving to the end of the runway. She spoke to him over the mike.

"How long?"

"An hour and a half with a tailwind, two if it's the other way. Why?"

"According to the weather report, the tide is turning on that coast in just over an hour from now. Fog clearing, half-moon."

"Sounds interesting." He smiled at her, boosted power, and roared down the runway.

The Chieftain turned in to land at Doonreigh, darkness falling, and taxied up to the hangars and Nissen hut. Barry had been into Docherty's bar box and had demolished half a bottle of Paddy whiskey on the way, sitting on his own in the cabin. He hadn't taped his face with anything from the medical box, had simply swabbed it with raw whiskey. When the Chieftain rolled to a halt, he unlocked the Airstair door and went down the steps. The fog had cleared, but it was raining hard.

"Back on the ould sod," he said.

Docherty, getting out behind him, said, "Ten thousand pounds cash in a supermarket bag you promised, Jack."

"And me forgetting. Isn't that the terrible thing?" Barry pulled out his Beretta and shot him twice in the heart. A few moments later, he was driving away.

As darkness descended, the sky cleared and there was the light of the moon as Dillon flew over the Irish Sea.

Hannah said, "Will we make it, Sean?"

"Ah, keep the faith, girl." There was strange intimacy between them.

He was low now, no more than fifteen hundred, and there was the coast, the cliffs of Northern Ireland, black in the moonlight, and Dillon checked the chart book on his knee and turned slightly to port.

"That's it. Dead ahead now." He descended to six hundred. "Only one problem. The tide's coming in fast down there."

He crossed the cliffs, the castle below. "Is that it?" she asked.

"Spanish Head as ever was."

He turned out to sea again, banked, and dropped his undercarriage. "Here we go. Try praying. It might help."

Whitecaps were pounding into the surf and there wasn't much beach left there. Dillon leveled, no more than fifty feet above the water, then dropped her in. The wheels bit into wet sand no more than two feet below the water, the Cessna careered forward, then nosed up to the strip of beach left.

It was very quiet when he switched off and removed the headphones. From that position, the sea looked relatively calm in the moonlight. Dillon smiled. "Nice view."

"Don't do that to me again," Hannah Bernstein said. "Not ever. Can we get out?"

"It's a thought. Any minute now and you'll get your feet wet, so let's go."

They crossed the beach and found a path that climbed up between two cliffs. When they reached the top, the castle was quite close.

"What now?" Hannah asked.

"I'd have thought that was obvious," Dillon said. "We'll make for the lodge," and he led the way.

• • •

Old John Harker was in the kitchen at the cottage, waiting for the kettle to boil, when there was a sudden draft on his cheek. He turned and found the door open and Dillon there, Hannah at his shoulder.

"Remember me?" Dillon said.

"My God!" Harker said.

"Has his lordship turned up?"

"Ten minutes ago. How did you know?"

"I know everything. Now this is how it is. Get your lantern and take us up through the garden. I'll decide what to do when we reach the castle."

"Whatever you say." Harker hesitated. "Is this the end of him?"

"If I have anything to do with it."

"Thank God for that." Harker took an electric lantern from a peg. "That secret passage from the panel in the library. It comes out in the front hall. Let's get to it, then."

Barry, in the study off the main entrance hall, helped himself to a large whiskey, swallowed it down, then went upstairs to the library. He stood, drinking the whiskey, and glanced up at the portraits of his ancestors. All Francis, but not himself. He looked at the one in Confederate uniform. He seemed to be smiling in a kind of amusement.

"Bastard," Barry said. "Arrogant bastard, but a good soldier."

He toasted the portrait and behind him the door opened and Dillon and Hannah entered. Dillon was unarmed, but she carried a Walther in her left hand.

"Sean, is the Devil on your side?"

"Only some of the time."

Barry smiled. "God knows how you got here."

"Just like you, only I landed on the beach."

"And how did you leave things at Compton Place?"

"All dead, your lot, Blake and Hedley Jackson a little damaged, that's all."

"And Lady Helen?" Dillon shrugged, and Barry said with a strange kind of urgency, "She's all right, isn't she?"

"Her heart isn't good. She had an attack."

"Christ, Jesus," Barry said. "She had me dead to rights, my gun jammed, and she sort of fell down."

Hannah Bernstein said, "I am Detective Superintendent Hannah Bernstein of Special Branch of Scotland Yard and I must warn you that . . ."

Barry flung his glass at her, ducked as she fired, and was through the panel and away.

"Let's go," Dillon said and ran across to the door and she followed.

They reached the entrance hall and the front door stood open, Harker on the porch, the lantern in his hand.

"He ran past me. Took the path down through the trees toward the cliffs."

Dillon went off on the run, Hannah following, and Harker went after them.

Barry ran, head down, through the trees, the Beretta in his left hand, not really knowing where he was going anymore. The sky was overcast, there was a rumble of thunder on the horizon, and lightning flickered.

Helen Lang. He couldn't get her out of his head, and why was that? He came to the track leading down to the Soak Hole. Dillon followed, Hannah behind him and old Harker with the lantern.

The sheet lightning flickered, the water raged below on the beach, the Cessna engulfed. Barry stumbled on and then he was at the Soak Hole, white spray exploding in a hollow roar. He paused at the steps down, turned, and leveled the Beretta as Dillon arrived on the run.

Dillon swept Barry's arm to one side and met him breast-to-breast. "A long time coming, you dog," Dillon cried, grabbed his right wrist, and twisted it up like a steel bar. Barry screamed as the bone cracked and Dillon ran him headfirst down the steps and let go. There was a last desperate cry, then the Soak Hole fountained again.

Old Harker held the lantern high. "God help us, but what kind of a man are ye?"

"I sometimes wonder myself." Dillon turned to Hannah. "Access Ferguson on your mobile. Tell him to arrange for Lacey and Parry to pick us up in the Lear jet."

"Of course." She put a hand on his arm. "Are you all right, Dillon?"

"Never better." The Soak Hole fountained again. "He was a bad bastard, Jack, and the sea's taken him, so there's an end to it," and he turned and followed Harker up the track.

The following afternoon, he sat with Hannah and Ferguson outside a private room at the London Clinic. Hedley came out, smart in his chauffeur's uniform and wearing a sling.

"How is she?" Ferguson asked.

"Not good. She's asked for Mr. Dillon."

Dillon got up, paused, then went into the room. She was propped up in bed. There was a drip into her left arm, various other wires attached to electronic equipment. A nurse was sitting close by.

Dillon moved to the bed. "Lady Helen."

She opened her eyes. "You got him, I hear? So Charles told me."

"That's right."

"So, the end of the Sons of Erin, all of them, even the Connection, and you know what?" She closed her eyes and opened them again. "It hasn't brought Peter back."

He took her hand. "I know."

She smiled again. "Mr. Dillon, you think you're such a bad man, and you know what? I think you're one of the most moral men I've ever known. Hang on to that thought."

Her eyes closed, her hand slipped away, and one of the machines made a strange noise. The nurse took over and Dillon walked out.

Ferguson and Hannah stood up. The Brigadier said, "She's gone?"

"But not forgotten," Dillon said. "Never forgotten." He put a hand on Hedley's shoulder. "Let's take a walk in the garden. I could do with a cigarette."

EPILOGUE

THEY DROVE UP from London to Compton Place a week later, Ferguson, Hannah, and Dillon, in the Daimler. The weather was terrible, heavy, driving rain.

"What did the Prime Minister have to say at the end of the day?" Dillon asked.

"Extremely sorry about Lady Helen, of course."

"Aren't we all?"

"But content with the outcome. I mean, it could have been bloody awful."

"Instead of which, it didn't happen, sir, is that what we're saying?" Hannah Bernstein, in black coat and trouser suit, sounded cold, forbidding.

"Now look, Superintendent, sometimes we have to think of the good of the cause."

"That's what the IRA say," Dillon told him. "Drummed into me from the age of nineteen." He put the window down and lit a cigarette. "Sorry, my love," he said to Hannah.

She put a hand on his knee. "Feel free, Sean."

He said, "So, the Prime Minister and the President heave a heavy sigh of relief and thank God for the foot soldiers. You appointed me public executioner again, only this time Hannah and Blake had to play their part."

"It's the name of the game, Dillon," Ferguson said.

Dillon turned to Hannah. "Do you ever wonder what it's all about? Because I do."

They were entering the village now. The parking lot of St. Mary and All the Saints was almost full, and there were cars parked along the village street.

"My goodness, but they are giving her a send-off," Ferguson said.

"Well, they would. I've learned enough about her to know she was greatly loved." Dillon checked his watch. "Forty minutes to the service. I don't know about you, but I need a drink. Pull in at the pub. If you don't want to join me, I'll see you at the church."

"No, I think a drink might be appropriate." Ferguson glanced at Hannah. "If you agree, Superintendent."

"Of course, sir."

The Daimler dropped them at the pub entrance and drove away. They moved inside and found it already full, not only with villagers in their best suits and dresses, but many visitors. Hetty Armsby in a black suit served the bar, helped by two village girls. Old Armsby sat on the end stool, also in a black suit, neck scrawny in a stiff collar.

"Good Lord," Ferguson said. "Two Earls, a Duchess, and damn me if that's not the Commanding Officer of the Scots Guards over there and the Commanding General of the Household Brigade. I'd better say hello."

"Good old British class system," Dillon said, turning to Hannah. "I'm going to force my way to the bar. Wait for me here."

He made it and said to Hetty, "Would you happen to have any champagne in your fridge there?"

"There might be a half bottle." She frowned. "Champagne?"

"At a funeral?" He lit a cigarette. "I want to drink a toast to probably the greatest lady I've ever known."

Her smile was instant and, impulsively, she reached over and kissed him on the cheek and there were tears in her eyes. "She was the best, right enough."

She produced the champagne. "Two glasses," he said.

A familiar voice said, "Make that three."

Dillon turned and there was Blake Johnson, his left arm in a sling. "My God," Dillon said. "Where in the hell did you spring from?"

"There's still an American air base up here at Crockley. It was a last-minute decision of the President's. Sent me over to carry his personal wreath."

He took one of the glasses of champagne and Dillon carried the other two. Blake kissed Hannah on the cheek. "Superintendent, as always, a pleasure."

"Nice to see you, and very gracious, but that's not why we're here. To Helen Lang, a great lady." She raised her glass and they all touched before drinking.

From behind, Charles Ferguson said, "And so say all of us."

The Church of St. Mary and all the Saints was so crowded that they had to queue to get in the door. There was a man in his forties with a woman of the same age, Hedley Jackson beside them. Hedley whispered something, the couple glanced across, and the men held back.

"Brigadier Ferguson? I'm Robert Harrison, Lady Helen's nephew."

"Of course. You're taking over as chief executive of all the family business interests?"

Harrison was actually crying. "She was a great woman, just great. She used to come over to Boston when I was a kid. We all loved her."

"These are colleagues of mine, Superintendent Bernstein, Sean Dillon, and Blake Johnson from the White House."

Harrison stared. "The White House?"

"I'm here as the President's personal representative," Blake said. "He's sent a wreath."

"My God, I don't know what to say." Harrison got his handkerchief out. "I guess I'd better get back to my wife."

Dillon was not a religious man. He remembered the Roman Catholic church in County Down in Ulster as a boy—incense, candles, and the holy water, the uncle he'd had who was a priest and too good for this world—but standing at the back of that old English church, the service meant very little to him. The hymns, the organ music, the eulogy on Helen Lang's life by the clergyman seemed to make no sense. Strange, like Dillon, she was a Catholic, but the Lang family was not. Yet at the end, what difference did it make?

He was happy to get out, stood at the side of the path in the rain, and lit a cigarette. For the moment, he'd lost the others, and Hedley appeared with a large black umbrella.

"Another cliché, Hedley," Dillon told him. "A funeral and the rain pouring down."

"You sound angry, Mr. Dillon."

"I just feel she deserved better."

"You got that bastard for her."

"The one good thing."

They stood to one side as the bearers emerged from the church with the coffin and moved toward the part of the churchyard where the Lang family mausoleum was.

"A hell of a woman," Hedley said. "You know what she did for me?"

"Tell me."

"The lawyer phoned this week. One million pounds in her will and her house in South Audley Street."

Dillon tried to find the right words. "She loved you, Hedley, she wanted to take care of you."

"It's only money, Mr. Dillon." There were tears in Hedley's eyes. "Only money, and what good is that, when you come down to it?"

Dillon patted his shoulder as the coffin moved on and they followed with the crowd, and when he turned, Ferguson, Bernstein, and Blake were with them.

The coffin went into the mausoleum, the vicar spoke, the bronze doors closed, the rain was relentless. Already a new plaque was here beneath the one that said "Major Peter Lang, M.C., Scots Guards, Special Air Service Regiment 1966–1996. Rest in Peace." It said "Helen Lang, Greatly Loved, Died 1999."

Hedley said to Dillon, "I suggested that, as there was no one else here. I knew she wouldn't want anything fancy."

"Remarkable," Ferguson said. "A wreath from both the British Prime Minister and the President of the United States. You don't see that every day."

The crowd started to disperse, they walked down to the church parking lot. There was an American Air Force limousine there, a uniformed sergeant at the wheel.

"Straight back, Blake?" Dillon asked.

"I've got work to do, my fine Irish friend, you know how it is."

"Oh, I do."

"Goodbye, Brigadier." Blake shook hands, kissed Hannah, got in the rear of the limousine, and was driven away.

• • •

People dispersed, the cars drove away. Ferguson said,
"That's it, then."

They walked to the Daimler, the driver opened the rear
door, and they got in, Dillon taking a jump seat opposite
Hannah and Ferguson. He pulled the glass panel behind him
closed.

"Do you ever feel tired, my love?" he asked Hannah.
"Really tired?"

"I know, Sean, I know."

The Daimler moved away. "So now what?" Dillon asked.

"There are still problems, Dillon," Ferguson told him.
"The Middle East, Africa, Bosnia." He shrugged. "Only the
Irish dimension has changed, with the peace process work-
ing."

"Brigadier, if you believe that, you'll believe anything."

Dillon leaned back, folded his arms, and closed his eyes.

JACK HIGGINS

THE EAGLE HAS LANDED

THE 25TH ANNIVERSARY OF THE THRILLER CLASSIC!

"First rate...a fascinating adventure story."
—*San Francisco Chronicle*

"The master's master of World War II spycraft storytelling...A superb and mysterious tale."
—United Press International

"Higgins is the master."—Tom Clancy

__0-425-17718-1/$7.50